We Had No Time to Be Afraid.

The broken water seemed to reach out to us greedily. The raft moved crazily, tipping sideways, shuddering from end to end.

I could see nothing but the thick spray; it filled my mouth and nostrils so that I could scarcely breathe; the roaring of the water was everywhere. . . .

Tsorl raised his head and cried out; before I could look, the raft was launched into the empty air. It came down with a jolt that made me breathless. The raft spun dizzily, then gently, surely, it was urged forward. We floated so gently it felt as if we had died and been carried off on the wind, bodiless spirits. Overhead we could see the stars, and all around us on the dark sea there rose the shapes of the islands.

Books by Cherry Wilder

The Luck of Brin's Five
The Nearest Fire
Second Nature

Published by TIMESCAPE BOOKS

Most Timescape Books are available at special quantity discounts for bulk purchases for sales promotions, premiums or fund raising. Special books or book excerpts can also be created to fit specific needs.

For details write or telephone the office of the Vice President of Special Markets, Pocket Books, 1230 Avenue of the Americas, New York, New York 10020, 212-245-1760.

THE NEAREST FIRE

Cherry Wilder

A TIMESCAPE BOOK
PUBLISHED BY POCKET BOOKS NEW YORK

A Timescape Book published by
POCKET BOOKS, a Simon & Schuster division of
GULF & WESTERN CORPORATION
1230 Avenue of the Americas, New York, N.Y. 10020

Published by arrangement with Atheneum Publishers
Library of Congress Catalog Card Number: 79-22114

ISBN: 0-671-44703-3

First Timescape Books printing July, 1982

10 9 8 7 6 5 4 3 2 1

POCKET and colophon are trademarks of Simon & Schuster.

Use of the trademark TIMESCAPE is by exclusive license
from Gregory Benford, the trademark owner.

Printed in the U.S.A.

CAST OF CHARACTERS

IN ORDER OF APPEARANCE

TIATH AVRAN PENTROY *The Great Elder of Torin, leader of Clan Pentroy*

AMMUR NINGAN *Ammur, the High Steward, his chief assistant*

MATT MATTROYAN *A Merchant of Rintoul and Itsik*

YOLO HARN *A young miner from Tsagul, the Fire-Town*

OLD HARN *Her foster parent, retired construction worker*

MORRITT HARN *His sister, a retired porter*

LEN HARN *Another foster-child*

WARKOR
CLEE *Miners employed at the New Cut*

TENN *Overseer*

RED
GRABBER *Prisoners sent to Itsik prison settlement*

DYALL THE ROPE WARD *First Mate of a salt boat*

GWELL NU *"Mad Gwell," the Forgan or Healer of Itsik*

COTH *A sick aid, one of Gwell's helpers*

TSORL-U-TSORL *Former Deputy of Tsagul*

KAREN SCHWARTZ *Scientific Officer of an Earth Bio-Survey team*

LISA CHILD *First Officer*

SAM FLETCHER *Captain*

NANTGEEB *A Diviner and scientist known as "The Maker of Engines"*

MEETAL GULLAN *First Officer of a troop of armed Pentroy vassals*

OBAL *A Pentroy house-servant. Musician and Witness or telepath*

SCOTT GALE *Navigator of the Bio-Survey team, also the Luck of Brin's Five, a Moruian family*

MAMOR BRINROYAN *Captain of the trader* Beldan

DORN BRINROYAN *Eldest child of the Family*

ABLO BINIGAN *Ablo the Fixer, an Outclip or extra member of Brin's Five*

LEETH GALTROY *Head of Clan Galtroy*

URNAT AVRAN PENTROY *A Dwarf. The Luck of Av's Five, the Great Elder's family*

BOSS BLACK *Governor of Itsik . . . a half-blood of Clan Pentroy*

ALLOO GULLAN *A Pentroy vassal*

BRIN BRINROYAN *Mother and leader of Brin's Five*

ROY TURUGAN. . . . *Harper Roy*

NARNEEN
TOMAR *The younger children of Brin's Five*

TILJE PAROYAN DOHTROY *Friend of Tsorl. Dohtroy representative on the Speaking Chain*

VEL RAGAN *Vel the Scribe. Friend of Tsorl*

GUNO WENTROY *Head of Clan Wentroy, also on the Speaking Chain*

JETHAN LUNTROY *A younger member of Clan Luntroy. Their representative on the Speaking Chain*

THE CLANS OF TORIN

The clans of Torin are groups of noble families who hold ancient rights to the land. Once there were more clans, each with a private army of vassals and free supporters, now there remain only five: Pentroy, whose lands lie in the north; Wentroy, who farm the Troon basin south of Otolor; Luntroy, whose lands lie about Rintoul; Galtroy, whose lands reach eastward to the Salthaven; and Dohtroy, whose lands are in the west by Tsagul. A sixth clan, Tsatroy, also from Tsagul, was destroyed some fifty years earlier.

The clans play a large part in the government of Torin. Each clan selects a number of members to make up the Hundred of Rintoul and the Hundred, in turn, choose the Council of Five Elders. The power of these bodies is checked by the overlapping rights of the town councils in Rintoul and Tsagul, which are not made up of "grandees" as the clan members are called.

The present five clans have intermarried for many generations but, since any child born of a grandee mother is itself a grandee, new blood is sometimes introduced into the clan families. (A famous "out-cross," for example, is the pair-marriage of Per Peran, head of the Southern branch of the Pentroy, and Ocar Peran, an architect of Rintoul: they are mother and father of Murno, the popular hero known as Blacklock.) Moruians believe that grandees look different from ordinary folk; they point out their aristocratic hands, their pallor, their height. This is not entirely true; it is not possible to see at a glance just who is a grandee and who is not.

THE LEADERS OF THE FIVE CLANS

Pentroy

TIATH AVRAN PENTROY *Leader of Clan Pentroy and Great Elder of Torin.*

Dohtroy

ORN ORNROYAN DOHTROY *Leader of Clan Dohtroy, a member of the Council of Five. Nicknamed "Margan," the Peacemaker.*

Wentroy

GUNO GUNROYAN WENTROY *Leader of Clan Wentroy and member of the Council of Five. Nicknamed "Guno Deg," Old Crosspatch.*

Luntroy

NOON NOONROYAN LUNTROY *Leader of Clan Luntroy. She is a retired flyer, rumored to be a friend of Nantgeeb the Magician. She takes no part in government.*

MARL UDORN LUNTROY *The Luck of Noon's Five sits on the Council of Five as Luntroy representative. Blind Marl, who lost his sight in childhood, is in fact a member of Clan Luntroy, not an adopted Luck of humble birth.*

Galtroy

LEETH LEETHROYAN GALTROY *Leader of Clan Galtroy. She is very conservative and her clan acts closely with the Pentroy.*

The Speaking Chain

This ancient form of folk-meeting was used more often in the past; it can be summoned by the leader of any clan. A famous Speaking Chain was summoned by Relrin Pentroy, Tiath's formidable ancestress, in the plain by Otolor. It lasted half a year and thrashed out the matter of whether Otolor should become a free city. Any grandee can represent its clan on a Speaking Chain: Tilje Paroyan Dohtroy, widow of Orn Margan's brother, stands up for Clan Dohtroy in this present story, and the Luntroy Clan is represented by Jethan Noonroyan Luntroy, a child of the Clan Leader's family.

CONTENTS

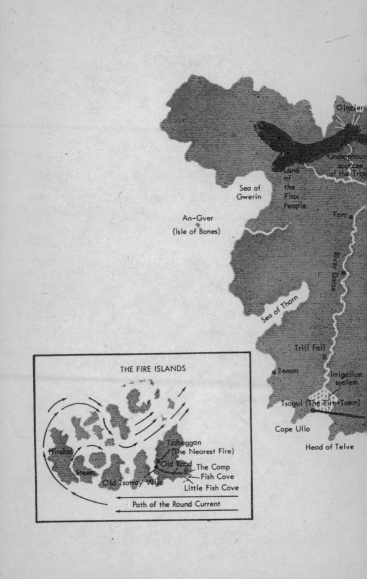

Glacier

Underground
sources
of the Trp

Sea of
Gwerin

Land
of
the
Flax
People

An-Gver
(Isle of Bones)

Forr

River Darte

Sea of Thorn

Trill fall
X

Benon

Irrigation
system

Tsagui (The Fire-Town)

Cape Ullo

Head of Telve

THE FIRE ISLANDS

Hirroko

Shean

Tsabeggan
(The Nearest Fire)

Old Road

Old Tsatray Villa

The Camp
Fish Cove
Little Fish Cove

Path of the Round Current

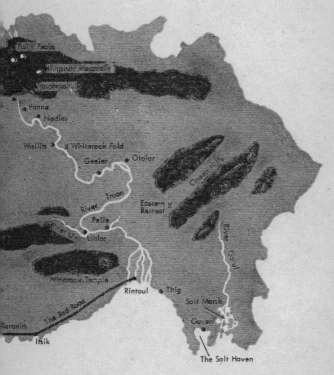

THE CONTINENT OF TORIN

Twin Peaks

Highrock Mountain

Thunderous

Fanne

Nedlar

Wellin   X Whiterock Fold

Geeler   Otolar

Froon

Omark Hills

River

Eastern X
Retreat

Petle

River Galul

Linlor

Windrock Temple

The Red Road

Rintoul   Thig

Salt Marsh

Garunin

Goven

Isik

The Salt Haven

Great Ocean Sea

THE
NEAREST
FIRE

Prologue

THE CONTINENT AND THE WORLD ITSELF have the same name: Torin. Long ago, on the fringes of recorded history, there were two continents, but the blast of the fire mountains, a tremendous volcanic catastrophe, destroyed the warm green land near the equator and left its remains . . . the Fire Islands. The Moruia of Torin still speak of "the fire that split the world."

The remaining continent is divided by two rivers, which run from the northern mountains to the sea. The lesser river, the Datse, is narrow and dark; it brings life to the arid lands of the northwest. Towns and villages cluster its high banks and spread into the river's canyons. The Datse breaks up into rapids and waterfalls, places of wild beauty, where the traveler must drag a boat overland or urge it through a side canal. At last the river flows into a complicated network of these canals, built according to a master plan. Around the channels the farmlands spring up green and the wool-deer thrive; the precious water is carried on in tunnels and sluiceways to the copper, silver and tin mines. This is the irrigation system of Tsagul, the Fire-Town, the most ancient settlement upon Torin.

By contrast, the great river Troon flows slowly through

a fertile countryside; it abounds with fish and game. Barges and smaller craft ply the length of the broad, gray river from the mountains to the sea. The towns along its banks can grow into cities. The Troon has a natural irrigation system at its mouth, the lovely delta lands, rich with bird farms, fishponds, flower plantations. On the edge of the delta rise the spires, the skywalks, the basket ways of the city of Rintoul, the "golden net of the world."

A city does not sleep, and Rintoul slept even less than the cities of other worlds; under the light of Esder, the Far Sun, armies of cleaners and porters came out to do their work. It was the year 271 of the New Age; spring was shading into summer; the last comet of the year just passed still burned overhead, a reminder that the heavens held wonders. A small party of human beings had come to the planet Torin, and one of them, Scott Gale, lived among the Moruians and was the chosen luck of the family Brin's Five. Now Scott Gale was sailing to the islands to rejoin his human companions; his departure had not passed unnoticed.

High up among the skyhouses of Rintoul the light of many candlecones shone out from a round window mullioned with golden rope. Inside there might have been grandees at play: listening to music, poring over their art collections, hearing the words of a fortune-teller. Instead the soft light fell on scrolls, skeins, willow paper and vellum covered with written characters; a huge woven map of Torin stood on a frame in the midst of the round room. This was a workroom in the skyhouse of the Great Elder, Tiath Avran Pentroy, a room full of secrets, where only a few persons ever came. Ammur, the High Steward of the Pentroy, kept the five keys of this room strapped to her skinny arm high up under her rich ribboned sleeves and did not remove them even when she slept.

The room told of civilization and luxury, but the two beings who stood in the room would have appeared strange to human eyes. Their loose limbs, their large eyes, the odd furred patches on their pale skins, the way in which Ammur Ningan folded long thumb and forefinger into the cup of her narrow palm: these were Moruian attitudes. Tiath Pentroy had risen in anger from a leather chair; his hooting voice echoed through the chamber.

"Dead? Withered away? Have you killed him then, you old wretched slave . . . ?"

"Accident!" The Ningan's voice rose up in a quavering squeak like the wheeze of a tree-bear.

"Tsorl-U-Tsorl died of a festering chain wound. The Healer of Itsik amputated a leg but it did not save him."

"I would not have had him dead." Tiath looked from the window over the white gulfs of the city and the sea beyond. "It is an evil omen," he said.

He raised one long hand and moved it before his face in an odd, scissorlike gesture, snapping his third and fourth fingers apart and together. He made the averting sign to ward off evil.

"Highness," said Ammur softly, "I thought it was your will."

"I have spent my anger," said Tiath. "He was innocent in the matter of Scott Gale's airship. Nantgeeb, the Diviner, stole it. Tsorl was a scholar and a maker of engines. Only Nantgeeb could match him."

"Tsorl was a threat at one time," persisted Ammur. "You sent against him—"

"I gave no order. I am not to blame," said Tiath with calm self-deception. "Tsorl would meddle in politics. The firestone clinger that burned his creature, Vel Ragan, was thrown by some overpaid troublemaker."

"Besides," he added, "if *we* had sent an assassin, Tsorl would have been dead long ago."

The Great Elder moved to the frame in the center of the room and walked around the map, occasionally picking at a thread. "We are expecting a visitor," he said.

"At this hour?"

"It is a person used to watching the sea and doing business at the docks," said Tiath.

"You are trying to surprise me," said Ammur Ningan. "You should let me arrange these things."

"Your powers are failing," said Tiath bluntly. "You got nothing from the secret mission to Nantgeeb's retreat. I hope your spies were right about the devil, Scott Gale. . . ."

"He sailed for the islands two days ago aboard the trader *Beldan*. He is sailing to the island called Tsabeggan, the Nearest Fire."

The Ningan came and stood beside her liege, and they stared at the western hemisphere of Torin. The woven map was very old; the contours of the mainland and of the islands had been embroidered fancifully in heavy relief. There were signs of alteration: the brown threads that outlined the lands in the west held by Clan Dohtroy had been unpicked several times and sewn in again, replacing some earlier thread. In the north, at the base of the mountains, a black thread outlined the sliver of Pentroy land in the northwest. There were a few lonely patches still outlined in flame-colored thread and one of these was on the large island called Tsabeggan.

"Tsatroy . . ." murmured Tiath. "The Fire Clan is no more. They were a pack of brave fools. See how well our peaceful friends of Dohtroy did from the destruction of Tsatroy; their lands almost doubled."

"I was on Tsabeggan once," said Ammur Ningan. "I was at the Tsatroy villa attending your Great-Aunt Relrin."

"Good," said Tiath. "You have some idea of the terrain."

Ammur's furry eyebrows twitched, but she asked no question. She followed her liege around the frame of the map. In the eastern hemisphere the colored clan threads blossomed all over the rich lands by the river Troon and reached far into the east, by the Salthaven. Pentroy owned the north, Wentroy green outlined the fertile land of the middle Troon basin; in the south around Rintoul blue thread picked out the holdings of Luntroy; and disjointed patches of Galtroy crimson stretched away to the east. Tiath laid a hand on the ancient temple at Windrock, which stood in the desert, almost on the edge of the map, the dividing line between east and west. He bent down to examine a small, shaded patch on the coast, still on this dividing line: the prison settlement of Itsik.

Far in the north, among the embroidered humps of the mountains there was a strange marker stuck into the map. Tiath plucked it out and twirled the metal pin between his fingers.

"We can move Scott Gale's flag," he said.

The small square of white synthetic fabric was printed with a circle of green leaves; it was the flag of the planet Earth. Tiath continued around his world again, with the stiff figure of the Ningan striding after him, and planted the alien flag firmly on the island of Tsabeggan.

"There are his fellow devils," said the Great Elder. "There is the ship of the void, twice, three times the size of that marvelous contraption that landed him in the warm lake on Hingstull Mountain. We must have them . . . we must have the ship and the man family . . ."

"Gale is already on the sea," said Ammur. "What is your plan, Highness?"

"To get there before him!"

"How will that be done?"

"You will know when you see our visitor. . . ." Tiath settled in a hard, high wicker chair and waited. When a quiet knock sounded, the Ningan opened a round window in the main door of the workroom and peered out.

"Let him come in!" she called in a formal singsong, operating the locks.

She turned back to Tiath Pentroy and gave her master a wintery smile.

The visitor stood blinking in the light. He was a sturdy Moruian of middle age with skin tanned by the sun and dark red hair elaborately dressed. He wore rich clothes: tunic, overtunic, extra sleeves, boot covers, a "flying vest" and a long, dagged cloak. Only the Ningan's silken baghose and embroidered jackets came close to this finery; the Great Elder wore a plain black robe without ornament.

"Matt Mattroyan," said the newcomer, "merchant of Rintoul and Itsik. At the service of the Great Elder."

"Mattroyan," said Tiath pleasantly, "we need the help of your ships."

"I have a fleet of ten large ships and a score of smaller vessels, Highness. What are your needs?"

"A rounder," said Tiath promptly, "a simple rounder to tow my barge to Itsik."

"Itsik?" echoed the Merchant. "What would bring your Highness within wind of the tannery and the tallow plant worked by prisoners?"

"I could be traveling overland from Itsik to the temple at Windrock," said Tiath.

"Well, a rounder to tow your barge is easily provided," said Mattroyan, his florid face growing puzzled.

"Do you know there are strangers on Torin?" asked the Great Elder.

"I have seen one," said the Merchant. "I have seen the one called Escott Garl, at the Bird Clan Air Race."

"Three more of his kind nest in the island of Tsabeggan," said Tiath crisply, "and I need a vessel of yours to come to them."

"That might be arranged, Highness."

"I need your ship of honor . . . the *Esnar*."

"But Highness . . ." stammered the Merchant, "that ship . . . the *Esnar* . . ."

"It is a steam vessel," said Tiath, "reeking of fire-metal-magic. I know that well. How swiftly could it reach the islands sailing from Itsik wharf?"

"Three or four days, Highness."

"So soon? A sailing ship takes thirty days from Rintoul to reach Tsabeggan."

"Longer if the winds are bad." Mattroyan grinned. "Highness . . . this will be an unusual transaction. . . ."

"Most unusual," agreed Tiath, "but you will be suitably rewarded. Sit down, Merchant Mattroyan; we must explore every detail of my plan. Ammur?"

"With your permission," said the High Steward, "perhaps we should read the omens at the start of this venture?"

"Excellent!" said the Great Elder.

Ammur came forward carrying a bowl of dark wood so old and smooth it was hard to tell whether it had been carved out or whether it was a very large gourd. It was filled to the brim with short strips of fabric of every color and texture, some embroidered with a character. She set it down on a stool between Tiath and the Merchant and held up a thick rod of amber-colored resin.

"Do you read omens before a voyage?" asked Tiath.

"Of course, Highness," said Mattroyan. "I use wind petals mostly, or the sands. This is a very fine resin-rod and bowl. . . ."

"An ancient treasure. . . ."

The Ningan rubbed the glowing rod briskly with a small patch of animal fur and plunged it into the bowl of fabric. When the rod was withdrawn it was thickly covered with the colored strips; the Ningan shook it once, twice, until only a few strips remained. She gathered these off the rod one by one, reading their meanings in a penetrating singsong.

"Fair wind, changing wind, the number seven, offers of friendship, fire-metal-magic . . ."

"Is that what it says?" asked the Great Elder.

"Here is the strip."

"Perhaps it is for the *Esnar*," murmured Mattroyan.

"Perhaps it is."

"A good catch," continued the Ningan, "or we might read that as 'a successful plan.' And two 'wild strips' here at the rod's end."

"What does that position signify?" asked the Merchant.

"Something that may or may not come to pass," said Ammur Ningan.

"Give the reading!" said Tiath.

"A dead person," said Ammur softly, "and a sailor."

"It is a simple enough warning," said Tiath, amused. "Take care that none of your crew fall overboard, Mattroyan. No dead person can interfere with our plan."

Ammur set aside the resin-rod and the bowl. Then all three, the Great Elder, the High Steward and the Merchant, began to talk. The sound of their voices went on and on, a natural sound, like the night wind curling about the sky-houses of the city.

1

A New Voice

DORN, THE YOUNG SCRIBE, has asked me to tell the story of my time in the islands. I will explain how I came there and who traveled with me on the Great Ocean Sea; I will describe the strange beings we found there. They were not Moruians, neither are they devils or Spirit Warriors, but rather they are "of a new mark," or of a different pattern, beings somewhat like ourselves. When I talk of them in this way, it seems too cold: they are my friends Karen-Ru, Lisa and Sam Deg. Their fourth member, whom they mourned as dead, is Scott Gale, who fell in with other Moruians in the mountains and joined the family called Brin's Five.

Dorn Brinroyan tells me that all this is part of the history of our world, Torin. He works hard at these tales; I have seen him sitting in his tower room at the New Academy longing for the mountains as he tells of them. If this is the work of a scribe, I am not at all sure that I am the right hammer for the rock . . . but on the other hand I have spent many hours doing uncomfortable work.

Mine is a new voice. I cannot speak of the mountains, of the river Troon and its wild creatures. I have not spent much time in the "beautiful high-woven city of Rintoul."

I was not a member of a Five, I did not weave; I would not know the ancient traditions of our world, "the old threads," if I tripped over them in the dark. I am a miner, the child of miners. My name is Yolo Harn. I come from Tsagul, the Fire-Town.

Tsagul, whatever anyone says, is not a bad place. It is an ancient city, older than Rintoul, and has its own laws and its own legends. We are the fire people, the Tsamuia, who lived in caves not in tents, who made pottery and worked metal from the beginning of the world. When one of our children was shown from its mother's pouch, it was held up naked in the light of the fire and a bronze amulet was laid on its breast.

The fear of fire-metal-magic, which lies like mist over the land of Torin, is not our fear. It was laid upon us by the rich clans of the southeast and their vassals and the wandering weavers who live on their lands. They have kept our roofs low and our people poor . . . and so on. This was the mixture of legend and politics I had from Old Harn on winters' nights by our fire. I don't know, even now, how much of this is true.

I do know that Tsagul is a solid workaday town laid out by generations of folk who knew their business. The houses, round or flat, are warm in winter and cool in summer; the drains work when they are not blocked. There are trees on Canal Prospect and a huge park to the west around the old Tsatroy palace. Overhead the coppery trails of the voice wire run from the City Hall and the sickhouse and the jail to the pitheads in the west and the north. To the east runs the red road, broad and straight, heading for Rintoul.

There is more traffic out of Tsagul along that road than ever comes in. All day long the wheeled carts and gangs of porters bear out metal, already worked or red raw the way we grub it from the earth. Rintoul could not exist without Tsagul.

I am a Child of the City. I know every inch of the streets, which begin as broad swept ways and end as teeming blocked lanes. I have climbed onto the rooftops as the Great Sun set to see the fleet sail home. I have heard the miners singing through the streets in the bright light of the Far Sun, carrying their baskets to the early shift. I have watched the gliders take off from the catapult in Wing-Up-Way.

I know how to trip the traces of a pedal cab, then rush up and help the Hauler get them set again, for a credit. I have been in the crowd on Market Round before City Hall to hear the Deputy speak and old Margan Dohtroy, the local grandee.

I was a Child of the City: that was my official designation. My parents, my mother and her partner, were killed in a cave-in on the old Tsatroy copper shelf when I was four years shown. I was raised in a waif-house on Tin Lane, by the docks, by Old Harn and his sib Morritt.

They were kind folk, and they became my true family; I took their name and will not set down the name of my poor young pouch mother and my young father. Morritt Harn had been a "mountain-mover" down on the wharves . . . one of the omor who carry huge high loads balanced by a head strap. She was running to fat when I first came to them but still strong enough to lift a small mountain. Old Harn . . . What can I say of him?

He had nearly lost the use of one hand, which was thin and hooked like a bird's talons. His eyes were long slits of coppery brown in his bony face. He worked three days out of five at City Hall emptying the rubbish baskets and earned further credits for waif-keeping. He had to work because there had been a snarl-up over pensions for the irrigation workers.

Old Harn was proud and clever; he had worked harder than any three persons during his long life. He was wise and he was foolish. He drove me mad with his talk of "uvoro," of freedom, when his proudest possession was a medal for special service on the irrigation projects. No pension, just a medal. He railed at grandees and pit-bosses, yet he worshiped the Deputy, Tsorl-U-Tsorl, as if this were Telve the fire spirit in person.

"One of the best," he used to say, "the Deputy is one of the best."

A great deal of what I did came from Old Harn. He was a rare bird; he was indeed "one of the best." His will, his dreams of freedom, carried me a long, strange way, all the way to the Fire Islands.

There was one other waif at Harn's house. Len was a male, older than myself, and I loved him as if he were my true sib. I ran after him and was pleased if he let me ride in his wheeled cart. He seemed to me enormously strong and clever. I can see now that he was always discontented. He remembered his own family and spun me long yarns about them.

It hurt Len to be a City-Child, a waif; he felt dishonored. When Len told me of his house, the good food, the woven pictures, the mats, the trips to fairs on the river Datse, I was vaguely discontented myself. I remembered my own parents: I remembered sitting up in the sleeping bag, eagerly, as these two young persons came striding into the room with their baskets. I had a bad memory too that turned into a nightmare. I sat up in the darkness of early morning and no one came. I sat alone for hours, and the neighbors would not set foot in the house because it was accursed. I was alone with only furtive knockings and footsteps outside the door.

Once, when I thought of this bad time, I ran to Morritt as she sat at the hearth mending fishnets for a few credits. I hugged her and said, "Was I always in this house?"

She gave me a strange look that hardly suited her fat, cheerful face. "You are the fish who swam into our net," she said. "You were brought to Harn's house by the warm south wind."

"Slag!" grumbled Old Harn, chewing at his bara seeds. "Slag and ashes! The child knows well enough how she came here."

"Do you think no one can spin fancy yarns in this house except yourself?" Morritt asked, grinning.

In the darkness beyond the hearth, Len sat and watched and said nothing.

When he was fourteen and I was nine, Len shipped with a salt vessel plying far beyond Rintoul. He promised to come back and bring Morritt a fine mat and a bag of salt, but we never saw him again. I was sad and hoped for whole years that he would come. The ache and the waiting became part of me; there was a loneliness behind my eyes that kept me a little apart from other people. I believed that every good thing must end, that every beloved person was taken and did not return. There was a children's singing game that we played in the streets on summer evenings and the chorus rang true for me:

"To wel welangar,
To tsa ulstarn."

"Every tall tree withers away,
Every fire is put out."

I ran wild in summer through the burned streets; in
winter I sat arguing with Old Harn by the fire. I went to
school, if you could call it that, four mornings out of five
at the Free Round on Canal Prospect. At thirteen I was the
tallest in my tally. The recruiters came, and I signed up for
the New Cut Mine. Old Harn had hoped for something
better: apprentice silversmith or maybe a job with a stone
mason. I was happy to be out of school, swinging along
to the New Cut—which was fifty years old—with my new
basket.

For four years, until my luck ran out, I worked at the
New Cut, and these were the happiest years of my young
life. I had my friends, my workmates at the mine, and I
had credits to give my family. We really did have mats and
good food and a trip now and then.

We went to the fairs up the Datse and to the Tsatroy
Old Park. There I saw the flower pools and the menagerie;
I wandered with my sibs through the wide courtyards of
the old palace and laid good luck skeins upon those two
white monuments, the cairns of Tell and Geran, the young
children of mad Elbin Tsatroy. I joined in the festivals of
the Fire-Town: I danced the Great Round in spring and
saw the Lighting of Torches for the New Year.

I started on loading at the mine and went quickly on
to hauling. Morritt, who knew the tricks of the trade, oiled
my aching muscles and fed me the strength foods. I ate
egg pasty, salt meat, fish cake, green nettles . . . even "red
devil." This is a kind of blood sausage seasoned with fire-
weed; it comes from the scrub deer they farm on the Datse
and it is a luxury . . . one credit for a fist length.

It was taken for granted in our house that I should become an omor . . . a worker who carries no child in her
pouch and founds no family. There has been a lot of
nonsense talked about the omor here in Tsagul and in the
rest of Torin. The bush weavers find a childless female a
pretty strange creature; the other city workers are jealous
of the omor's strength. They mutter about secret cults and
magical ceremonies.

I will say this: anyone can be strong given good food
and training at the right age. This great increase in strength
and muscle often occurs when a worker comes from the

country to the town and does different work and eats city food. Strong muscles will grow, and part of it is wanting to be strong. The other part, for an omor, is not a matter of magic but of medicine, whatever the scribes have written.

The omor have sub-guilds or circles, where likely youngsters of about sixteen receive the mixture of two herbs, the drink called Watten. It causes sterility; after one year of the Watten Cup, the drinker is an omor for life. She will never give birth to a child to carry in her pouch. That leaves one or two questions unanswered. An omor may take a mate or join a family, or she may live unmated like the hermits in the desert. It is not quite a matter of choice ... it is a choice far beyond our eyes. My luck ran out, however, before I had this choice. I had taken one drink of the Watten Cup, no more, at the Circle Blue, among the omor who worked at the New Cut.

II

I was more than sixteen years shown, tall and strong. I had moved from hauling to cutting on the seam, and I was sometimes employed on the crushers. I had two friends, Warkor and Clee, and we worked as a team. Clee was about my age, he was thin and dark and strong-willed; Warkor took care of us both—she called us her cubs. I like to remember those two out of all the miners, but there is one other I recall: Tenn the Overseer.

This was an oversized brute who made our lives a misery. Everyone knew Tenn for a mean creature. There was a loose pile near our adit and a go-slow one morning until it was shored up. There was an argument that developed into a quarrel, then into a near riot. Our team had no real part in it.

One moment I was standing with my team holding my basket and minding my own business, the next the Overseers came in "to restore order." Tenn began beating Clee with his whip handle; I took up a stone and struck one blow. I can still feel the blow as I struck; I knew instantly that Tenn was badly hurt, maybe dead. My luck had run out.

I don't like to set this down. The pen shakes in my hand. I still turn cold with fear and see the faces of my comrades on that wintery morning. I still see the bloody stone

where I cast it aside. I feel bitter shame for wounding
Tenn. He was Tenn Tennroyan, head of a family, a miner
like myself. How can I call him a brute if I am not one myself? Oh, it was an accident, a starfall, a knot in the thread
of life, but I was deeply dishonored and felt that my own
life had come to an end.

I stood there unable to move while Tenn was carried
away; I was arrested and taken to the mine "rest house,"
then to the city jail. I spent days shivering and staring at
the wall in spite of the extra blanket Morritt brought me.
I can't remember what I said to the scribe who had been
sent to speak for me by the miners' guild. My case was an
embarrassment: the whole thing had come at a bad time
and had political overtones because of the wrangling about
pay and the go-slow at the pithead.

Destiny is the cobblestone that trips us on the way to a
feast; it is the one brick that holds up the wall; it is the
silver amulet that turns up in the belly of a fish. This was
a three-comet year. As I shifted my gaze from the cell wall
to the cell window, I might have seen a comet fly past or
Scott Gale's small airship blast across the continent to the
mountains and descend into the Warm Lake on Hingstull
Mountain.

At this time too Tsorl-U-Tsorl, the Deputy, lost his
fight with the Council; he was not the first good Deputy to
be flung out of office or the last. Tsorl was dismissed and
charged with stealing city funds. He was dishonored; there
was talk of a death-pact between him and his team of personal helpers. No one knew what had become of him.

Old Harn did not know of this at first. He sat about in
the cold anterooms waiting to intercede with Tsorl for me,
for Yolo his foster child, but he never saw the Deputy.
Tsorl had gone, and Old Harn went home to Tin Lane and
began to cough. He died toward the end of the winter.
I could hardly weep when Morritt brought me the news;
I was alone in my cell of misfortune with footsteps beyond
the door.

My case had been dealt with more or less fairly. I was
sentenced to ten years in jail for wounding; it was a light
sentence because of my youth. It might have been lighter
still if I could have paid compensation to Tenn, who was
an invalid, and his family. But I had nothing. The sentence
sounded to me like a lifetime, but this was partly a young
person's impatience with periods of time. I knew that the

dishonor of such a deed would last far beyond any sentence.
I sat in my cell and was taken out every day to the work-
rooms of the jail to learn weaving at a mat loom. There was
talk of passing the sack for me at Circle Blue to raise some
compensation and lighten my load. But the time was so bad
nothing came of it; before New Year, they reasoned, there
will be an amnesty.

There was an amnesty, and this is a thing I remember
very well. About twenty days before New Year, the prisoners serving "fives" or "double fives"—those of us who
had been recently sentenced—were brought down to the
dining hall. There were about a hundred persons; we stood
there while the Head Ward read from a skein. It appeared
that our gracious neighbors, the clansfolk of Rintoul, that
golden city, had need of vassals. The noble trade partners
of Tsagul, in particular Clan Luntroy, were on the look-
out for strong workers to take the bond.

Our numbers were reduced even further; I was nudged
into the "strong" group. I looked far up the curtain walls
of the old jail and saw on a balcony in one of the folds a
flash of color. The scene was very gray: we wore gray
cloth, the walls were gray; so, I guess, were our faces. But
on the balcony leaned a couple of grandees in flame and
purple and blue. Beside the Head Ward stood two senior
vassals with the flax flowers of Luntroy on their chests.

Luntroy is not a clan with a bad reputation in our part
of the world, but the fiery colors of those pale-skinned
fools watching us kindled at last a fire in my brain. We
were being tricked into exchanging one jail term for a lifetime of bondage. The clansfolk were playing on our sense
of dishonor. I thought of the new-made vassals trundling
back with their masters over the long red road that leads
from the Fire-Town to Rintoul.

My name was called early; I saw the Head Ward smile
at the senior vassals. I knew I was accepted before they
gave me the word; they were conscious of doing me a kindness. I cleared my throat and spoke up in public for the
first time in my life.

"Good Citizen Ward," I said, loud enough to reach the
balcony, "what will happen if I do not take this bond?"

The Head Ward was dumbfounded and angry; there was
a flapping of skeins at the high table.

"By the fire, Yolo Harn," said the Ward, "anyone so

careless of Luntroy bounty and the good name of Tsagul
might well do a term at Itsik!"

Itsik . . . a filthy place to the southeast where prisoners
are sent for punishment. The work is foul and backbreak-
ing, and the smell is unbearable; it is compounded of hides
and tallow and the tanning vats and rotting fish, but worst
of all is the stench of dishonor. The whole room, prisoners,
vassals, even the grandees broke into nervous laughter.
I thought of Old Harn and his damned medal, and I knew
at last what freedom meant.

"As you decide," I said firmly, "for I will not be a vassal.
I don't accept this amnesty!"

The Head Ward cut my name from the skein with the
flick of a knife blade. Luntroy had one less vassal; a link
was forged in the chain; a brick kept the wall standing; the
stars whirled fiery in their courses. I was sent to Itsik
fifteen days before the New Year.

2

Itsik

I HAD THOUGHT OF WALKING TO ITSIK by way of the red road for it lies between Tsagul and Rintoul, but instead we went by sea. Two other prisoners went to Itsik at the same time as I did, and we were marched down to the docks as night fell. It was a long walk through the warm sunset streets; I felt as if I were marching back through the byways of my own childhood. There were the familiar alleys, the scurrying children, the gliders at rest in their hangars in quiet Wing-Up-Way.

The guards paused for a snack at the corner of Mill Way and passed out fresh bean bread and small beer to their charges. A few children were still at play, and they sang the song that I remembered. It was part of a long singing game called "Crazy Elbin," addressed to the mad old grandee Elbin Tsatroy. "Where are you going, Crazy Elbin?" asks the song and the reply rings out . . . to the Mountains, to Rintoul, to the river Troon, to the Salt Marshes. The verse that appealed to me most was the one they sang now:

> "Ban ulrin, ban ulrin,
> Dan O dan, dandar . . ."

> *"Going to the islands,*
> *So green, green, green . . ."*

As we were marched off again the chorus rang out, dark and mocking:

> *"To wel welangar,*
> *To tsa ulstarn . . ."*

> *"Every tall tree withers away,*
> *Every fire is put out."*

I walked now at the end of a rope behind two older prisoners called Red and Grabber. Every prisoner in the City Jail chose or was given a new name, a gavje or bad-luck name. I was called Cub. Everyone knew what I had done . . . my crime and the reason I was being sent to Itsik for half a year. I had no idea what Red had done; she was a tall, bony omor, and I had a notion she was in jail for theft, thieving from the docks. Grabber was a short, misshapen creature, and although he stumped along patiently now, with a grin on his broad face, it was obvious to everyone that he was mad. Every so often he went into a kind of slow frenzy and grabbed whatever was nearest to him, especially if it moved, and hung on until someone threw water in his face or felled him to the ground.

We shuffled through the crowded docks, and a few voices called farewell to Red out of the shadows. There was no one who knew me, and I was glad. Morritt had come to me before the amnesty, full of hope, smiling again. She had work with a family out of town, on the Datse. She told me to keep up my spirits; the time would pass more quickly than I thought. I was happy for her and happy that she knew nothing about this next piece of dishonor that I had woven into the skein.

We were led up the gangplank of a big low-slung craft and settled under an awning on the afterdeck. The ship was just about to cast off; the anchor was winched up, and the sails, dank and black, were already set. The guards had gone. The Captain did not come near the little knot of prisoners, but presently, as the ship edged down the harbor, the Rope Ward, or second officer, came aft with a couple of sailors.

He peered at us in the light of a lantern; he was a young

male, very tall, with long blood-colored hair in a plait down his back and an enveloping canvas cloak. He did not look unfriendly.

"Hold on tight if the weather gets up," he said.

"Don't tell that to Grabber for the fire's sake," said Red hoarsely.

"Oh, is that him?" asked the Rope Ward.

Grabber groaned and rolled his eyes. He was already seasick, although the boat was only halfway down the broad bight of the harbor.

Suddenly I stood up. I was drawn to my feet by a great feeling of joy that overrode everything else. A tow-haired sailor by the rail had turned his head, and I saw that it was Len.

"Len!" I called. "Len Harn. . . ."

I was hardly conscious of the Rope Ward and the other prisoners watching me; it was Len, my dear sib, exactly as I had seen him in dreams. I did not know or care how I looked, in prison gray, grown out of recognition, almost, for now I was as tall as Len and more heavily muscled. The tow-haired sailor walked toward me, peering in the dim light, and I saw that he knew me. He did not speak.

"I am Yolo . . ." I said, still brimming with my discovery.

"I am Len Alroyan," said the sailor; "there is no Len Harn."

"Len . . . do you know me?"

"I know we take prisoners to Itsik!"

He turned his back and walked away.

I sat down again, and the pain I felt seemed worse than anything in my life. Even the horror of what I had done to Tenn the Overseer, my crime, did not match this terrible sorrow. I bent my head and felt tears run down my cheeks. If I had not been tied with rope, I might have plunged into the sea and made an end of my wretched life. I felt a hand on the shoulder and saw that it was the Rope Ward.

"I think you are a good sailor," he said, "and if the weather gets up you can take a turn on the ropes."

He was trying to comfort me. I managed to reply, and he went away with the lantern, leaving us in darkness, with a fresh breeze tearing at the awning.

We sailed out of the bight of Tsagul into a growing storm. The salt boat wallowed in black waves that washed right over the decks; clouds hid the Far Sun when it rose.

I forgot everything but the wind and the waves and their battle with the ship. We moved to the gutter at the length of our ropes so that poor Grabber could be sick, and soon he had nothing left. He lay on the deck groaning more loudly than the ship's timbers.

The conch that counted the hours could scarcely be heard, but I judged that it was about the first hour of morning when the Rope Ward sent a sailor to untie me. She offered to take Red, too, but the omor was almost as sick as Grabber. I followed the sailor into the waist of the ship and was set to rolling a huge sail that had been thrown down unreefed. I did this, with other sailors, then I was given a place at the long sea-brake, a kind of wooden fin that we held at angles to the ship to still her wild passage into the open sea.

I managed to shout to my neighbor, "Where is Itsik?"

"Flaming miles to the southeast!" she roared. "We are so far off-course we will come to the Islands if the storm doesn't let up!"

We wrestled for hours with the sea-brake and were given strength from a leather drinking skin of thin tipsy mash, passed from hand to hand. Then a cry went up, and we ducked for cover: a scream of breaking wood came from high overhead and a length of the foremast, tall as a young tree, crashed to the deck. The Sail Ward and the Rope Ward waded in with axes, cutting it free.

Still the wind did not abate and we sailed on, fighting with the sea-brake and the tackle, washed up to our ears with the icy sea and deafened by the wind and the rain. At last a smear of light appeared in the east and the wind suddenly died away. The ship hung in the water like a rotten log in the light of Esto, the Great Sun.

I hung gasping over the rail and watched the colors return to the world. The sea became greenish gold, then an oily gray-green, and the sky overhead was blue-white. Far to the southwest hung a thick green haze.

"Yes," said the Rope Ward, at my side, "those are the Fire Islands."

"Have you sailed there?" I asked.

"A few times."

We stood quietly at the rail, and he gave me bara seeds to chew. The chill of the night had passed, and the deck was steaming in the heat of the new day. I pointed ahead;

something moved on the surface of the water, too low for
a boat but not a piece of flotsam.

"What's that?"

"Muck raft," said the Rope Ward. "Towed out from
Itsik, or even from Rintoul, and put into the Round Current."

He told me the path of the great Round Current that
moved in an arc from the continent of Torin, through the
islands and back again. He stared at me curiously for a
moment, and I saw that his eyes were green.

He said, "Yolo Harn, you sail well. You've been a help
to us this voyage."

"I don't get seasick." I grinned.

"The muck rafts go all through the spring and summer,"
he said. "I knew a sailor once, sent to Itsik for wounding.
He stowed away on one of those things. . . ."

"And he came to the islands?"

"I reckon he had a good chance."

"But the rafts will be searched if it is so easy!"

The Rope Ward laughed.

"It's not easy! The Itsik folk are afraid of the sea and
of the islands and suffocated by their dishonor. There are
mainly runaway vassals at Itsik. But you . . ."

"Well, I'm surely no vassal!" I said.

He put a hand on my shoulder and turned back to his
work.

"Better go back to the awning," he said.

I found that I was bone weary, but as I struggled back
to my place on the afterdeck, I understood a strange thing.
The Rope Ward liked me in a special way that no one had
done in my life before. I was puzzled and not displeased;
I thought of his green eyes and felt his hand warm on my
shoulder.

I reached the tattered awning where Red and Grabber
lay sleeping and crawled under it. I slept soundly on the
steaming deck of the salt boat as the crew made shift to
bring it about and head back toward Itsik.

II

The weather held for the next day and night, and we
sailed into Itsik under a clear sky with the two suns shining. The sight of the place surprised me. I had nothing but

a confused idea of filth and stench and dirty work buildings like a bad pithead. Itsik was clean and neatly laid out
in a series of half-circles, one beyond the other. Between
each crescent and the next was a high stockade. The first
stockade shut off the tip of the peninsula, leaving it open
only to the sea, by the paved docks. In the next crescent
there were thick groves of bara trees with glossy dark
green leaves and stems that were rendered down for oil.
Beyond that there seemed to be folds for wool-deer, a small
village, with weavers' tents strung over the redwood trees.

The smell was certainly real. Even now in the early
morning it hung over Itsik like a cloud. There was already
a shift working in the big tannery shed on the left of the
main compound. Red, who had served at Itsik before,
pointed out the tallow works, and on the right the mess
hall, the sleeping huts, the sickhouse. I asked about a
small inner compound behind the sickhouse.

"Punishment Block!" Red spat on the deck. "But don't
worry, it's mainly used for the Specials."

I didn't ask any more questions because I thought the
Specials might be mad persons. Grabber was very subdued
still and as sensible as he ever was, but I didn't want to
upset him. I had one hope . . . to get away from these
two as soon as possible and work beside someone else.

We stood at the rail unroped and carrying our gray
pouches of personal possessions slung across our bodies—
these are called "mothers" in prison slang and the word so
used is highly indecent. To my surprise Len came up beside me as we stood there. He was gruff and embarrassed; I
wondered if the Rope Ward had made him speak to me,
but I believe it was his own memory of Harn's house. He
pointed out the officers' block and the flensing shed, right
down on the dock. Workers were hacking away at tall
blocks of some whitish substance. Suddenly I saw
bones. . . .

"Great fire!" I whispered. "Is that a sea-sunner they have
killed?"

"Winds forbid," said Len, "they are sacred beasts. That
is a toben, a kind of large fish."

We talked at the rail for some time, quietly and naturally.
I could hardly believe that this was Len and that I had
lived through the long years since he went away from
Harn's house. But it was Len, and he had hardly altered:

he was still that proud, boastful child. I seemed to have
grown much older.

Before we parted, he slipped me a small package wrapped
in a square of brown oiled silk.

"Hide it well," he said. "In your boot, maybe. You can
trade it better than silver credits. It is brown bark,
'smack.'"

Smack was precious. It is a spice that adds taste to food
and makes the smack-eater a little tipsy. I thanked Len as
warmly as I could. The ship had docked; I came to Itsik
and did not look back at the ship to wave farewell to Len
or to the Rope Ward.

The wharf had become more crowded; workers were
loading hides and tallow onto the salt boat. I was surprised
again, this time by workers' clothes. These cargo movers
were all strong, with the sullen look of prisoners, but their
clothes had the look of ragged finery, the castoff clothes of
grandees. Clan colors—Wentroy green, Galtroy crimson—
blossomed on their striped cloaks; a few had tousled wigs
of fake hair or leather vests trimmed with fur.

A guard wearing an old Pentroy banner over his cloak
collected us and took us to be hosed down. In the receiving
depot there were more of these colored clothes, clean and of
such a weave as I had seldom seen, but I kept my own
gray and was marked out as a Tsagul prisoner.

Grabber had fully recovered from the voyage. Just as
the sickhouse team arrived to check us over, he went into
a fit and seized a clothing rack. Red and I stood back as the
guards tried to pry him loose. A sharp, querulous voice
rang out.

"Stop that, you fools! Let it alone!"

An extraordinary creature bustled into sight: a female,
short, wiry, with long skeins of dirty white hair tied in
bunches. She wore an old vented robe kilted up about her
skinny legs, and her patched half-cloak was hung around
with bunches of herbs, grips and scissors and shell knives.
I recognized the brown of Clan Dohtroy, our own local
grandees, and the crest of Dohtroy, flower and gourd, was
embroidered on her shabby pectoral.

"Who's that, for the fire's sake?" I whispered to Red.

"The Forgan of Itsik, our Healer," said Red. "That is
Gwell Nu—mad Gwell . . ."

Gwell Nu approached poor Grabber and examined him
briefly. She twitched a shell knife from her belt, and I saw

her make a scratch on his arm—which he did not notice at all—and rub in some salve. In a few heartbeats Grabber was fast asleep. I looked at the Healer with respect. If Gwell was mad, it was a kind of madness that worked like good sense.

She was pleased to see new arrivals from Tsagul and greeted Red like an old friend.

"What's this then? Cub? Yolo Harn?" she cackled when my turn came. "You may call yourself what you will, my dear. Always pleased to see strong young workers from the Fire-Town. How goes good Orn Margan Dohtroy? Peace to the good liege's house. Keep to yourself . . . don't mix with this rabble from the Rintoul clans. I'll see you right, child."

She knotted at my skein.

"Woodcutting detail!" she called to the guards, and closed one huge tawny eye in a hideous wink.

The guard called back cheerfully: "Privilege! You're doing favors for Dohtroy landfolk!"

"You can count on it!" said Gwell Nu. "A worker from Tsagul like this Cub here is worth two of your Rintoul runaways!"

So I came to the cleanest work on Itsik through the privilege of Clan Dohtroy, and I put aside my principles to the point of wearing a brown hood, the Dohtroy color. In the crazy world of Itsik it helped to do such things. For Itsik was like a history of Old Torin acted out by a troupe of street players.

It was designed and run by clever builders and makers of engines, who were themselves often former vassals, some of the half-blood, children of a grandee male and a "common" female. The prisoners, who did the work of Itsik, were mainly vassals dismissed from service or sent for punishment. These benighted creatures, right from Boss Black, the Pentroy half-blood who ruled from the second compound, to the humblest runaway, still kept their allegiance to the clans that had cast them out and sent them to the place of dishonor. Even the common criminals, the scourings of the city of Rintoul, found it wise to choose a clan and wear its colors.

We worked hard on Itsik, by the light of the sun and of the Far Sun. We had our own strength foods: toben fish or tough salted meat from the old wool-deer killed for their hides. I did well on Itsik in spite of the petty clan battles and the endless gossip about noble families. I led my wood-cutting team in five days and soon took control of our mess mat. My workmates were the younger prisoners, young vassals, misfits, dazed by the long hours, the bullying and the dishonor.

I did well on Itsik, and I hated the place more deeply and bitterly every day. Every blow I struck, every exercise of power, every shouted command, reminded me that I was Cub, the successful bully. I had been sentenced for wounding, and I was condemned to repeat my crime in some small way every hour that passed. The stink of Itsik, for me, had nothing to do with hides or tallow or toben blubber.

One morning in Esder light, before the Great Sun rose, there was a bad accident in the bara plantation. A heavily laden skip full of the glossy leaves and oily branches came off its wooden track and landed on a work party. I did what had to be done. Hauled the skip aside, gave the alarm, chivvied my poor shocked team into uncovering the victims. I did what I could for the injured; one omor was badly cut with her own axe—I staunched the flow of blood. I worked like a devil until Gwell Nu and her aides came to help, and I went on helping them all morning.

As I washed my hands from the gourd in the first sickhouse, Gwell Nu snuffled beside me.

"You did well, Yolo Harn, my dear. You did almost too well!"

"Too well?"

"Perhaps you will be recommended for a guard, my dear; what do you think of that? A guard, a helper, who remains when it is out of time and works at Itsik for credits."

My face must have betrayed my horror at this idea; Gwell Nu laughed sadly.

"It is not a bad life," she said.

She filled two beakers with water, added a pinch of herbs and handed one to me. We sat on a high sleeping platform—this first sickhouse was half empty.

"A guard may live in the second or even the third compound. Many of them found or join Fives. They love to follow the old threads."

"I'll bet they do," I said grimly.

"It is an honor difficult to refuse," she said. "I have known a sentence to lengthen, a day here, ten days there, until the half year became a year—and the offers were repeated until the prisoner accepted."

"That is vile injustice."

"Most things are," said Gwell Nu.

I knew how she had come to Itsik. Years ago she had run off up the Datse and left the house service of old Ton Dohtroy. This grandee was well known in Tsagul for his kind patronage, yet he had cast aside and wasted this wise servant.

We drank the water, and it was sweet and delicious with the herb she had added.

"Cheer up!" she said. "I will order you to be my Night Watch. I need one with a strong back and good nerves."

I went out and broke four rules immediately so that I earned five lashes. I hoped that I would receive no rewards for good behavior in this place. I spent a few more shifts woodcutting, then I became Gwell Nu's Night Watch. She usually employed a "Dohtroy" omor for this task, and indeed all her helpers tended to wear brown. The sickhouse work was interesting and it did not make me queasy: Itsik is not an unhealthy place and most of the cases were work accidents. I relished the talks with Gwell Nu in the long, silver-lit night hours.

"What are the Specials?" I asked, one night. "I have asked, but I get no straight answer."

"Truly, my dear, your old devil of a foster father, Harn, would call them political prisoners," said Gwell Nu. "There are never very many. One or two come in under Secret Hand . . . a clan method for shutting a person up secretly, no questions asked."

"Gwell Nu, when the clans do so much wrong, how can you cleave to a clan?"

"Dohtroy is not a bad clan," she said.

We had no secrets.

"Escape on a muck raft, my dear? Well, it might be possible if you have something to bribe the guard on cargo duty."

"I would not be stealing from the cargo shed."

"It would be a cover . . . a round of food pinching on the dock."

"Gwell Forgan, do you know anything of the islands?"

"Not much. They are hot and green and a few primitive Moruia live there. On the island of Tsabeggan, the Nearest Fire, there is a stone villa, raised in old time by the distant mothers of the Tsatroy clan."

"Tsatroy was once a great clan, so Harn told me, and now there are only small pockets of their land remaining: the old Palace in Tsagul, this villa, which I had not heard of . . . and Sarunin, the place of ashes. . . ."

"Every fire is put out," said Gwell Nu. "I heard of the Last Battle at Sarunin from an old Tsatroy vassal serving out its time when I first came here."

It was a cold, sad tale, one that I thought I knew well: long after the clan wars, in fact only ten or eleven fives of years ago, the clans Tsatroy and Pentroy fought over a land dispute. The Tsatroy host were encamped in a valley between Itsik and Tsagul, not far from the present course of the red road. In a day and a night the whole army died in its camp, accursed, some said, or poisoned; the Tsatroy leaders burned and buried their dead, then went into the fire themselves, died burning in their silken tents. The place was deeply defiled, and the curse had never been lifted.

"Gwell Nu," I asked now, "what killed those poor warriors?"

"Red-wither," she said promptly. "Summer Plague. I am sure it was that. The Tsatroy lieges did right to burn out the camp as a purification."

"I wonder if it was this thing that turned the wits of Crazy Elbin," I said. "What became of her? Perhaps she did run off to the islands as the singing game tells us. . . ."

Gwell Nu gave me a sad, sly look.

"No, my dear, not so far. Elbin Elbinroyan Tsatroy lies in a firestone grave behind the Special Compound. She spent her last days there, the poor old Highness, courtesy of the Pentroy."

"Gwell Forgan," I said shuddering, "come with me. Come away from this terrible place. . . ."

"Child, I am too old, and I am needed here. Where would the poor dears get another Forgan, even a mad one?"

"You are not mad!"

"If I stay on Itsik, who knows?"

It was a day at the end of spring, a day of light rains. I came on duty as Night Watch and found Coth, a male sick aide, cleaning up after an operation. I knew it must

have been a serious one because Gwell Nu sat on a sleeping
platform tired out, flexing her thin hands.

"Keep watch on it," said Coth. "She wants it to pull
through, but for all her skill I think the poor devil is done
for."

"Where was it cut?"

"Left leg amputated below the joint. An old chain
wound that had turned ravenous."

We were in the cutting tent: not really a tent but a
wicker-roofed oval house, like all the sickhouses. I went
and laid cooling chest cloths wrung out in herb water on
the patient. An old male with no clan markings. A cloth
full of sleeping medicine still covered the face. I wondered
vaguely if this were some new arrival, then went about my
watch. I went up and down the sickhouses and gave out
cool drinks or settled some patient more comfortably. I
came back to the amputee and worked on him again. He
lay like the dead, but his skin was cool, dry and healthy.

In the loneliest hour of the night, with clouds hiding
the Far Sun, I came back to the cutting tent again and
found Gwell Nu rested. She had made a sweet drink.

"It will live, I think," she said. "It is strong as Telve the
spirit warrior."

"New prisoner?"

"No, my dear." She grinned. "Not very new. It is one of
your Specials."

I was more interested. We stood beside the sleeping
platform, and Gwell Nu lifted the covers and stared at the
stump of the left leg, bound and daubed with healing
plaster. I stared at the strong arms, with metal bracelets,
the leather vest; something began to sing in my head.
Gwell Nu saw me staring, and she reached out and lifted
the cloth from the face. I felt breath hiss into my mouth.
It was impossible, but it had happened. All the links were
forged in the chain, and I saw my destiny clear and in-
escapable in that moment. The special prisoner had a strong,
handsome face wisped with gray hair on the cheeks. I
had heard him speak more than once. It was Tsorl-U-
Tsorl, the former Deputy of Tsagul.

3

The Way to Freedom

GWELL NU LISTENED WITH HOODED EYES when I told her the identity of the patient. I was full of plans, but I did not tell them all, there was no need: she guessed what I wanted to do. We spent another night and another going about the normal work of the sickhouse. Tsorl-U-Tsorl was not permitted to wake fully.

"What kills after a cutting," explained Gwell Nu, "is a kind of bodily fear. He must have sleep."

I sat by the Deputy's sleeping platform, and once or twice his eyes rested on me. He spoke in a deep, rumbling voice, broken words and phrases from his dreams. He cried out, "Gargan, you devil!" and sketched a blow with his open hand. Gwell Nu was watching.

"You see . . . he is in the secret hand of Tiath Gargan, the Strangler!" she whispered.

The name of the Pentroy Great Elder filled me with fear.

"Gwell Forgan, the rafts sail in three days. . . ."

"I don't hear you, my dear, I don't hear you," she chirruped.

She went flouncing off through the sickhouses, the instruments bouncing about on her shabby finery. Mad or not, Gwell Nu could be maddening. I sat beside the Deputy and he murmured softly: "Tsabeggan . . . the Nearest Fire . . ." as if he had heard my thoughts.

The following night when I came on watch, I thought there had been another operation for Gwell Nu was curled on a sleeping platform as if exhausted. Presently she called me.

"I reported to Boss Black on the condition of the Special patient."

"He is very strong. It is the best cutting you have done; he will live."

"I am not quite so hopeful." She grinned.

Suddenly a fit of anger seemed to shake her.

"He is condemned," she said. "My work was for nothing. He is marked down to die . . . the term is 'to wither away.' He will not be sentenced, he will simply die. . . .

"In fact," she announced, "although I shall miss my good Night Watch, I think this Tsorl is scheduled to die this very night."

"Oh Gwell Nu!" I understood her plan, and it filled me with excitement and gratitude.

We were alone in the sickhouses all through the night hours, and we managed it easily. Tsorl-U-Tsorl was surprisingly light for us to carry; we put him in a little room where Gwell Nu slept sometimes and stored her medicines. In the first light of the Great Sun, I wheeled the death cart to the Special compound, and a sleepy guard led me to the burying ground at the back. There was no sound or movement from the other huts in the block, and I guessed that Tsorl had had the place to himself.

The burying ground was beyond the stockade on a strip of land reclaimed from the sea. The ground was sandy and soft, only a few gray creeping plants grew there; a wind from the sea was always blowing, and a few seabirds drifted overhead.

The graves of the Specials were scarcely marked, but on one grave, not the oldest, some person had laid a skein of mixed red and orange. A single character was woven into the skein . . . the fire symbol. I knew who lay in this place and I called to her proud mad spirit. "Crazy Elbin . . . Nahoo, Enu Elbine . . . Give us your blessing, old Fire Mother, for we are coming to the Islands!"

The guard helped me prepare the grave: I dug a deep pit, and we wheeled out charily a metal container in a waterbath. We emptied the steaming firestone and clay mixture into the pit. Then I heaved in the long hide bundle that Gwell Nu had stitched so well "against infection." The guard went away, complaining that the whole business had spoiled her breakfast. I buried the hide bundle, which contained nothing but bara branches, as quickly as possible. Gwell Nu had prepared a skein, and I laid it on the grave. The skein read simply "Release for the prisoner," a common grave thread on Itsik, and one symbol of Tsorl's name . . . the fire symbol again, so there were two of these glyphs lying side by side. I read this for a good omen.

There was much to be done. I waited until the day shifts were at breakfast, then went to the kitchens and boldly loaded up with food. If any questions were asked, I was to say that Gwell Nu was ordering a special strength meal for all the sickhouse patients, as she was sometimes allowed to do. As it was, no one asked; I could have walked away with two carts full. I took my laden cart and wheeled it toward the sickhouse then turned aside and hid it in a stand of bushes by the stockade.

Then at last I went to my own sleeping place and slept with the other shift workers. I always worked a double shift so I was allowed to sleep a double shift, all the day in fact. For a long time I tossed and turned, eager for the night to come, and I was up again about the time the Great Sun set. I went down to the docks at their busiest time.

I had checked out the muck rafts many times since I came to Itsik, but now as I stared at them I felt a thump of fear. There were two rafts, sturdy and long, about ten body-lengths one way and twenty the other. Both were already fully laden with a mountain of food waste in the center in a rough enclosure of branches. Vats of stinking waste from the tanneries stood near this midden; on the sides, piled up high, were great clumps of bara straw, the coarse fiber that is left after the rendering of the bara trees for tallow.

There were three ships at the dock, and they suited my purpose well. One was a fruit ship from the Rintoul delta, and this gave me an excuse for bribing a guard to leave the dock—fruit ships were worth robbing. The other two ships, called *Tabel* and *Ullo*, were of the fleet of the merchant Mattroyan, a town grandee and great trader out of Rintoul. They were loading with hides and would sail at first Esto light, towing the muck rafts to the Round Current before continuing on their journey east to Rintoul or west to the Fire-Town.

I hung about and passed the time of day with Red, who was a leading stevedore. I took a chance and asked which guard might be on middle watch. She nodded at a Wentroy vassal and thought she guessed my purpose.

"Bribes like a charm," she said hoarsely, "and so do I, come to that. Come on, Cub. . . ." I gave her a credit's weight of smack from Len's package. I had not used a crumb of the stuff since I came to Itsik.

A crowd had gathered at the bow of the *Tabel,* where the cargo doors opened onto the dock. A mat had gone down, and there was a gambling ring in progress. Vassals love to gamble—perhaps they believe that only chance can help them—and the Itsik prisoners would gamble away the very food they ate. It looked as though the Mattroyan sailors were willing to take their credits if they could. I joined the crowd and saw that there was a game going on, but the main interest was a tall omor paying out bets and telling a strange tale.

"Murno Pentroy, Blacklock, everyone's favorite—second place!" she cried. "I have it on my skein here. Match this token or I cannot pay!"

A Luntroy vassal, a prisoner, matched the skein and received credits, asking plaintively: "But the winds took the good Jebbal? I made sure she would outfly flaming Blacklock this spring."

I knew then they were talking about the Bird Clan, a great air race held up country every spring for young clansfolk and others with more wealth than sense. We had already heard more than one garbled report of this contest, and the Great Air Race, as far as I was concerned, was a great bore. I was looking through the crowd for the Wentroy guard when the tale became more interesting.

"Tell us about the devil who won!" begged the crowd.

"I saw it," said the omor proudly. "I stood in the escort of our good Ullo Mattroyan, the Merchant's child, when she flew her fine machine *Tildee* into third spot."

"But the winner! The winner!"

"It was tall and strong, of a size with Blacklock. It had curly hair, dyed red-brown, but the natural color was said to be black."

"Pah, it wore a wig!"

"By the fire it did not. Persons close to it said it was a

male, and it had the look of one. Strangest thing was the eyes. . . ."

"Where did it fly from?"

"From the black heart of the void!" cried the omor. "I heard the spirit warriors, the twirlers, give out its history in their dance. 'A hero flew in a silver ship from beyond Derin, the Far World.' "

This was exciting stuff but it made me uncomfortable. I seemed to hear Old Harn's voice whispering, "Slag and ashes! Superstitious nonsense! Nothing can fly from the void. The twirlers so-called are religious tricksters, no better than beggars."

"It wore goggles to hide its eyes," the omor was saying, "and one time I saw it bare-faced. You could have tripped me with a thread. The eyes were small and round and bright blue."

The crowd gasped with awe and disbelief; I shuddered at such an unnatural thought. It seemed too fantastic for the omor to have invented. Then as I spotted the guard I wanted and moved to his side, the omor said something even more frightening.

"It has a nest of its own kind in the islands."

I made some sound of fear, and the Wentroy guard said: "Cheer up, Cub Dohtroy, they won't come to Itsik!"

"I hope not," I said. "Friend guard . . . I see there is a fruit boat and it has put melons in the main shed. . . ."

"Greedy young beggar," said the guard. "What are you after then?"

"If a certain person on the middle watch were to take a walk about the third hour of morning . . ."

"I don't walk for nothing." He grinned.

We haggled then, and I gave him a pinch of smack and closed the deal for four credits' weight. I went off to supper with the day shift, wrestling with the fear of what I planned to do that night and with a host of new fears. *A nest of devils in the Islands.*

But the hatred of Itsik was stronger than any fear. I looked cautiously at the prisoners eating their supper and the thought of not being with them the following day was enough to make me dare anything. Indeed I felt so kind that I was on the point of giving away my food or at least not taking more than my share, as was expected of a bully. This was too unusual: I snatched a fistful of bean loaf and made the whole mat cringe for the last time.

Gwell Nu was waiting with instructions and a bag of medicine. She had an even stranger look than usual and laughed when I came into the sickhouse.

"You look mad as myself," she said. "You are afraid, my dear."

"Not too much afraid."

"This is a mad venture," she said, "and if you and this old fellow are drowned in the first good-sized wave, it will be my doing."

"We will not drown."

We went about our ordinary work and tended to the Deputy, who slept quietly in his hiding place. I said to Gwell Nu at the first hour of morning:

"Have you heard about this Strange Being who flew in the Bird Clan Air Race?"

"Yes," said Gwell Nu, "I have heard about Strange Beings, from Boss Black himself, but I cannot believe any of it."

"This person is a Moruian . . . a fake?"

"What else? Consider, child, what it would take to come here from the void. We have strong engines and might have even stronger ones if the clans wished it, but we would be hard put even to fly around the globe of Torin."

"These beings might have much stronger engines!"

"I cannot believe that there are creatures so much more clever than the race of the Moruia. And if there were and they could fly around Torin high in the air, higher than glider or balloon, why would they land in the Islands? Why not approach Rintoul?"

"Have you heard that too . . . they are in the Islands?"

"It is all fluff and rubbish," said Gwell Nu gently.

"Perhaps they would be afraid to come to a great city. . . ."

"You will find no devils but perhaps a few Moruians, the Islanders. Make friends with them. If Tsorl is the strong spirit you say that he is, then he will make a life in the Islands or send word to Tsagul with a spice vessel; he has powerful friends, I guess."

When the time came to set out, we parted without tears. Gwell Nu was my spirit mother and my friend and a person of great wisdom; I think she *was* a little mad, in the way that diviners and holy persons are mad.

I went deliberately about the most difficult part of the escape. I brought the food cart out of the bushes and laid the Deputy upon it in a sleeping bag. He stirred a little but made no sound. The cart was easy at first, but it became very heavy; I wheeled it in shadow, on grass, to a first cross lane on the long way to the wharf.

There is no regular patrol in this part of the compound; guards are used on Itsik mainly to discourage theft. Few prisoners escaped: there was nowhere to go. If a prisoner tried its luck by land, it was marooned between the two cities in a harsh countryside without water. The nearest springs, so it was said, were in Sarunin, the Place of Ashes, forty weavers miles away and heavily accursed. Escapers were usually found gasping on the red road or dead by a thorn bush.

There is no regular patrol, but I almost lost the game when a party of guards came from the tallow works. They were a long way off on the same cross lane, but with Esder faintly shining through the clouds onto the pale soil of Itsik, they would have seen me at once. I had to jerk the heavy cart back into the shadows. I waited as long as I dared, then crossed the lane and went on, gasping, in a dangerous patch of dappled shade. My luck came back a little as we came to the dock, for the clouds overhead thickened and the night was almost dark.

I brought the wretched cart between two old store huts to the metal fence that was woven around the docks. I waited until I heard the conch on the nearest Mattroyan ship sound the third hour. Then I heaved at two fence posts and bent and tugged at the netted wire until it bent down. I urged the cart over it with a terrible creaking. Food bags fell down and I picked them up again. I came to the dock at last and made a short desperate run for some thick shadow, where I sat and felt the Deputy's limp hands and listened.

The dock was not silent even at the dead hour of morning; far away was the food shed and the guard hut. My Wentroy guard was taking his walk, I hoped, and on board the *Tabel* a wakeful sailor on its watch was playing a pipe. The sea sucked and gurgled around the moored ships and the muck rafts; a little light wind whistled around the docks, eerie as the pipe music.

At last I took food bags and the two fine leather water bags from the sickhouse and stole across to the nearest muck raft. It rode low in the water, below the level of the dock. I stepped down lightly, and the raft hardly quivered;

its logs of seasoned redwood were solid as the dock itself.
I crept to the center of the raft and burrowed under the
rough cloud of bara straw. It made a good hiding place,
dry and comfortable. The raft smelled bad, it reeked, but
I was so used to the foul air of Itsik I hardly noticed it. I
went back and forth three times more, and on the last trip
I carried the body of Tsorl-U-Tsorl over my shoulder in
a long-bag-lift.

It was the longest distance I had had to move him, and
it was as far as I could have managed. I climbed down,
aching, onto the raft and lifted him from the dock; my legs
gave way, and we lay on the deck of the raft. We had not
made much noise, but there were voices aboard the *Tabel:*
the watch was being changed. Another voice spoke loudly
in my ear.

"Where . . . ?"

Tsorl was awake, staring at me with eyes full of fear
and anger.

"Quiet for your life!" I whispered. "Tsorl-U-Tsorl, you
are safe. Trust me!"

"Who are you, by the fire?" His eyes were wild. "What
is this stinking pit?" he demanded, loud enough to fill me
with alarm. "Call the guard, damn you, my leg burns with
pain. . . ."

"Quiet . . . listen to me!" I whispered.

"Call the guard! Must I call? Where am I?"

The voices on the *Tabel* had not stopped; I was terrified
that we would be heard.

"You are being rescued from Itsik!" I knelt by his head
and held him gently by the shoulders above the fastening
of the body bag.

"Get your hands off me!" he said fiercely. "Fire will
smite Pentroy . . . my leg . . ."

He struggled; there was only one thing I could do. I
brought out the sleeping cloth from my jail pouch and
clapped it over his face. Gwell Nu's medicine overpowered
him so that he writhed for a few moments, then lay still.

As I dragged the sleeping bag under cover of the bara
straw, I heard a voice from the ship, "Just the night wind,
friend. . . ."

I lay in our warm pouch under the straw and dozed with
my head close enough to the Deputy so that I could listen
to his breathing. I heard the sound of water under the raft,

the creaking and squelching of the muck, the scampering of feen, the little creatures that infest food stores.

I was very tired and my muscles ached, but I believed sleep was far away. I sang in my tired head to drive away fear, and it became the old singing game. "Nahoo, enu Elbine, ban va der?" "Ho, Crazy Elbin, are you going far?" And the answer came softly into my mind.

"To the islands, to the islands,
Green, green, green . . ."

I saw the old grandee, tall and thin as a tree, her face blasted with madness, whirling a silken cloak embroidered with fire symbols. The cloak whirled about until it hid the world and became the night sky filled with suns and stars and comets. I was wide awake, and the movement, rocking and swinging, was all around us. I peeped out from the straw and saw the surface of the Great Ocean Sea, near enough to touch and gold in the light of Esto. Far ahead I could make out the skinny rump of the *Tabel*, the Mattroyan vessel, towing the raft toward the Round Current. The tow rope, dark brown with age and thick as my arm, swung and looped in the bright water like the body coils of a sea-sunner.

Nearly free! We had nearly done it, and I would have leaped out onto the deck of the muck raft and danced for joy. But there were perils ahead and astern, where the other ship, the *Ullo*, towed the second raft. I checked the Deputy, who was sleeping naturally, and crawled a little astern until I could see the *Ullo* more clearly. It was under one sail and a head of steam!

The fire-metal-magic of the Mattroyan fleet was half-known everywhere, but I had never seen it operate. A tall chimney made from a hollowed tree stood in place of the mainmast—in fact it *was* the mainmast with its top removed—and I could make out some sort of metal boiling vat on the deck, stoked by the crew. The *Tabel* was plainly a sailing vessel and gradually, as I watched, the *Ullo* steamed ahead and their muck raft passed our own. We must have been no more than a few hours out of Itsik.

A long groan echoed through the tangle of bara straw, and I crawled back through the concealing tunnel I had made and came to the Deputy. His eyes were open, and I saw that at last he was in his right wits.

"Who are you?" he asked hoarsely. "Are we on some sort of ship?"

"We are on a muck raft, and we must stay hidden for our lives."

"How did I come here?"

"I am bringing you out of Itsik, Deputy."

"I am Deputy no longer," he snapped. "Who are you working for? What did they pay you?"

"I did it by myself, aided by the Itsik Healer. I serve no one."

"How could you carry me? Let me get a look at you! What is this damned tangle of straw?"

"Bara fiber. I carried you because I am half-omor and strong enough. I come from Tsagul."

Tsorl laughed, but his laughter was full of pain. I mixed him a small sweet drink, as Gwell Nu had instructed me to do at this time, and I managed to persuade him to drink it.

"Tsorl-U-Tsorl," I said, "there is something bad that you must know. Are you strong enough?"

"I have had so much bad treatment that not much can harm me," said the Deputy.

He spoke with great bitterness, and he did not pay any heed to me as I spoke. His eyes were not mad but they slithered over me and were gone; he lived still in some other world of his own pain and his own worries.

"Your left leg had a chain wound that became ravening," I said. "The Forgan was forced to cut it, below the joint."

He turned pale and his eyes rolled in his head.

"I can feel it still. . . ."

"Only the spirit leg. It has gone."

Then he began to rail and curse his fate, blistering the air with fiery oaths and swearing that some foul butcher from Itsik had lamed him for the Pentroy. I lost my temper.

"Be ashamed! Gwell Forgan saved your life with her skill!"

"So you say!"

"And saved it again by letting me take you from Itsik. You were meant to die, to wither away secretly in captivity."

He gave a sigh. "That I believe. I'm sorry I cursed this healer."

Tsorl sat up a little and stared at the sleeping bag. "Why did you take me from Itsik?"

"My name is Yolo Harn. I brought you out for the

memory of Old Harn, my foster parent. He would not
have had you there, Deputy."

"Harn? I don't know the name."

He lay back frowning. I had not expected him to recall
Old Harn, and I was glad he did not lie and pretend that
he did. I gave him food, then later I crept to the edge of the
raft covered by the straw and cleaned my hands with wash-
ing sand. I changed the dressing on Tsorl's leg; it must have
been painful but he made no sound. The healing was going
on well; the Forgan's work was excellent.

We lay under the straw, peering out now and then at
the sky and the two ships. The raft was escorted now by
huge lumbering pairs of vano, the legendary birds of the
Great Ocean Sea. They were not bold enough to settle
while the raft was under tow but they came flapping in
one or two at a time, swooped on the food waste, then
wheeled off again.

So we traveled on in clear, calm summer weather,
sleeping a little. The *Ullo*, far ahead, had already cast off its
raft into the current and steamed west to Tsagul. I could
not see the distant curl of smoke from its chimney without
a twinge of homesickness for the Fire-Town. On the following day, about midday, we felt the swirl of the Round
Current under our own raft. The *Tabel* cast off the rope,
and we saw her tacking awkwardly out of the current and
working east. The raft was caught in an eddy and spun
around a few times like a leaf, then the current swung us
solidly toward the southwest.

Slowly I stood up and brushed aside the bara straw. The
vano, bolder now, came and settled in pairs and fives on
the food waste in its pen. Far to the southwest the islands
were a thick haze of green; they seemed to float in the air.
I moved to the Deputy and helped him to stand upright. He
stared at the wheeling birds, the sea and sky, and for the
first time he looked like that leader Old Harn had known.
In fact he was very weak and his sound leg trembled. I
cleared a space on the deck and made a rough support of
compressed straw and branches. When he was settled comfortably, we let the suns shine on us.

Presently Tsorl began to speak again in that unheeding
way of his and I listened.

"To the islands then," he said. "Maimed and then set
adrift. No one to follow my trail. But by the fire we're not
done yet!"

He laughed aloud.

"To the islands . . . Tsabeggan, the Nearest Fire. Find them, if it is not a dream. The little airship was real enough."

"Tsorl . . . ?"

"What? What is it?"

His face was lined and his hair streaked gray, but his eyes were lively, very dark, almost black. As he glanced toward me I recalled an old tapestry that hung in the City Hall at Tsagul, a hunting story with old warriors, one dark and fierce as Tsorl.

"Do you believe that there are devils in the islands?" I asked.

"There are strangers on Torin, if that's what you mean," he said impatiently.

"Nothing can fly through the void!"

"They have done it," he said, "and I have seen one of their ships."

"There was a sailor on the *Tabel* who claimed to have stared one in the face!"

"What? Only one? Where was it?"

"It was victor at a big race up country."

"Otolor!" he said eagerly. "By the fire, Yolo Harn, you are an ignorant townee wretch. Tell me the tale."

I told it to him, and he smiled at every word.

"Poor devil," he said. "It was saved from that ship, the same one I examined. It must live a charmed life . . . may the fire of Telve protect it still. It has won the Bird Clan Air Race—but will it escape the clutches of the Great Elder? Tiath Gargan will have it if he can, unless that other, the damned Magician, takes a hand!"

"Aren't you afraid of these creatures?" I cried. "How can you speak of them so calmly—if it is true and not clan gossip."

"I am afraid," he said, "but these are reasonable creatures, thinking beings. A person who can pass among Moruians at the Bird Clan air race is no monster!"

"Would you speak to it?"

"I will speak with them!" he said firmly. "If there are any on that island, I swear I will speak with them if I have to crawl the length and breadth of Tsabeggan."

His determination was oddly comforting; I began to be less afraid. Tsorl looked at me more closely.

"How old are you, Yolo Harn?"

"This is the seventeenth year from my showing."

"Bring me water," he said. "Let us talk. How will this thing be done?"

I crawled under the straw into our tunnels and fetched water. I felt very strange, lightheaded from the escape, free and yet downcast. It was my own fault, I reasoned, for not thinking far ahead. I had certainly not rescued this harsh old ruler to be my friend; I had done it for Old Harn and for the promptings of destiny—but I had not reckoned with being alone on a raft with one ruling spirit.

Tsorl drank up and smiled at me.

"I have remembered Harn," he said. "Drath Harn, worked on the irrigation projects, came to the rank of Team Leader. Rated high for endurance. Some kind of wasting in his left hand."

"That was Old Harn."

"Didn't he work odd days at City Hall?"

I did feel better now that he had remembered. I sprawled on the deck in the sunshine and told about Old Harn. It became the story of my own life and my bad luck and how I came to Itsik. All the time Tsorl prompted me to go and smiled but not falsely, so that I felt he saw me for the first time. I had an image of him at last as the Deputy speaking to the citizens of Tsagul from the balcony above Market Round. I could imagine him before that, urging on his faithful workers as they dug the canals in the waste northwest of Tsagul. Tsorl-U-Tsorl. One of the best?

"That is the tale of Harn," I said, "and my own tale. Now it is your turn. Tell me how you came from Tsagul into the hands of Tiath Pentroy, the Great Elder, and how you know there are strangers on the island of Tsabeggan."

It was hard for him to take. He had all the habits of a leader and did not expect those he worked with to speak back. But he tried: I was necessary to his plans. He smiled and shook his head.

"Yolo Harn," he said, "I cannot go over this. Too much of it is like an evil dream . . . let me tell you another time. Ask me something else."

"What was your childhood then? I have told you mine."

I had no real curiosity, for I thought I knew his story; he seemed by his voice and manner the child of rich townees or merchants of Tsagul. I was encouraging him to talk.

"My father was a teacher and scholar," he said. "He

knew much about plants and herbs and the behavior of metals and the movement of the stars. He was employed privately by a rich family in Tsagul who lost their money. It was a common enough story. A day came when there was nothing left; the elders of the house were dead or absent, the servants all run off with what they could carry.

"My father was left with the charge of the two children of the house, a young female and her younger male sib. He took them away into the country. He rescued them from the creditors and raised them at his farm on the Datse, a place called Trill Fall.

"He made a family with the young female, my dear mother, after her sib fell sick and died. They were most perfectly happy together and pouched one child, myself. My mother's health failed too and she went from us when I was eight, nine years shown. My father lived on alone on his farm for many more years.

"When I was fourteen I came down to Tsagul and took examinations as a scribe and a metal worker; from the first I worked for the city. Patronage was still a force in those days, but I had no dealings with Clan Dohtroy—the most patron I had was Tsabbutt Krell, a former Deputy and leader of the reform party.

"I had long ago decided, standing in my father's orchard when I was about twelve years shown, to have no name and no family allegiance but my own. I became Tsorl-U-Tsorl, and this I remained."

It was a strange story; it had the ring of truth, but I felt that it was closely edited. Much of the color and interest of the Deputy's life had been taken out of it. I thanked him for the tale and fed him more medicine. I walked around the raft and stirred up the feasting vano birds. They were so slow I could have caught them in my hands.

I sat at the front of the raft and looked at the surface of the Great Ocean Sea, crisscrossed and patterned with light and with shadows of the little creatures that swarm in thousands just under the water. I saw a strange-looking creature looking back at me when the raft passed over calm water. Long, thick, dark brown hair worked into a rough plait, skin burned red-brown by the Great Sun. All the badges of despised Itsik were on me, from the "measuring strings" that bullies wore around the muscles of their arms to a star skin-sewn in brown thread on one wrist. I still had my gray tunic but over it I wore a fancy brown leather vest laid aside by some grandee; my boots were trimmed with fur.

I stripped off then and there and plunged into the sea. I dried myself in the sunlight. Far to the south a toben fish sent up its triple jet of water and air; the green haze of the islands was so close that it had settled on the surface of the sea. Soon I would see mountain peaks and solid green land. Freedom. It was the earth and the sky. I was a creature new shown, a sea-sunner hatched from an egg of pearl in the depths of the ocean. If I had freedom, if I could keep this wild and blessed freedom behind my eyes from this moment, then I could endure anything.

4

An Adventure and a Reward

WHEN WE SLEPT IN THE BARA TUNNELS on the second night of the raft voyage, the islands were already filling the horizon to the west. This was the hottest season of the year and the hottest part of the globe of Torin; even the sultry summers of the Fire-Town seemed cool by comparison. The steamy breath of the islands could be felt, and we longed to be free of the festering heat of the muck raft.

I woke suddenly in the darkness under the straw.

"Wake up!" Tsorl was tugging at the straw to wake me.

"What is it?"

There was a movement of the whole raft, a regular rocking as if some giant foot was pressing us down in the water. I thought at first that we had come to land and caught upon some rock. Then we both heard the noise, and it was so strange that I felt a thrill of terror. But as the sounds continued I became interested. What could it be?

There was a background noise, a slow, regular, windy sound that reminded me . . . yes, it reminded me of the big bellows sometimes used at the New Cut Mine to blow dust from a dirty seam. Then there were slurping sounds from above our heads as if the garbage were being churned

61

up, and strangest of all there was a piping and whistling
and growling like a giant pouch pipe . . . like voices. . . .

Tsorl was trying to crawl out of the straw to get a look
but I held him back.

"I'll go!"

I crawled a little way from the tunnels where we slept
and made my way quietly onto the open deck. The Far
Sun shone as brightly as I had ever seen it: I could dis-
tinguish colors—the dark coppery green of the scales, the
delicate fishy blue of the underbelly. A long body, twice
the length of the raft; fins tipped with silver that folded
and fluttered like birds' wings; strong suckered feet that
grasped the raft and could have submerged it with one
push. High overhead I beheld the sea-sunner calmly and
methodically eating the food waste from the enclosure.

The head was broad and flat; I could see the muscles
bulging, with a flash of dark rainbow scales, at the corners
of the long jaws. There were spiny projections, a low,
folded crest on the skull; the eyes were deep and folded,
mere threads of light. It was a sight full of fear and wonder, yet as I watched the huge creature whistling and
grunting as it gobbled the food, the mystery of these great
sacred beasts was lessened. It was terrifying but only because of its size; it was as natural and even as beautiful
as a huge tree or a mountain.

The sunner was completely unaware of me. The vano
birds, disturbed in their sleep on the waters or the raft
itself, were flapping about protesting at this new scavenger
who was likely to clear the raft of all the food. As it
moved and changed its position the raft rocked dangerously
but I guessed the sunner would not let it sink. The coils of
its body floated and moved easily in the water and acted as
a kind of rudder. But the drift of the raft had slackened
and I knew a real danger: we were being urged out of the
Round Current. There was a clear demarcation in the
ocean to the east and if we left this great trail of moving
water we would rest becalmed and not come to the islands.

I went back toward Tsorl and found him close at
hand; he had made his own window in the bara straw to
watch the sunner. We crouched whispering in the darkness.

"We will be out of the current," I said.

"Then we must get the beast off the raft," he growled.
I had no weapon but there was a branch of a redwood

tree, harder than the bara, that I had put aside for an oar. We went to the open deck where I had been standing; Tsorl moved nimbly after me, but I knew he could not be free of pain.

The sunner had scarcely altered its position. I clutched my branched club and moved boldly around the deck until I stood in the bright Esder light about twenty feet below the huge head well within range of its eyes. I reached into the garbage pen, took up half a melon and shied it at the right eye. I shouted with all my might.

The sunner gave a high whistling squeak as the melon struck its eyelid and reared back a little. The raft tilted and rocked . . . and the sunner looked at me. It cocked its head on one side and opened its left eye so wide that I felt I had been caught in a bright beam of green light. An impossible three note cry, a sound between whimpering and questioning, came from its fearful mouth: "Wo-wo-wo."

Instinctively I ducked down behind the fence of the enclosure. There was a moment of silence, a new series of small movements rocked the raft. I stood up again and shouted again and saw the sunner with head flattened over the pen waiting for me.

"Wo-wo-wo?" it yelped softly.

"Go off! Get away, you damned monster!" I bellowed. The sunner roared aloud; I ducked my head again.

"Wo-wo?" the sunner whispered.

Up I bobbed again like a spring-toy; the sunner was bent forward expectantly *with its eyes tightly shut.* I could not help it—I laughed, I laughed because I knew what we were doing, and I shouted again through my laughter. The sunner opened its eyes and gave a whuffling roar, a sound of pleasure. I ducked out of sight a third time.

"By the fire that split the world, what are you doing with that monster?" cried Tsorl.

"Playing a game!" I said. "It is like a child—it plays 'Look-See.' "

"Yolo Harn, you are mad. . . ."

"Wo?" whimpered the sunner. Its sighing voice echoed around the raft and over the shining sea: "Wo-wo-wo?"

I bounced out onto the open deck, and the sunner guffawed with delight. I began walking with an elaborate striding walk like a street player toward the far side of the raft. I swung around and shouted at the sunner. Its coils moved in the water as it swarmed over the raft to get a better look at me. We went so low in the water that a wave washed around my feet and Tsorl cried out as the same wave reached him. In the shadow I saw one of the sunner's suckered feet clinging to the edge of the raft.

"Go away!" I shouted again. "Sunner, go away! You will drown us!"

I ran along the tilting deck and beat with all my might at the dark green foot. The sunner howled with pain and reared up right over me. I saw the gaping jaws, the pinkish underside of the head. I summoned all my courage simply to back away instead of collapsing on the deck and putting my hands over my head.

Far away across the sea there came a loud and terrifying cry. I lost my footing and rolled, nearly into the sea. I saw the second sunner, more than twice the size of this one looming above our raft, plowing through the water. Its body coils churned the water and made a silver wake larger than the wake of the *Tabel*. The cry was repeated: a sheet of sound, a lightning flash. Then abruptly, with a last whimper, the smaller creature dived off our raft and swam away.

I picked myself up and crossed the slippery logs to find Tsorl. He was sitting on a pile of straw staring out to sea, where the two sunners, mother and child, or so I thought, were making course to the south.

"They could be tamed," he said. "They are intelligent beasts, and the young ones could be taught to serve us."

"They are free," I said.

I thought of the lives of the sea-sunner: roaming the Great Ocean Sea, foraging among the ice mountains and the fire mountains, dwelling in the vast, landless spaces of the world.

It was not a time for us to rest. We sat silent until the thin light of Esder was turned to a rich gold and the Great Sun rose. The islands were very close.

"I have a map of the islands," announced Tsorl, "and I came by it in a strange way . . ."

"Tell me. . . ."

"You're very brave, Yolo Harn. Do you know that?"

"It was a baby sunner, however big."

"Well," he said stiffly, "I am grateful to you . . . for everything."

I fetched some of our food and drink, and Tsorl-U-Tsorl began to tell his tale at last, as some kind of reward for my silly game with the sunner.

II

"It was the day of my death," he said. "I had made the pact. I was perfectly serious. My friends who shared in my dishonor at the hands of the Council of Tsagul were all determined to accompany me. The red cord was ready to bind our hands."

"Which friends?" I asked softly.

He gave me a vague look past my left shoulder, but he told the names.

"There was good Arn Lorgan, the Bridgemaker, and his partner Lateen, who was one of my scribes. There was Tilje Paroyan Dohtroy, whom I loved as my true sib, my partner almost; there was the scribe, Vel Ragan, who had been scarred in my place by a firestone assassin soon after the Irrigation Projects were complete and we had trouble with the Hundred of Rintoul. Vel was the youngest—too young for such a pact.

"When my dismissal came, we sat together, all five, and seemed to be a family. Perhaps the wine we drank made us ready to die, perhaps it was my bitterness, my spirit governing them."

I remembered all the persons of whom he spoke; Old Harn had admired Arn Lorgan almost as much as the Deputy himself. I had seen the two scribes, Lat Arnroyan and Vel Ragan, with his terrible scarred face, coming and going at City Hall. The Highness of Dohtroy surprised me most; she was a handsome, proud creature, who was carried about in a palanquin in the streets of Tsagul during the ancient festivals.

"We were to meet at the Dohtroy villa to the north, by Deerfold Ponds," said the Deputy. "Tilje was to have everything in readiness. The forenoon was hot. I went with Vel Ragan and dropped off at City Hall—a last visit to make gifts to the staff. If Old Harn had been working that day he would have received something, but I don't remember him in the line.

"I sat alone in my old workroom; none of the Council came near me, not even my former supporters. The Hall was rather empty at that hour; no new Deputy had been elected. A scribe, an old female, I don't know her name— Fell or Feth—she came running. The Voice Wire from the landing field; I answered the call and heard some startled officer from the tower.

"A Pentroy glider had come in from Otolor, and the passenger was being flown into the city by relay machine to see me. When I heard the name I knew something was afoot: it was Ammur Ningan, the Pentroy High Steward. Tiath Avran Pentroy trusts few people. It is the old hawk's failing; he cannot delegate his power. But this Ningan is his most powerful creature . . . and she was coming to me, unattended save for her pilot."

"I have heard of that one on Itsik." I laughed. "It is the one called Tav Ru, Old Darkness."

"The vassals do it too much honor," said the Deputy. "It is a damnable creature—Old Grayness were a better name. Ammur is the scribe of scribes, dry and wrinkled as an ancient scroll covered with symbols we cannot understand.

"I sat alone in the workroom that was no longer mine and thought of my dear friends waiting at the villa. Then the glider landed on the roof of the Hall, and the Ningan demanded personal audience with Tsorl-U-Tsorl from the startled scribes and officials. She stood before me travel-stained, her finery bedraggled; I was more puzzled than ever.

"We sat together with the pilot guarding the door and I heard of the small ship that had been captured on Hingstull Mountain. I longed to see it and examine the metal of which it was made. I read the skein from the Great Elder couched in flattering terms. We had met once, and I had presented him with all my treatises on metals. I had never given up hope of a better deal for Tsagul, and now the Great Elder himself seemed to promise it if I examined this vessel.

"Ammur Ningan fussed about the workroom cracking her fingerbones; she was anxious for me to come at once, to fly to Otolor within the hour. Tiath Gargan is a harsh liege. She had no doubt that I would come; it was simply a matter of timing.

"At last I gave my word and sent the two Pentroy travelers to be fed and taken care of in the Hall. It was the day of my death, and I had promised to go on this absurd chase. The cups were ready at the Dohtroy villa, my old friends were awaiting my approach. I must dishonor them if I broke the bond . . . but destiny was at work here, surely? Why had I been recalled from death, as if Telve had stretched out a hand to me?

"I did what had to be done—sent back to my lodgings on Canal Prospect, where an old house servant was putting my things in order, and asked for a small pack of clothes and my metal-testing gear. I summoned a Witness and gave it instructions and credits. I waited alone, with Ammur Ningan ready to depart, until the Witness flew to the villa and established the mindlink between myself and my poor friends. I broke the bond.

"I broke the bond, and it has haunted me since then. I believe I have a debt to my poor friends, but I doubt that it will ever be paid. Perhaps I should not have planned to take them with me into death. Perhaps I had a desire to live. I flew out of Tsagul so swiftly that it seemed like secrecy. I remember I asked Tilje Paroyan to meet me in Rintoul. But I saw none of them again. . . ."

"Dishonor is a weak thread," I said. "I have heard too much of it. I am not sure about Destiny, but I know it is better to live than to die. Tsorl-U-Tsorl, I have this to tell you: Arn Lorgan, the old Bridgemaker, is dead. Harn spoke of his funeral rites."

"May his soul bird fly far," said the Deputy.

"What?"

"It is his own expression. He was mountain-bred—in fact I believe he came from Hingstull or thereabouts."

"I am not sure what is meant by a soul," I said, "but to become a bird would not be too harsh a fate."

"I wonder where you got this obsession with freedom?" He smiled.

"Go on with your story," I begged. "Come to the airship."

"I flew that day to the outskirts of Rintoul, the delta lands," he said, "and went aboard a small sailboat. I met Old Thune and his assistant, scholars from Rintoul—superstitious fools, half-afraid to touch metal but more afraid of the Great Elder. Ammur Ningan returned to the city. I have often wished she had accompanied us.

"We came to Linlor in the Wentroy lands and presently a cargo barge came down the Troon, shrouded and secret. Under the covers was this thing—this airship. It was small, built for one or two passengers about the size of a Moruian. It was a miracle of design and execution. The people who made this craft are many great fives of years ahead of us in every branch of knowledge.

"The metal was an alloy; it contained things known on Torin, such as iron and graymetal, and other things not so well known, though I might have isolated them. This was the outer casing. I was the only one who dared set foot inside the small round vehicle. The method of propulsion was totally strange to me, but there were talking systems and arrangements for air and light that resembled things we have here—things known by a few. Things known, I must admit, by that damned magician, Nantgeeb, the Maker of Engines."

"I know of that one, too!" I laughed. "It makes engines for Blacklock, Murno Pentroy, who flew in the Air Race."

"Nantgeeb almost caused my death!" said Tsorl. "I was absorbed in work on the foreign ship. I believed that the flyer was dead by now; frozen on the mountainside or drowned in the Warm Lake. I remember. . . . It seems childish now, but I behaved without foresight. . . . I remember that I was irritable because we had no word from the Great Elder. He was bearing down from the north on his housebarge.

"We came with our strange cargo to a tiny hamlet on the east bank of the Troon, a place called Pelle. I remember sitting at the eating mat with Old Thune and the younger scribe, then we all woke suddenly in bright twin sunshine. We had slept at the eating mat for more than a day, and the crew of Pentroy vassals had slept too. The silver ship was gone from the deck.

"I don't know to this day how the sleeping was managed: probably sleep-medicine in the food. We had bought fruit and fish on the river and at Pelle. The ship? The wretched vassals claimed that it had been 'spirited away.' In fact it must have been a very well-planned engineering feat: the ship removed by hoist and sailed up the local stream."

"How did you know it was stolen by the Magician?" I asked.

"Rumor and guesswork! The villagers had been bribed, but they were bribed again: it did seem to be the work of this Great Diviner. I was relieved. At first I thought the ship might have been stolen by treasure-seekers to be melted down and destroyed. By the fire, I missed that ship! It was the finest and most interesting set of mechanisms that I had ever seen. I bitterly envied Nantgeeb, who had it now to study at leisure.

"We made a search around the village, then sailed on as fast as we could to Rintoul—the vassals were half dead with fear of the Great Elder's wrath. I could not believe that the scholars and I were in physical danger; it had been no part of our business to guard the silver ship. I would have done well to share the vassals' fear and make a run for it. Indeed I think some vassals took to the river and the delta lands.

"I intended to make my report to Tiath Pentroy and put in a word for the crew; who can guard against sleep-medicine? We sailed to the city wharf, and there was Ammur Ningan to meet us with a contingent of household servants, even members of the city watch. She was more gray than ever, a wraith in the cold morning light, her long face pale with fear and rage. The poor scholars and I were quickly overwhelmed. I cursed myself for a fool and an innocent; by comparison with these clan creatures, the very Council at Tsagul are cautious and law-abiding.

"I was flung into a cell below an ancient building in Rintoul: the so-called Sea Flower room. I saw that I had been horribly betrayed and could hope for no justice. I considered that my chances of surviving were very small. I raged fiercely and demanded audience with the Great Elder. I was determined not to die without a fight and to proclaim my name and my whereabouts to all the prisoners and guards in the building, in case a message might be brought to Tilje Paroyan or my other friends in Tsagul. I sat in chains and could not tell night from day.

"Then he came, the old Strangler, Tiath Gargan himself. What a figure he cuts! The whole world seems to cringe at his step. And so reasonable, almost soft-voiced. When I see this monster parading about as the greatest power on Torin, I don't wonder that our flying machines are poor contraptions. His arrogance has strangled all his good qualities."

"I did not know this terrible ruler had any good qualities," I put in.

"There is no doubt of it," said the Deputy. "He has been the power in Clan Pentroy, if not the Great Elder, ever since he was a young flyer. He has brought order and peace and made many wise decisions, though at cost very often to the people of Tsagul. He has done this for six fives, for thirty years."

"Was this long after the last battle at Sarunin?"

"Yes, a long time," said the Deputy. "This is the so-called golden number anniversary of the Last Battle. Eleven fives, fifty-five years, have passed since that time. Tiath was a child . . . about two years shown, I was not yet born, by one five of years. I have often thought of Sarunin. Something might be done with that unhappy ground."

"It is dreadful . . . accursed . . . a place of ashes. . . ."

"It is a pleasant valley," said Tsorl.

"Finish your story."

"I spoke with Tiath Pentroy, pleaded for the vassals. They had been hung, out of hand. The scholars? I believe they tried to incriminate me in order to save their own lives. No matter—I hope the miserable creatures survived.

"When Tiath was stirred to a display of wrath I shouted even louder; I drowned in rage and struck out at him. He had broken his promises on the skein he sent to Tsagul; I cursed him in fiery terms. I was beaten to the ground by the guards and lay in darkness, bleeding and neglected. After some time I found myself in the compound at Itsik. I became sick again with the wound in my leg. I have a hazy memory of being examined by an old female, strangely dressed: that would be our mad benefactor, Gwell Nu."

"You have been ill-used, Deputy," I said. "I wish an assassin would deal with Tiath Gargan!"

"I wish he would be defeated by law," said the Deputy.

The Great Sun had risen, and it marked our pathway, the Round Current, stretching toward the green tree wall of the islands. Tsorl took off the worn leather vest that he wore over his red tunic and felt inside a shoulder flap. He drew out a thin fold of paper.

"I learned many things inside the small ship," he said. "First: it can join to a much larger ship, or so I read one diagram. Second: there are at least four strangers on Torin."

"How do you know that?"

"A kind of silk-beam copy was tucked behind the instruments. It showed four figures in silver body-bags or flying suits standing beside the small ship."

"But tell me . . . the faces . . . the eyes . . ."

"The figures wore heavy helmets. But the ship stood among our own forest trees . . . in the islands," replied Tsorl. "I also found this map and kept it hidden. That vile Ningan believed me so secure I was not even searched."

He spread on the deck a large square not of paper but of tough, fine material, not woven, more like fish skin. He pointed this way and that, and finally I did see: there was the ocean and there were the shapes of the Fire Islands.

"It looks like another silk-beam copy," I said.

"You have the glimmerings of intelligence, Yolo Harn," said the Deputy, "besides strong muscles and rash courage."

I rose to my feet and stood tall over the square of blue skin holding an imaginary silk-beam lens to my eyes.

"It was taken from above!" I said. "From so far above the surface of the sea that the islands were spread out like a map!"

"Yes," grinned Tsorl, "and somewhat higher than any balloons or flying machines of ours can fly."

"What are those markings?"

"Words and numbers . . . I cannot get even a thread of their working. But one thing I believe I understand: those small crossed lines."

A group of small crossed lines, not unlike the written symbol for the sound O, stood on a large island.

"That is the island of Tsabeggan," he said, "and that is the camp of the strangers."

"If you say so. How do we sail there? Does the Round Current show on this map?"

"A little."

Tsorl pointed out a series of curving flecks in the sea between the islands.

"The rafts may be carried in here," he said, "between these two islands."

"Hindan and Steen."

"Those are their names. The narrow strait looks dangerous. I believe there are rapids and broken water there."

"What becomes of this trash on the raft?"

"You've seen what happens to it!" The Deputy laughed. "It is flung or scraped off, eaten by vano or sunners. If any is left when the rafts emerge from the inland sea beyond Tsabeggan, then the sailors scrape it off before taking the rafts into tow—back to Itsik or to Rintoul."

"Tsagul sends out no rafts!"

"I take credit for that!" exclaimed Tsorl. "I hate to throw dirt into the sea, but I think we must do it right away. We must lighten our load before we run between Hindan and its smaller neighbor."

It was midmorning now and a fair day, hot and cloudless. Tsorl's amputated leg was healing swiftly and well; he practiced with the ring-walker that Gwell Nu had sent with us. It was a series of hardwood rings that could be locked into position; the lower end had a half-ring, two wooden feet; the upper end could be adjusted, one ring at a time bent down or unfolded, according to the height of the lame person. Even with this device Tsorl was slow, and I kept him from lifting.

I took my redwood pole and used it to heave the barrels of tannery waste overboard. The pen was already half-empty from the young sunner and the vano; the raft rode lightly over the water.

Hindan was the largest of the Fire Islands, so big now that it did not seem like an island at all. We could see the ranked trees on the shores and, high above, the cone of its fire mountain, tipped with black rock. The island of Steen was hovering in a green mist; we could not see any strait or "broken water." All around us on the surface of the sea lay the signs of the islands: branches, huge leaves washed thin as green lace, sodden logs, clusters of strange fruit.

I had worked hard all morning, and after doling out our water and fruit and blackloaf I slept. Tsorl sat among the remains of our bara straw and stared at the coast of Hindan. I slept on and on into the afternoon, and Tsorl woke me not long before the setting of the Great Sun. I saw that he had made all fast—tied down every food bag. He pointed ahead without a word; all I saw by Hindan's coast were rainbows, round and curved patches of light, dancing upon the surface of the sea where the Round Current flowed swiftly between the islands.

Broken water! As we came up, more swiftly now, the raft began to rock and heave. We saw the rapids, white as bared teeth, and further on the coast of Steen in the narrow strait—so narrow that it was like a dark tunnel overgrown with vines, filled with roaring foam.

There was enough left of the excellent rope I had stolen from Itsik for us to make two loops upon the deck of the raft, woven into the thick, ancient ropes that tied

the logs of the raft together. We squeezed under these
loops and lay flat, shouting encouragement above the
growing sound of the water. We had no time to be afraid;
the broken water seemed to reach out to us greedily,
stronger than the Round Current itself. The raft moved
crazily, tipping sideways, shuddering from end to end. We
were carried with great speed into the boiling strait between
the islands.

For a long time I could see nothing but the thick spray;
it filled my mouth and nostrils so that I could scarcely
breathe; the roaring of the water was everywhere. Trees
and thick swags of knotted pine scraped over the raft and
threatened to tear us from the deck. This went on and on
until I thought it would never stop. When I lifted my
head, I had glimpses of the raft being tossed from one
side of the channel to the other. It was scraped underneath
by the teeth of the rocks and sometimes caught and sus-
pended on a taller crag that lifted out of the rapids. Then
the raft would pause and spin slowly, half out of the water,
with the pair of us clinging to the deck like sucker fish.
Each time the raft came down and was rushed on its way.

At last Tsorl raised his head and cried out; before I could
look, the raft caught and hung again, then it was launched
into the empty air. The stern tipped up so high that I
thought it must turn over and hold us drowning beneath it,
but once more it came down with a jolt that made me
breathless. I looked back and saw that we had been carried
over a plane of rock that made a waterfall. The raft spun
around dizzily at the base of this fall and then gently,
surely, it was urged forward again by the power of the
Round Current. We floated in the inland sea between the
islands.

The coast of Hindan rose to our left, and the rocky
beaches of Steen were already falling behind on our right.
Strangest of all, the night had fallen during our ordeal;
it was the brief time of Runar, the little darkness. We
floated so gently it felt as if we had died and been carried
off on the wind, bodiless spirits. Overhead we could see the
stars, and all around us on the dark sea there rose the
shapes of the islands.

It was cold at first; we lay exhausted and exchanged a
few words. Then the natural heat of the center of the globe
of Torin stole over our soaking raft and ragged scraps of
equipment. I came out of my loop and checked the sup-

plies. The light of the Far Sun rising showed a raft stripped
bare; the pen contained hardly a breadfruit rind for a
sunner to nibble. The vano, those scavengers of the ocean,
had been left far behind. Not a shred of the bara waste
remained. Our trusty waterskins, which I had tried to re-
plenish a little when it rained, were still tied in place but
one had been pierced by thorns and drained, the other
contained a few cups of stale water.

"We must come soon to Tsabeggan," I said, "or we will
be thirsty."

"Before the Great Sun sets tomorrow," said the Deputy,
"or even earlier. We might have trouble beaching this
raft."

"You are sure which of these islands is Tsabeggan?"

"Of course! Don't teach your grandmother to weave
leaf patterns!"

"That is an old thread! At the New Cut Mine we said:
'Don't tell the ancient how to pump bellows.' "

Tsorl laughed aloud. We sipped our stale water, and I
lay back looking at the starry sky. I thought of my vision
of old Elbin Tsatroy, flinging the stars around upon her
cloak, and I described it to the Deputy. He laughed again,
more gently.

"That is a fine dream, Yolo Harn," he said, "but the old
Elbin looked nothing like that tall and eerie figure."

"You have *seen* her? What did she look like?"

"She visited . . . passed through Trill Fall on her wanderings when I was a child," he said. "She was every inch
the grandee, I remember. A small, neat, birdlike person
with black eyes like a hawk. She seldom spoke . . . this
was part of her madness. She whistled to her two old body-
servants to make them do her bidding. She had them carry
a tapestry bag of offerings for those she met on the way;
she would dip into the bag and present something. It was
a gamble: a piece of jewelry might come out or a worth-
less tin cup."

Tsorl laughed again, sadly, and held up his right arm.

"This arm band came from her indirectly. She gave my
father a brass candleholder from her bag and he melted it
down and made me this bracelet. I have never taken it
from my arm except to insert a new slip of metal as I
grew."

The real picture he gave me of Crazy Elbin was not so
striking as my dream, but it haunted me from that time.

I peered ahead at the inner sea and the passing shapes of the islands, gray-green now in the light of the Far Sun, and prayed to the old Fire Mother, saying that we were coming to her villa on Tsabeggan. I did not think too much of the strangers we might find there, but they moved through my dreams that night, blinking their round eyes, which were blue as crystals of copper salt.

When the Great Sun rose, we were in the very midst of the inland sea and making a steady pace back to the west in the Round Current. We looked keenly to the islands for inhabited places, and once we saw a wharf and a clearing, used by spice traders. On two islands far off to the northwest we saw smoke; perhaps these were encampments of Islanders—primitive Moruia—who are told of in legend.

The raft might have been beached easily several times on beaches of sand or pebbles below the vines and tall fever trees. We made out few redwoods or bara trees but any number of the lace leaf vines with leaves wide enough to use as a cloak and the greenwings with their huge, tough leaves like feathers. The fever trees had slippery trunks covered with scales and they glowed in the darkness of the forests with a blue luminescence.

Tsorl looked ahead to the island of Tsabeggan—an island nearly as large as Hindan and standing very tall. Its central mountain was a perfect cone, but surrounded by ridges and lesser mountains. As we came up to it after midday, the Round Current, which had served us so well, began to play tricks. We moved faster and began to curve away from the green headland on Tsabeggan.

I had lost my good redwood pole, but I tore a long plank from the pen in the center of the raft. I tried to row in toward a white sand beach under the headland. Tsorl took a plank and we both rowed hard; we struck the shallow shelf of the bay and scraped our raft toward the land fingerbreadth by fingerbreadth with the current tugging us away. I made a rope fast, plunged into the shallow blue water and dragged the rope up the beach. I hauled with all my might and Tsorl scraped away with his pole, and suddenly, as if the Current had had enough of our foolery, a wave caught the raft and washed it into land.

I pulled, and the raft rode right up onto the sand and nearly landed on top of me. The Deputy flung himself down on the white sand, and we laughed together; then at once we were silent. Tsabeggan was a most beautiful island, far enough to the west to have grass upon it as well as forest and more redwoods among the fever trees. We heard the sound of the sea, the cries of a family of flame birds weaving their ragged nests in a tree on the headland. But even in those first moments we heard something else: a hum, a thump like a heartbeat that reverberated through the whole of the island.

Tsorl put his ear to the ground in one place, then another.

"What does it sound like to you?" he whispered.

"An engine," I said. "Something a lot bigger than the crusher on the New Cut!"

A long metallic sigh echoed through the trees, and the engine was still.

5

Tsabeggan

TSORL-U-TSORL HAD A WILD LOOK as if he would struggle off into the woods that instant in search of the engine, but in fact we were tired and hungry creatures, castaways without shelter, food or drink. I had a small gourd at my belt, and I looked for water. Fifty paces away I found a thin trickle of water coming down the hillside under a cover of vines and bushes. Under the leaves—anywhere but in the sun's light—there were flying insects and creeping things, and I knew that some of them could sting. I filled the gourd and we had drink, with a pinch of Gwell Nu's sweetening herbs.

I went exploring again at once. I had seen a strange thing not far from the place where the water trickled down. It had nothing to do with engines or devils; it was a flight of narrow stone steps built into the cliffside, leading to the top of the headland. I went up ten steps, scaring a fat land-sunner.

The creature was slow and not used to hunters; I stood still until it settled again behind a rock, then I pounced. I had hunted land-sunners at Itsik in the bara plantation, but this was a larger specimen. I killed it with a blow from a rock, then saw that what I had snatched up was not a rock. I carried the dead sunner to the beach, and while I skinned and cleaned it, Tsorl examined the brick.

"A fire symbol baked onto the clay," he said. "Those steps lead to the old Tsatroy villa. What are we supposed to do with that hunk of meat?"

"Raw sunner is not bad," I said.

"Get some dry leaves, Yolo Harn," he said, "and we will make a fire."

I found this hard to believe, but he was the Deputy after all, a scholar who had perfected the Voice Wire and other useful inventions. I gathered the dry stuff, and Tsorl produced from his shoulder pocket a lens rimmed with metal—a burning glass. Making a fire, making the leaves catch fire from the rays of the Great Sun was not difficult, in fact the leaves blazed up so quickly they were consumed and I had to fetch more. We soon managed a good blaze, and I cooked the sunner meat wrapped in its thick skin with seawater and herbs. We ate and drank and dozed in the sun.

Before the Great Sun set I climbed up the old steps. They were sunken but not overgrown; the land here had been cleared, and the forest had not grown right back. I came to the top of the headland and stood in awe. This was the work of my own people, the Fire People, and they built as well as the Torlogan, the Great Builders of Torin. A tall weathered arch of brick and stone rose facing the sea and over it in open stonework was the fire symbol.

Inside the arch was a circular courtyard paved with old brick, now overgrown with grasses, waist-high in some places. It was a calm and beautiful place; I could see where the living quarters had opened off the courtyard, but the woodwork and tent hangings of this summer villa had long since fallen or rotted away. I went to fetch Tsorl and found him already plodding up the steps with his ring-walker.

I offered to help him, but he waved me aside. He came to the top of the headland and stood for a long time, staring at the tall archway until the rays of the Great Sun, setting, streamed through the open work of the fire symbol, until it burned like a live flame.

"I never thought to stand in this place," he said at last, "but here I am, Tsorl-U-Tsorl, citizen of Tsagul, and I greet the proud spirits of the Fire Clan."

We cleared a round unroofed place, perhaps an old

storeroom, and I gathered lace leaves to make a kind of tent. We lit another fire with embers from the first, which we had banked up on the beach, and covered it with leaves to make smoke against the swarms of insects that were coming out. I had a vial of ointment from Gwell Nu, and we smeared our faces and limbs; it worked fairly well, but in the islands, so I found, everyone becomes a little lumpy with stings. I slept, closing my mind and trying to drive all phantoms from my dreams; but when I woke once or twice, Tsorl was walking about, restless, as if he communed with the spirits of this lonely place.

When the Great Sun rose again, there was a stirring of creatures in the forests of Tsabeggan and on all the islands of the inner sea. A thousand flame birds flew up shrieking; small animals, the weljin or tree folk, came swinging out in their morning chorus. I stood in the grassy courtyard and felt a kind of joy. I was part of the island as it woke, as the morning wind moved the trees and vines and ruffled the grasses.

I was alone, Tsorl was nowhere to be seen, and there were no voices but the voices of the birds and animals; best of all there were no strange sounds. I wished that I could remain alone, part of the island, a creature sleeping or hunting according to the hour, a creature so free that it had no name. . . . Then I heard a sound: Tsorl came through the archway.

He had been down to the beach and caught four fish in a net of lace leaf, and he was as pleased as if he had built a new canal system for Tsagul. I looked sideways at the Deputy as he stirred up our fire: he was old, almost as old as Harn, he was crippled, and his honors, his power, had vanished completely. He was like one dead, as if he had truly been buried in the special compound at Itsik. Yet the flame of life had never burned more brightly in him; he was brave and strong, and I was the one who shrank away from the world.

"I have our bearings," he said. "The old jetty where they brought in the building material for this villa lies to the west. There is a road, and I think it must have led right down to a dock."

We walked through the fallen rooms of the villa and saw more steps and a ramp that led into the forest. There was the road, and it was still not overgrown. It ran under a light roof of vines like a broad grassy trench.

"I must go and hunt," I said, "and keep eyes open for your strangers."

"Take care," said the Deputy.

"You think they are very dangerous?"

He laughed aloud.

"They might consider *you* as dangerous!" he said. "You do not see yourself, Yolo Harn. If you take the bully-strings off those muscles, it does not mean they are not there. You could be a wild islander striding among the trees, hunting who knows what game. Do not frighten the strangers. It is just as important not to frighten the strangers as it is not to be afraid of them."

"What shall I do then?"

"Be quiet and watchful. Look for the camp on level ground. There will be a metal ship, who knows how large, and you will see it or hear it easily through the trees. See them first and come and report to me."

I looked at the beckoning roadway and the forest and felt no more than a twinge of my usual fear. I could hardly believe that there were strangers on the island; it was a dream, a miscalculation; they had all flown away again. I had a new redwood pole and my knife and my prison pouch slung across my body. Tsorl watched as I slipped into the trees, but I looked back only once.

I am not much of a hunter; my best results have come by chance like the land-sunner on the stone steps. I hoped to find another sunner or maybe a scrub-deer or even a breadfruit tree. The killing of a weljin would not only be difficult but distasteful—they have sweet voices like children and swing from the trees by their tails. I went along beside the road moving as quietly as possible and spent long periods in stillness, watching. I saw birds, including a walking bird that I might have tried for, but the forest was too thick for sunners.

I turned aside and went toward the foothills, the rising ground at the base of Tsabeggan's small, perfect fire mountain. If I bent down, I could glimpse the summit and the rising bluffs through gaps in the forest roof. The trees and vines were strange: redwood trees but with fewer stripes on their trunks and branches, fronds of every color from white-green to deepest blue-green that grew straight from the thick mold on the forest floor, vines that glowed of their own light in dark corners from a slippery coating on their matted stems.

The walking bird, large and brown, broke from cover again almost at my feet and ran off uttering a soft chittering cry. I looked at the pile of brushwood it had left; my luck had not run out—this was its nest. In the warm, feathery place I saw seven eggs, yellow with brown flecks. I stole four, wrapped them in brush and packed them in my prison pouch.

I went on into something like a clearing where a tree had fallen and taken some of the forest covering along with it. I looked back toward the roadway and could just see it, a lighter place among the trees. The sunlight was hot, and there were rocks; it was the place for sunners. I watched and sure enough, there was a frill-necked creature motionless on a rock, soaking up the warmth. I stalked it, struck and missed; it went into an impossibly deep crevice, and I was left ready to curse.

The sounds of the forest came back as the sounds of my scrambling footsteps died away, and one other sound came back. It had been going on for some time, I realized, and I had paid no attention to it. It was a sound I knew well: the sound of a hammer striking upon rock.

I listened for a long time, but the sound was unmistakable; I began to work my way toward it. The forest was unchanged, there were no rocks, then suddenly there was a long shaft of sunlight that lit up a fragment of an old wall, a Tsatroy wall, and in the sunlight a Moruian child with ordinary streaked blond hair patiently tapping away at the wall.

I was forty paces away; a pair of weljin overhead cried out and the child, the islander, flicked back its hair and saw me. It began to run toward the roadway, a little thin creature in some kind of brown tunic.

"Wait!"

I called and laughed and ran. The child could not run very fast; it was only a matter of a few paces before I could catch it.

"Wait, child. Don't be afraid!"

We ran, and I deliberately held back a little; we leaped together down onto the roadway, even broader at this point. The child stumbled and fell, almost at my feet.

"There now," I said, "you've taken a tumble! I won't hurt you, Island Child. . . ."

I seized the thin arm, and the cloth covering it was surprisingly thick and closely woven. The child turned its head and strained away from me in a spasm of fear. The fear leaped out at me and became my own fear. For this was not a child, not an islander. It was a thin, slight creature with a round pale face under the childish fall of hair and its eyes, yes, its small round staring eyes were a pale sky blue. . . .

I released the thin arm and stumbled backward. We stared at each other, each straining to master our fear. I believe we knew even then that each meant the other no harm, but the presence of some being absolutely strange brought its own absolute fear.

The stranger rose slowly to its feet, eyes fixed on me, and stood erect in a special position. Its small whitish hands were held away from its body palms outward. This meant little to me, but I deliberately laid aside my pole and my knife on its thong. I placed my own hands flat on my chest in the position that meant "no weapons."

I stared, reporting already in my mind to Tsorl-U-Tsorl. What I saw was a creature of a similar shape to a Moruian, but with the proportions altered, the body lines different, the set of the muscles and bones quite odd. Shorter than myself by about a head, slight but well-balanced. It stood astride on heavy matte-surfaced boots of some unknown substance with metal fastenings running over the front of the foot. It wore tight brown trunk hose and a loose greenish tunic of close-woven cloth marked with heavy seams and curious square pockets.

A slender neck and a round head under the childish hair. Suddenly the creature spoke. It raised a hand, placed it upon its chest and uttered two sounds. The voice was so strange that I could not take in the sounds at first. A voice not deep but resonant and musical; yet the sound of the human voice is a harsh music. Two sounds repeated, a two-sound word?

"Ka-ren. . . ."

I did not understand. I stood bewildered, then summoning all my courage, I held out my hands in the sign of first greeting and lowered my head politely. The creature was pleased, it smiled a perfectly recognizable smile and showed small white teeth. It nodded its flaxen head, held out its hands and bowed its body.

It repeated the word: "Ka-ren!" It pointed toward me and I took a step backward.

I spoke up and said: "Ta van!"

It is a formal greeting: Good wind. The stranger tried to copy the sound but could hardly do it, and for the first time we smiled together, we laughed.

The stranger moved slowly and took from one pocket a small gray box. It spoke into the box, and to my surprise a voice came out of the box, replying. I had a moment of panic, but then I thought of the Voice Wire. This was some such thing surely, even though it was wireless. The conversation lasted only a moment, and I thought the creature, my stranger, shut off the crackling voice in the midst of some excited speech.

Then it turned away from me and took a few steps on the Tsatroy road, using a gesture I understood well enough. It beckoned me to follow. I stood there, wondering, then I did follow, leaving a good distance between us. I took up my knife again, but left my redwood pole lying on the path. I reasoned that if the strangers were all as small as this one and as well-meaning, there could be little danger.

6

First Contact

WE WANDERED ON STEADILY, and I saw that the trees gave way to a wide clearing, the place of the Tsatroy dock. It was like a field now with the grasses grown tall and a few clumps of lace leaves and vines that had grown up again. The scene would have been strange enough—the clearing, the remains of the Tsatroy paving and walls, the secluded harbor of Tsabeggan—but the strangers had turned it into a place strange beyond dreams.

The grasses were crisscrossed with paths; everywhere there bloomed white and red and yellow patches upon the grass tips. The trees and vines were tied up with squares of paper; transparent domes, small balloons of every size popped up beside the paths. The grass had been bent down in one place and there stood the tent. It was round and pearly blue, and the fabric was divided into triangular sections. Its size was enough to make me step sideways; it was as large as a good-sized round house in Tsagul.

As I watched my stranger go into the clearing, I understood the meaning of the paths; the strangers, all of them, were fanatical about walking on the grasses. Everything that grew upon Torin was precious. If they could have managed it, they would have floated above the ground so as not to disturb a single unknown grass frond. My stranger tiptoed along a narrow path, and I followed, very carefully.

To right and left I saw the heads of grass tied up in colored pieces of fine netted cloth. Under the clear domes there were seed heads, flowers, perhaps families of insects. One large dome housed an ordinary pair of lace-spinners, good-sized browns that might have fetched a few credits at a fair up the Datse. On a platform by the dock stood another creature, even stranger than the first, calmly making a silkbeam of the strangest specimen of them all—myself, Yolo Harn, picking my way into camp.

The second stranger was taller than the first, as tall as myself, slender, dressed in the same costume of trunk hose, boots and square jacket. Its face was longer: Moruians look upon Lisa Child as the "beautiful" human, but this is because her face most nearly approaches a Moruian face. At this moment the thing I noticed was the color of her skin: a warm, silky color between dark brown and black.

I found another platform laid down in the grass where I would not tread on any dome or pocket, and I simply stood and stared all around me in a circle as far as my eyes could see. My stranger at the sight of its companion ran on and stood beside it, a little for protection, I could see, for its fear of me had not gone. The two of them bowed to me and talked to each other in nervous, noisy whispers. They went over the same business as before—hand on the chest and a two-sound word.

"Karen!"

"Lisa!"

There was a kind of explosion inside the blue tent. It sounded to me like a wild beast, a mountain wolf or even a small sea-sunner. As I watched, trembling, the noise was repeated, it grew louder . . . it was a voice, a terrible human voice! Out of the blue tent bounced a broad, strong, hairy, pink-faced stranger making a terrible noise and wrestling with another silkbeam.

The others cried out together, *"Sam!"*

The noisy one checked in its stride, pulled off its hat, bowed at me and let loose another noisy whisper of absolute amazement. Then it slapped its own hairy chest and said, "Sam." And I understood. Sam. Karen. Lisa. The first things that the strangers had thought of were their own names.

I felt foolish and shy, but my fear was under control. I laid my hand on my own chest and said as loudly as I could:

"*Yolo Harn!*"

They were very pleased. We smiled together and tried to say each other's names. Lisa turned from her silkbeam on its thin legs and began some ritual with a brown box that stood waist-high on the platform. Shallow trays came out of the box, and I saw that they were full of food: the strangers were preparing a meal. I sat politely on my own platform—a square of hard blue fabric like the tent—in the midst of their grass garden and stared.

So it was the beginning, the time in camp, and already it was captured on the film in their silkbeams, the camera. I have seen that particular film many times with the sound-track of the human voices and a few sounds of my own. Karen-Ru confided later that they were not sure whether I would be frightened by the camera; there had been tribes of forest dwellers on their home world who feared that the camera stole away their souls if it made a likeness. I had no such fear, but it was very strange and in the end a little sad to see that string of pictures.

There is the clear island day, the fantastic campground, the road leading out of the dark forest. Karen comes down the road, jerky, frightened; then slowly, steadily with the deliberate walk that also betrayed wariness and fear, along comes Yolo Harn. Tall, thin, oddly muscular, colored by the sun . . . a close-up of the face, and the camera lingers then flits away, as if frightened by what it saw. As the camera pictures the newcomer picking its way on the paths, there is a burst of speech in the background: Karen whispering to Lisa.

"*Are you getting him . . . peaceful, I'm sure . . . oh heaven, I'm shaking all over . . . hope I did right. . . .*"

Lisa replying, "*Humanoid is right. . . . See the eyes though. Sure it's a male?*"

"*I think so, but very young . . . young boy. Smile . . . he's very smart.*"

"*He's civilized.*"

"*You think so? Out of the forest? Where is Sam?*"

Then a close-up of Karen speaking her name, and a shot of Yolo bowing. Voices of both girls in the background, speaking their names, and, overlapping, the muffled sounds of Sam in the tent. Part of Sam's missed because the

camera is on the newcomer, laughing nervously at Sam.
Sam at last, panting, cussing.

*"Where in blue blazes did you get this character, Karen?
Have you tried names? What about names?"*

He slaps his chest.

"Sam!"

And the newcomer, looking as shy as she felt, replies,
"Yolo Harn. . . ."

The Moruian voice: whistling, hooting, with two
changes of register, so I am told, for every human change.
The voice and face of a Moruian on film. I saw the film
and remembered the day, and when times were bad I
thought of that day very often. I stepped so quickly into
the camp; the humans were so eager to have me come. Yet
we cannot go back to that perfect beginning of our
friendship again. It is not the camera that steals away our
souls, it is time.

Lisa prepared a tray of food for me and Karen set it at
the end of the large platform. I came closer and sat on
the steps around the platform, as they all did with their
trays. Before much eating was done, I remembered that
I had something to add to their feast—as it was polite to do
—and I stripped off my prison pouch and handed it toward Lisa. All three humans left their meals to examine
this strange gift: an ordinary round pouch of rough tent-
weave wool and flax cloth with strange symbols worked on
the band joining its two circles of cloth. Strange symbols
that mean in fact, *"City of Tsagul Watch-House. Do Not
Steal This Pouch."*

The plain star-shaped opening on the back of the pouch
was something they could not fathom, and in spite of their
delicate handling I feared for the contents. I reached out
and showed how to untie the thong that held the star, and
inside they found, at last, the four large eggs packed in
brushwood. They thanked me extravagantly and handed
the pouch back, but I let them keep it.

I looked at my tray and found that I was very hungry.
Lisa had given me things carefully calculated not to make
me ill. Breadsticks. Leaf greens and berries and fruit from
the island trees. A delicious cold yellow drink of juice that
she made from a tiny cube. I gobbled all this up and
pleased the humans as if I were their child new shown.
Then showing her skill and the wonders of her cooking
box, Lisa blew the stuff from the eggs and while Sam

threaded them on a string, she cooked an egg pasty with salt on a hot plate, and we all ate some of it.

We rested after the meal, sitting around the platform, but the humans were governed by that devil of Sam's called "Routine." Presently they began to work, and one thing after another made me afraid. Lisa put the trays into her box, which created a hissing sound in its innards, then strangest of all she spoke to the box. I did not understand the sounds but in fact she said "Carrier to the tent!"

Sam moved aside, and the whole box rose up on metal treads and walked down the steps. I watched, frozen with fear, as the box picked its way down the steps and rolled smoothly along a path and entered the blue tent.

Karen saw my fear, and everyone made soothing noises but it was too late. I had risen to my feet and at last, through the screen of a grove of trees that had grown up in the center of the dock area, I saw the ship. If the carrier had made me afraid, this was something to make me crouch down, hands over head, like the roaring of the sea-sunner. Yet I was too proud. I simply stared and trembled.

All three humans reacted at once: Sam walked toward the ship and beckoned. Lisa and Karen held out their hands. They soothed again in their rough musical voices. Slowly, slowly I came around the platform, thinking of Tsorl and of the fire spirits for protection. I let them lead me, but without touching my hands, toward this huge, terrifying object.

It took up a good part of the second clearing, and the grass where it had landed was scorched and burned in a circle. There were the same paths laid down leading to it, and the grass was beginning to grow up again. My fear was unreasoning, I knew that, but the sight of that ship from the void, solid, silvery, painted here and there in strange bright colors, with its ports like bulging eyes, its antennae, vents, fins, locks, was overpowering.

It seemed from the first to have a life of its own; I could hardly believe that it would not rise up of its own accord and roar away into the air. I remembered a tiny thread of the same fear when I had visited the Tsatroy Palace in Tsagul and had seen a famous old war engine from the clan wars. There stood the fierce old siege catapult with a pile of stone balls and its rope wound tightly as if ready to hurl the stones at an enemy. I could not believe that it would not go off by itself.

Sam had some business inside the ship, so he approached it and a door opened: a ramp came down. This was not the magic it seemed at first; Sam was using his long-range unit, his "sesame box," another of the grayish boxes that played so many parts in the lives of the humans. I watched Sam go into the ship and hoped that he could control the monster and not allow it to make any loud noises. Still I could not stay close to the object of my fear, and when I turned aside it seemed to loom behind me, glittering. I went back to the platform and sat for a long time watching the humans, Karen, Lisa, and Sam again, when he returned from the ship.

It was easy to see that they were following some pattern in their work, that they did many tasks in order, but the tasks at first were a mystery so that their business was pointless as the scurrying of the inin, the ants of Torin. In fact, they gathered and checked their plant and insect specimens, they checked and adjusted the water and waste systems that served their tent. Sam performed many tasks concerned with the air and with the weather; he had a platform by the harbor in the upper branches of a large redwood tree. I could not sit idle while all of this was going on and I rose up and took the beautiful silvery digging spoon or spade out of Lisa's hands and dug four little trenches and a pit.

Time was passing, but we did not notice it; we were in a kind of harmony where our lack of speech hardly mattered. The Great Sun moved down the sky, I had three strange names and four or five strange words. Sam went up to his platform again and he called something urgently. The girls stood still and stared at the road from the forest. Then a voice rang out, and I started to my feet guiltily. He came out of the shadow, plodding, and plodded right to the edge of the camp.

He did not see me at first but stood and demanded in a voice full of anxiety, "What have you done with Yolo Harn?"

Tsorl-U-Tsorl was an awe-inspiring figure: an old warrior, or a sea robber, as the humans called him. He stood there, fierce, tired, hair bristling, his arm bands catching the light, his arms like polished brown wood. How he had come so far with the ring-walker I could hardly guess. I stepped up and called to him.

"I am here. They are all friendly, as you said!"

"By the fire!" he growled, "you had me worried. I found your stick on the path . . . sets of footprints . . ."

I ran to help him then and explained about walking on the paths. We began to approach the platform, and I saw that all three humans were standing close together with curious expressions.

"Deputy," I said, "smile for the fire's sake . . . they are afraid of *you!*"

He smiled then and raised his arm in a salute; he was the politician beaming from the balcony. It worked well enough, and we came up to the others. This time the naming ceremony went better because I was able to present Tsorl—in a formal greeting it is better not to say one's own name but to be introduced.

"Fine," said Tsorl, "they are friendly and to my eyes they do not look so incredibly strange. They see enough out of those little eyes. Where is the ship?"

He repeated his question with gestures to the others, and Sam began to get his meaning.

"It is over behind the trees," I said warily.

Tsorl, in his usual brisk manner, plodded straight off, eyes alight with curiosity. The humans were surprised, but they led us again, if Tsorl did not lead them, and back we came to where the shining thing stood.

"Deputy . . ." I plucked his tunic.

At last he understood.

"Yolo Harn," he said, "you are a native of Tsagul. You are a miner, born to work with metal. In fact you have seen more of metal and engines in your few years than most Moruians see in a lifetime. You are also brave enough to wrestle a sea-sunner . . . do not turn coward now at the sight of this ship!"

So I walked forward, gripping his hand, until we stood close to the metal monster. Tsorl was enchanted. He stared at the ship with burning concentration as if he would take in every detail of its construction at one glance. He limped up and laid a hand on its shining skin. Sam and Lisa came to his side and the three of them walked the whole length of the vessel exchanging words and gestures and nodding wisely. I took the opportunity to step a few paces back; Karen had remained behind too, and she smiled comfortably at me. I wondered if this person thought me a coward.

Suddenly Lisa uttered a sharp cry and turned back from examining a portion of the ship. Human voices whirled about the clearing; to my horror the one, Karen, at my side, let out a torrent of speech and began to weep. It is one of the things like smiling and laughter that we share most perfectly with the race of humans. I could do nothing . . . I could understand nothing. Tsorl limped back toward me, and I ran to him.

"Curse me for a fool," he said. "Yolo Harn, I have done a terrible thing. I have shown these poor creatures that I have seen the smaller ship. I saw the place where it fits onto the mother ship and showed them I understood its purpose. They are asking for news of their fourth member."

"But perhaps it still lives. . . ." I said.

"Try explaining that . . . without words!"

"Show them the map!"

"Not yet," said Tsorl. "We must try our best. How will this thing be done?"

The humans stood in a tight knot, comforting each other. Tsorl pointed and I helped when I knew what he wanted. The tent . . . we must go into the blue tent. We were all silent now, or whispering together, Moruians and strangers each in their own language. They led us down a path and into a second door of the blue dome.

I believed that nothing could scare me as much as the silver ship, and in fact the interior of the tent, a place of wonders, was cool and comforting. Some things were strange, but some I understood: the four screened places where the strangers slept, even the queer ballooning sleeping platforms and the shaped sitting benches. Tsorl looked about and saw what he wanted—maps. A larger copy of the one he carried hidden in his leather vest. Sam spread it on a part of the tent wall, and it stuck fast.

"I must sit down," said Tsorl. "Is that some kind of chair?"

Before my hand touched it, Karen was at my side helping to bring it to Tsorl. He sat before the map, but before he could point to it, Sam was taken with another useful idea. He called for our attention and began a long piece of play-acting. He pointed to first one then another of his friends and said their names. But sometimes he said the wrong names. The humans all joined the game and while we sat trying to take the meaning, they alternately nodded their heads up and down or shook them from side to side. They intoned the words: *Yess . . . No-oo*. Karen? *Yess*.

Karen? (It was Lisa) *No.* Sam? (It was still Lisa) *No.*
Lisa? *Yess!*

After a few rounds Tsorl and I were joining in, nodding
or shaking like wooden dolls. Yess. No-oo. The nodding
had confused us at first more than the sounds: the common gesture for *yes* is simply blinking.

"This is all very well," said Tsorl, "but they may be setting too much store by these quick negatives and affirma-
tives. The world goes along on 'maybe' or 'maybe not.'"

"Deputy, these ones come from a different world."

"I know it!"

He took up the ring-walker to point to the map, but
Lisa handed him a small white wand made of metal that
extended to the right length. Then we began the impossible:
explaining a matter of life and death to persons who had
not a word of our speech.

First Tsorl located the place in the mountains where he
believed the small ship had come down. I held on the map
a berry, for the ship, and we brought it down the river
Troon, clearly shown on the map, on a small folded page
for a barge. Question (acted with a small paper beaker):
Was the ship empty or was the stranger in it? Answer:
Empty . . . Yess. Ship on raft to Linlor . . . if we followed the map correctly . . . Tsorl goes aboard. Urgent
questioning about the pilot.

Tsorl pointed to Otolor, clearly visible because the Troon
is wide at this point and there is an island in the river,
which he tells me is part of the town. The stranger here.
Already we know it is called Scott, a name we can hardly
say; like other Moruians, we compromise with "Escott."
Escott was at Otolor after the barge with the ship had
passed by. A long complication here with eyes and ears;
human eyes are smaller than ours, but human ears are
somewhat larger, set forward and lower on the head. Question: Was Escott seen by Tsorl, by Yolo or Otolor?
Answer: No-oo, but news heard by Yolo and others of
Escott at Otolor.

A last desperate effort—Karen turned aside and could
not watch Sam's acting. Question: Is Escott dead? (Sam
measured his length on the blue floor of the tent and lay
there looking very dead.) Answer: ("Pray Telve it is the
right one," said Tsorl.) No-oo. More questions: *Where*
is this Escott? At this place on the map? Or this? We cannot tell them.

So they were given a thread of hope, no more, and they seemed to understand our difficulties. Lisa made a diversion with counting. We all came along well together for the simple count . . . one to ten-more-many, but Tsorl could not proceed with the two higher systems he knew, or with their higher systems. We battled on with the simple count, using tens of fingers. We spent some time comparing hands. The humans have a wide flat hand with five digits like our own, but there the resemblance ends. They have only one turner called "the thumb" to be set against the hand-cup or palm. We have, of course, the first turner and the second turner, our pointing finger, which can be set against the hand-cup too. Still there is something strong and full of craft about their hands, and they have put them to good use.

By the simple count, Tsorl tried to indicate the numbers of people in the two cities. We had already identified ourselves proudly as citizens of Tsagul, our good Tsagul, a gray-black smudge on the edge of the map. Rintoul stood out to the east, twice the size, a great blot on the delta of the Troon.

"By the fire, Yolo Harn, I am a fool," said the Deputy. "I have not shown them the map."

I saw with an anxiety that had been growing on me all through our queer, exhausting effort to communicate, that the Deputy was very tired and strained. His good leg was full of muscle cramps and the other still painful. I helped him take the map from his shoulder hiding place. We handed it to the newcomers, and indicated Linlor, where Tsorl took it from the small ship. I thought Karen would weep again, but they were all quiet, and it pleased them to hold the map once again because it had belonged to their comrade.

Then Lisa gave a warning cry, and I was just in time to hold Tsorl as he slumped off the long blue chair. His eyes were closed, he was fainting. I flexed his arms and sat him upright as Gwell Nu had taught me, then pressed the "waking place" under his ribs; he came to with a gasp. The humans brought water in a paper beaker, and I gave him some but I saw that what he really needed was sleep. It was too far to bear him back to our first camp at the Tsatroy villa right across Tsabeggan, and I did not believe that we should share the strangers' tent. For one thing it strained their hospitality and for another I was not sure about spending a whole sleeping period in such a new place.

"Tsorl-U-Tsorl," I instructed, "we will sleep out of this tent, maybe on the platform by the harbor. Sleep now. . . . I will put a sleep herb in this water."

"As you say, Yolo Forgan. . . ."

It was good to hear him attempt a joke. I had my herb pocket in my vest, and I put the pinch of herbs in his drink. My supplies from Itsik were holding well; the sleeping herb I used was Common Leen, which is the mildest, the strongest being Red Leen and Ullit or water-petal. The Deputy lay back in his chair and slept. I picked my way to the front door of the tent and looked out at the setting of the Great Sun.

Karen came with me, and I pointed to the platform. She called to Sam, and there followed one of their casual, everyday miracles. Sam walked out of the tent with a small blue package and presently, on the sandy ground beyond the platform, a small blue tent flowered.

I lifted Tsorl, and they watched me do it, as some sort of test of strength, but then they came forward again and showed that the very chair he had been using could be made into a carrying bed. I laid him down again and took one end of the bed while Sam took the other. We carried the Deputy to the tent and laid him in it. I went in too and sat beside him. The humans bade me good night, but shortly Lisa came back with a tray of food—more of that good yellow juice and fruit and a square of good-tasting salty stuff. I learned later that it was called "all-purpose protein."

Lisa was the Forgan of the strangers, and we had a session of pointing and strange words concerning Tsorl and his amputated leg. I managed to convey that it was not an accident . . . the leg had not, for instance, been bitten off by a large fish. Also, the surgery was not my own work but that of another "far away across the sea"; I hated even to point in the direction of Itsik.

I took out my folded storage cloth, which had places for all the medicines Gwell Nu had sent along with me, and Lisa saw that they were mainly from plants, some ground fine, some dried, some scraped. I sniffed the sleeping cloth, which had all but lost its power, and let Lisa smell it, then tried to show its use. When all this was done, she went away, back to the large tent where lights had flowered so that it glowed in the little darkness. For a last exchange I pointed to a smudge of light in the west, among the lingering sunset colors of Esto, and taught Lisa the names of the two suns: Esto and Esder.

Then I was alone. The Deputy slept soundly; I sat twanging and trembling like a harp string for hours longer. The sight of the common world: the sea, the trees, the Tsatroy cobblestones, all soothed me. This was my world after all, this was the good orb of Torin, the special place hung in the void by the making spirits for the race of the Moruia, the weavers, and the Tsamuia, the fire people.

Tomorrow, I thought, I will go to the cove, yonder, to the east of the camp and catch them some fish for breakfast in a lace-leaf net. So in the end I slept, but the lights burned on and on in the larger blue tent. The humans had had an astonishing day too. They made their reports; it was part of the routine. That night Karen wrote in her personal journal as follows:—

DAY 103. FIRST CONTACT, 10.35 BASE TIME
Anthropoid, young male, app. 1.86m, loose, agile, upright gait; all greater joints and musculature differing in detail yet to be determined. Heavy development of "trapezius" and "biceps"; hands with two protothumbs in apposition. Skin color red-brown, hair fine, brown; cranial shape long-headed with strange anterior development. Eye color mid-brown, eyes twice the size of human eyes, c. 50mm in length set into sides of the head. He can stand still and look in a full circle. Voice: uncanny fluting tone . . . Sam places a register above and below our norm.
CLOTHING: "Tunic" of fine unseamed gray cloth, ?wool/linen mixture, circular shape, worn with right shoulder free. Undergarment of gray cloth, overgarment of tanned decorated leather descending past the hips. Soft leather boots, side fastening.
His name sounds like "Yoro-harren." Intelligent, highly civilized. Not, as I believed at first sight, a primitive or forest dweller. This proved by Second Anthropoid. Older male. 1.76m, heavier build, graying hair on the head, traces of facial hair, growth of thick down on neck, shoulders and upper arms. *Left leg amputated below the knee.* This guy is definitely some kind of chief, leader, soldier. NAME: Tsaw-oo-Tsaw.

It seems crazy but they may have come looking for us. They are castaways, alone; they came here over the sea. Some kind of refugees from fighting? *Tsaw has seen the shuttle.*

Oh Scott . . . oh after this long time. I can't take much more of it, and I can't stop hoping. There's a world out there, now we know it, you were right. Maybe these are your "Moruia of Torin" that your granddad heard about in that old "alien-hoax" on a moon of Mars. After seeing the stonework on this island, and after seeing Yoro stand before me on the path and that game old Tsaw pointing at the map like some general, I can believe anything. I can believe they found you, and that you are safe and will come back to us again. Sam can't leave now, that is certain. We will extend communication with these two and work on a plan for taking the ship to the continent. Wherever you are, Scott, hear me, think of me, as I think of you. . . .

7

The Dream and the Awakening

TSORL HAD DONE WHAT HE SET OUT TO DO: he had found the strangers, their camp and their ship. Yet he had done it at the cost of his strength; he was very weak for days, as if the trials of the voyage on the raft and of his operation itself had finally taken their toll. He lay in the small tent or came out and sat in the sun and watched the activity of the camp.

The next morning, and on many other mornings, I went to the cove beyond the camp and caught fish. It was a pleasant cove with a thin crust of land protecting it from the open sea and the Round Current. The waters were teeming with fish that no one had ever disturbed; it was a fisher's dream place.

The humans were in one of their worry-nets about the fish. This was rare precious Torin fish, they argued; it should be preserved rather than eaten or captured only on film. On the other hand it was surely right that Tsorl and I, two castaways on our own home world, should have a right to its bounties and be able to eat the fish we caught. Another point was that the fish was delicious. The humans had plenty of food, but not much was fresh, and they valued freshness above everything.

Finally Sam came to the cove and saw the way the fish swarmed; he watched me with the lace-leaf net, baited with fat flies. Then he sat on a rock with a deep sigh of pleasure and took out a roll of tough white thread. He tied a fat fly to its end and cast it into the blue water. We sat side by side and caught, slowly and deliberately, about fifteen good-sized fish, more than twice the number I had taken before. When Sam reentered the camp carrying his catch, the two other humans shrieked and shook their fists at him, but it was only play-acting. We all had a fish feast that day, and afterward fished moderately for our needs.

We were still in a world of few words and some half-guessed thoughts. The routine the strangers kept explained itself by degrees. Tsorl, as he grew stronger, went to the ship and sat gazing at it for hours, with an expression like Sam when he caught fish. Even I grew bold enough to draw near and touch its metal skin. When some of its engines were tested and the whole of Tsabeggan seemed to thrum with the sound, I ran away and hid my head, but Tsorl drew closer, bristling with interest. Sam and Karen took him inside the ship the first time. I pretended to be busy with some digging but I was pleased when Tsorl came out again. Lisa looked at me and blinked one of her little slanted brown eyes as if to say: "There, you see; nothing to worry about!"

The next part of our life together, Human and Moruian, had to do with the machines in the blue tent. We went there at the strangers' invitation and saw moving pictures in a small box, about four fists by three and shaped like the tent windows—a square with the corners rounded. When we came to accept the colors and shapes of this film, we saw a world, the strangers' world. Sometimes the images or scenes followed one upon the other; people—were they people?—walked about in thousands, buildings crowded higher than the sky-houses of Rintoul, trees, or something very like them, thrust up to the glassy screen.

Better still, there were the sets of separate images: one man, one woman, one child, one tree growing out of the ground. We could control the images ourselves by pressing knobs on small gray boxes that felt like horn. We pressed the button and brought back the man, the woman, the child. We stared at them for a long time.

Finally Tsorl said: "Sam is a male, a man. Are the others, Karen and Lisa, really shaped in that strange way?"

"Yes, I think they are," I said. "Why don't we ask them?"

"Pah! You're an impolite wretch, Yolo Harn."

"Karen and Lisa will not swim where I am. They have a shyness. They are females."

"Shyness is not a characteristic of females on Torin," said Tsorl, "but I suppose you may be right. The point is why are they so shaped?"

It took several boxes of educational pictures before we found out. There was a terrible image on the screen. I leaped up clutching my own body and ran out into the sunlight. I thought I must become ill. The image, which I could not drive away, showed a woman with a full-grown child, ready for showing, still within its mother's body. How would it get out? How would it breathe? How had it been fed during the growing time? The humans could not understand why I was upset, and I could not explain. I did not go back into the tent for a day and a half, and then only because Tsorl called me urgently.

He had found an image of a strange animal. Yet not so strange. It was tall and resembled a smooth-furred wool-deer. It had a young one in its pouch. We were very pleased with the picture.

"Surely that looks something like the old ancestor, the Wild Enmor of the west, whose bones are found and preserved," said Tsorl.

"It is a dear creature," I said, "and looks rather like an old neighbor in Tin Lane who sold shellfish."

"I have almost solved the mystery," said Tsorl. "Look at this picture. . . ."

It was another animal—a monstrous hairy sort of giant weljin, going upon two legs. We switched between the two pictures, and the humans came to watch too. They were pleased at the sight of the hairy one; obviously they felt the same kinship with it as we did with the pouched one. Between "Yes" and "No," we came to a dim understanding. We accepted that the humans were not pouched and this was their ancestor; they found it difficult to believe that things worked differently with us.

"Short of having you strip off your clothes," remarked Tsorl, "I do not think we can get much further."

"I will do no such thing," I said. "Even a Moruian female has its shyness and modesty, Deputy."

"You know, of course, that our friends all think of you as a young male!"

"What does that matter?"

Yet perhaps it did matter. It made for less communication and understanding. Next morning when Lisa and Karen went off to their place on the harbor to swim, I followed them. They huddled in the water when I came close; they were clothed in strange wisps of cloth shaped to their strange bodies. I felt shy but I stood on the bank and took off all my clothes. Moruians always swim unclothed and the idea of wearing cloth in water by choice is very odd.

Lisa and Karen understood at last. They saw that I was a "pouched female without breasts," as they wrote in the reports. I was becoming accustomed to reading their faces, and I saw all kinds of thoughts flitting over them this morning. I dived in and swam about, and afterward we all sat in the sun on the bank. We were all very polite and did not stare or ask questions until we knew each other much better. But the mystery was solved.

Even now that the state of knowledge between the two peoples has advanced a long way, Moruians find the birth of human children a subject of profound discomfort and disbelief. Humans, so far as I can gather, think that Moruian birth is easy but a little primitive.

In these first days I went on an expedition with Karen and Sam to the other side of the island. We followed the old Tsatroy road back to the villa, and they marveled in their turn at the stonework. I collected all the poor possessions of Tsorl and myself. We went down the steps of the villa and there was our raft still beached. I felt that it was an old friend: the days on the ocean leading to freedom seemed far away, and I remembered them with a kind of sadness.

We had our food on the headland overlooking the inland sea and stared at the islands with Sam's seeing glasses. I could barely squint through the double glass, but the one-eyed glass, like the ones used by Moruian sailors, was easy for me to use and brought the islands very close. We saw more camp smoke, but that was the only sign of the true Islanders. No trading ships sailed among the islands; no Mattroyan steam vessel disturbed the air.

Tsorl had recovered his strength and with it his independence. We moved out of camp to a smaller cove

beside the Fish Cove. This was the human name of the
fishing place, and our camp was called Little Fish Cove.
Our friends begged us to keep the small blue tent, and
with our own few pots and mats and blankets, we made
ourselves very comfortable without any unseemly off-
world luxury. We ate the food we gathered ourselves, but
very often we gathered enough fruit or salad grasses or
crabs for the humans as well and shared their food at a
general feast.

By this time we spoke a strange mishmash of Moruian
and Human speech, still interwoven with hand and body
signals. Almost every day Tsorl and I sat before the screen
in the main tent and looked at the pictures. We noticed
that the screen had strong mind-powers of its own. Flash-
ing lights or certain notes of music or singing rang in my
head, and once or twice I found myself falling into a
trance or sleep.

The question of mind-powers had barely been raised,
but already we suspected the truth, namely that the humans
were "thought-blind." We watched them at a game called
"cards" and could not understand how a player could
keep his collection of numbers and pictures secret from
the others. We learned to play a child's game called "Snap"
and another called "Memory," and as we feared, it was
no contest. Working together or separately, Tsorl and
I simply knew what the little stiff pieces of card had upon
them.

The humans were enchanted with this simplest power
and tested us with another set of symbol cards. When
Tsorl, from any place in the camp, "sent" the cards to me,
I heard him plainly and scored a perfect round. When I
sent to him, the results were nearly as good. We tried
with Tsorl sending to the humans: Karen tested very much
better than the two others, but still it was a human score,
irregular, changing with her mood. I knew that my own
mind-powers were not strong and in any case they were
"green-thoughts," the powers possessed by a young person. Tsorl, however, though he set no store by such things,
had considerable mind-powers.

When I saw this, I begged him to keep sending his
thoughts to his friends on the mainland: to Vel Ragan, his
scribe, or to the proud Dohtroy highness Tilje. He agreed,
but without much hope.

"Yolo Harn," he said, "you have saved me, but at some cost. They will think I am dead."

Still the daily life, that old devil routine went on, and one morning I went into the big tent, all unsuspecting, at the summons of Tsorl and Lisa.

"Be brave," said Tsorl, "and we will solve the problem of communication."

"What kind of net have you made for me?" I asked warily.

Lisa had put a new attachment onto the screen, and part of it was a kind of wire hat with two soft parts to fit over human ears. After some persuasion and adjustment, I allowed them to fit it to my head and a strange voice, like the voices of the films, said to me gently: "Go up." On the screen was a curious moving symbol that I recognized as a stick-man; the stick-man climbed a stepped line and I realized that he was in fact going up. "Go up," murmured the voice in my ear and then, after a moment, "Go down," and the stick-man went down.

I looked at Tsorl and Lisa, and they motioned me to speak the human words. I managed this easily enough, and saw Lisa touch another switch; a little demon of red light danced on the screen and I felt it boring into my mind. I snatched off the wire cap and shook my head to clear away the voice.

"Please . . . " said the Deputy.

"It is a terrible thing!" I cried. "It is hateful and will turn me against metal forever. Deputy, how could you!"

"Yolo Harn," he said, "it is a Teaching Machine and contains what Lisa-Child calls 'speech tapes.' You could learn in a short time a version of their speech."

Lisa was persuading me too in words I could not understand.

"Believe me," said Tsorl, "I would do it first if I could. In fact I will do it . . . I will be taught by this machine, but more slowly."

"Why is that?"

"It is a kind of sleep teaching," explained Tsorl. "As I understand it from her, humans must take sleeping medicine as well as the light to use the thing at all."

"I know it would make me sleep, and I am afraid, Deputy."

"There is nothing to fear. I cannot do it properly . . . I think it is because I am too old and too stubborn. My mind fights against the sleeping; I go at an ordinary learning pace."

"Great Fire of Ullo!" I exclaimed. "How fast would I go? Their speech is as wide as ours . . . it would still take ages!"

"Not so long," he replied. "This is a shortened version of the speech to assist foreigners."

I sat there, sullen, with the wire cap still in my hands. Lisa caught my eye; she went to one of the store sacks in the tent and drew out a small brown package . . . another of their miracles. She indicated that the package was for me and said what was, for me, a magic word.

"Boat . . ."

I was being bribed, I knew it, but it was a very good bribe. The brown package was a small boat that inflated at the tugging of a ring and had its own "power-pack." I had already scooted all around the harbor in one of these marvelous boats and would have gone around the island if Sam had allowed it.

"There, you see," said Tsorl with some disapproval, "you are being given toys, like a child. . . ."

I answered like a child too; perhaps I had been acting the grown-up for too long.

"Would the boat be mine to keep?"

I acted this out to Lisa, clutching an imaginary boat-package to my chest, and she nodded a firm "Yess." I sighed deeply and sent a prayer to the fire spirits and made the averting sign to ward off evil. Then I settled the wire cap on my head and fixed my eyes on the screen.

The red light flashed and the stick-man began to walk up and down while the soft voice . . . I believe it was a female voice . . . sounded in my ears. In no time I was far away; I floated, I swam, I was a bodiless spirit. I knew nothing but the light and the pictures on the screen. The soft voice was everywhere about me, and my own voice repeated the strange words. "Go up . . . go down . . . go back . . ."

Even the light went away and I remained in timeless emptiness with the voice. Finally the voice stopped too; perhaps it said farewell; I was asleep.

I saw a haze of blue overhead like the summer sky, but it quickly turned into the roof of the blue tent. I had slept, lying back on one of the long chairs; the wire cap was off my head; the Teaching Machine slept too. Everyone was in the tent watching me wake up. Lisa held orange juice to my lips; Tsorl held out his hands in the gesture that inquired:

"Are you recovered?"

I blinked to reassure him and got up from the chair. I felt an overpowering desire to get into the fresh air.

"Do you want to sleep?" asked Lisa.

"No!" I said. *"I go out from tent."*

I staggered into the sunlight and took great breaths of air. I hardly realized why the others all followed me, clapping their hands to show pleasure.

I went onto the Teaching Machine every day for two camp-clock hours, and in twenty days I had learned Basic English. Tsorl plodded along, and as he went, he attempted more difficult things. He tried to prepare a list of exchange sound-symbols, English and Moruian; he spoke the Moruian word or expression onto another collecting tape when he thought he had a good equivalent. This was a work that fascinated him, but he often complained that it was not exact. Many of the translations of Moruian words, especially those dealing with traditional ways of life, our "old threads," have been hammered out and agreed upon as something that comes closest to the right sense.

Little by little I was able to speak to the humans and to understand what they said to me. But we did not speak enough or exchange the right words. It was a long holiday, a dream time; once I sailed around the island with Karen; once I led Sam and Lisa on an expedition to the central mountain. We exchanged songs, games, jokes; we swam and collected seeds and dried out bunches of leaves for Karen to pack into her "dry garden" folder.

Tsorl and I were able to retell the little we knew of Scott Gale; he was often in the thoughts of the humans. His musical instrument hung silent on the wall of his sleeping place in the blue tent. It was a wooden guitar, something between a harp and a box harp. He had been the singer among them, and his favorite melodies were very ancient songs of Earth. We spoke to his friends in tones of guarded hope, but Tsorl was not really so hopeful.

"Scott Gale did not keep hidden," he said to me, "but perhaps this was right. Half of Torin must know of his existence . . . he is bound to meet with the Great Elder sooner or later."

"What would be done with him? What would Tiath Gargan want with a Human?"

"What he always wants . . . power!" replied Tsorl-U-Tsorl. "Power to work his will, power to govern and control all that is on Torin. Tiath would hold sway over the winds themselves if he could. Pray Telve that Scott Gale keeps out of his net!"

II

Sam Fletcher was the leader of the humans, and he was, in his own way, a ruling spirit. He was cheerful and very quick-tempered; he shouted so that I had to cover my ears and urged us all to "Get on with it!" or to "Rise and shine!" He came by the name Sam-Deg, and I explained the sense of this as best I could. He was Sam-who-tells-others-what-to-do and Sam-who-is-cross-again, but as well as that Sam-we-like and Sam-we-do-our-best-for. Sam Deg. Yet under this brisk manner was a true leader, a stern and decisive person. For this reason, there was never a true meeting of thoughts between Sam and Tsorl-U-Tsorl, for the Deputy could not tell his misfortunes or make suggestions to this other leader. When Sam questioned him, he became elusive and pretended not to understand. They managed to communicate pretty well on matters of science, and Tsorl strove to understand in mere days the accumulated wisdom of all the years of Earth. He watched and calculated and listened until his head became heavy.

Lisa-Child was a kind and motherly person; she was the Healer among the humans and had control of many medicines and some healing machines. She massaged the crossness out of Sam Deg in the evenings by kneading the back of his thick, hairless neck. They were partners, they had a kind of pair marriage, like many in Tsagul, and far, far away, unbelievably far, so that it hurt my head even to think of it, they had a male child, a pale brown human that they called a boy, whose name was Zak. He was studying to be a Healer and to fly in a ship of the void like his parents.

When I thought of this separation, these monstrous distances, I did not know how any thinking creature could bear such loneliness. Yet I was far from any person I might have called my family; I did not know if I would

ever see my dear foster-mother Morritt again or Gwell
Nu who had taught me so much. I thought sometimes of
those true workmates, Warker and Clee from the New Cut
Mine; I saw in dreams the handsome face of that sailor, the
Rope Ward. All of them were far away. Tsorl's case was
worse; he was a mere ghost, and his friends and former
supporters could have no idea of what had become of him.

I had great difficulty in explaining to the Humans the
facts of my dishonor and my stay in Itsik, the prison
settlement. Even with Karen, who was my closest friend
among them, I found myself shy and tangled up. I had
been "in a bad place," I stammered. I had been doing "bad
work." I am sure this sort of talk puzzled her especially
compared with the other tales we told of the rest of Torin,
where we held nothing back unless our words were unequal
to the task.

Karen was the youngest of the Humans; her other name
was Schwartz, and no Moruian could manage this without
much practice. The name is from another Earth speech
and it means "black," so she became Karen-Ru. She was
a scholar whose chief study was plants, then animals . . .
everything that lived on the ground, in the trees, in the
water. The immensity of her tasks, the listing of so many
new things, might have driven her out of her wits, but she
remained calm and cheerful. She had endless patience; her
mind could range in an instant from wide thoughts about
the whole globe of Torin—which parts were hot, cold,
moist or dry—to the contemplation of two grass-bugs
climbing a stem of grass. She questioned me closely about
the most ordinary things. It makes me laugh now to recall
the halting descriptions of tree-bears, wool-deer, fish, flat-
bills, which came first into the records from Yolo Harn,
the Child of the City.

Of one rare creature I had first-hand experience: the
sea-sunner. Karen-Ru did not believe a word I said about
this huge beast; she nodded wisely as I stretched my arms,
but I could see that she thought I was telling a tall tale like
a fisher. I could have called upon Tsorl-U-Tsorl to back up
my story, but I did not, I was too proud. I used to walk
down to the ruined watchtower at the end of the old
Tsatory breakwater and look out to sea through a one-
eyed glass. I saw a few trading vessels pass far away, but
none came to the islands; the sight of these ships amused
and excited the Humans. Karen-Ru always liked to see a

ship, and at these times I knew she was thinking of her dear sib Scott Gale. She still hoped that he might return in a ship to Tsabeggan to rejoin his friends.

One morning, not long before our dream time came to an end, my patience on the headland was rewarded. I shouted to Karen and danced and yelled until the whole camp came running, thinking I had been bitten by a sand spike. There, far out to sea in the pale morning light, rode a pair of sea-sunners. I like to think they were my very own sea-sunners, the mother and its child we had met in mid-ocean. The seeing-glasses went from hand to hand, and all the Humans marveled at the sight. Karen-Ru was delighted with the great beasts. As we trailed back to have breakfast, we found Tsorl-U-Tsorl come from Little Fish Cove. He was sitting upon the platform all alone practicing sums with Sam Deg's little calculator box.

"Sea-sunners?" he said. "Yolo Harn can tell you all about them. She played a game with one."

Everyone was interested in the keeping of records. Besides the measurement of wind, tide and sunshine, there was measurement of such things as the amount of water in the air and especially air pressure—the way the air pressed around everything. It was higher, Sam explained, than the air pressure on the planet Earth, and the whole atmosphere of Torin more dense. It was easier for all flying things, from birds to flying machines, which we had described, to get off the ground on Torin. The Humans found our birds and insects rather large and slow-flying.

Besides the weather records, there were charts for every kind of human activity: their diet, their heartbeats, their blood pressure; Lisa began new records for Tsorl and myself, which always amazed her. Then there were records of the hours spent in any particular activity: the Camp Log, which Sam kept, and the personal journals, which every Human kept. Tsorl got the habit and kept a long skein of the days.

I alone kept no records; I wanted the time never to end, the perfect days to be one long, timeless day where we talked, ate, swam, fished and kept records forever, like those lucky folk of legend who went to dwell in Car-Der-Vanuyu, the Place Beyond the Four Winds. But in the legends it is told that the lucky folk found it hard to get into touch with their lives again when they returned to the world of every day. They sat as if surrounded by a mist; everything was very faint and far away; they saw everything a little smaller than it really was, like the figures seen through the wrong end of a seeing-glass. So it was with all of us in camp; the Humans could not really conceive of the size and sort of activity that went on upon Torin. Tsorl and I, because of our misfortunes, kept the world at a distance, too. I remember the first message that came to us through the mist. It was a very strange one, and it caused dissension and disbelief.

I woke in the light of the Far Sun and knew that Tsorl was out walking on the beach and that he had called me as I slept. I went out of our tent and found him staring into camp.

"Come," he said. "Something is doing. We must try for a message."

I was full of questions, but he said no more until we came near the Humans' blue tent.

"Go in, Yolo Harn," he said. "Wake Sam Fletcher without waking the others. Tell him he must come to the ship and bring its sesame box."

This was easy to do; when I wanted to I could move more quietly than anyone in camp. Sam was a good waker, quickly alert; he took up the sesame box—the door opener, named for an Earth legend. We went through the back door of the tent and found Tsorl standing before the ship. It looked stranger than ever in the light of Esder; its knobs and projections and its shining surfaces were fragile in the pale light; the forest trees looked more solid.

"What is it?" asked Sam, staring keenly at the Deputy.

"Yolo Harn must help me with words," said Tsorl. "How long since you, Sam, or Karen-Ru tried the wireless on the small ship?"

"You mean the shuttle?"

"The one Scott Gale flies."

"Karen tried every day for a long time, but I guess she has let it alone now."

"We must try again."

"This is crazy!" Sam was getting back some of his bounce. "Why now . . . in the night? Anyway Scotty doesn't have the shuttle anymore."

"No," agreed Tsorl. "It is in the hands of Nantgeeb!"

I understood and shivered with excitement. This personage, whom Tsorl called "the damned Magician," was a source of fear and wonder to me and to many others on Torin.

"Sam Fletcher," I said, "it is mind-power. Tsorl has been called."

"It's crazy . . ." muttered Sam.

He pressed the sesame box, and the door of the ship slid open above us and the ramp came down with a sigh. Sam led the way, and I helped Tsorl onto the ramp where metal cleats steadied his ring-walker. I went quite naturally into the ship and hardly knew I was in until the door sighed into position behind us. It was no time to be afraid, and in any case the ship was less frightening inside than it was out. We stood, at first, in a small space called a lock, then we went through a hole in the wall closed with folded plastic. I went through this first and assisted the Deputy.

There were soft lights glowing where Sam had touched wall panels, and I looked into two long rooms half divided by a metal sliding door. The walls were softly colored in blue and green and padded in places. It was a comfortable place, worn and well-used by the Humans, yet very neat and quiet. Everything—seats, tables, sleeping platforms— folded to the padded walls. We followed Sam along a metal passage to the front of the ship, our boots slipping on the floor for they had no magnetic strip like Sam's boots.

Sam operated more of the soft lights, and we came to the Control Center, the Comcen, which was a maze of gleaming surfaces. Everywhere the round dials and numbered slots winked like strange eyes. The chairs were long couches or metal rounds called mushrooms that rose from the floor at the touch of another live panel. I could see that the Deputy was familiar with this place and loved it and understood some of its uses, but it was too strange a place for me.

We picked our way across the room to one set of screens and dials and settled on a long couch. Sam began his magic with the dials, which hummed and glowed brighter at his touch. He made a series of light bleeping sounds, a language that the Humans possessed, and we were able to see the sounds as pulses of light, short and long, on a narrow screen by his hand.

"That is the call sign for the shuttle," he said repeating the sounds. "That is what we usually sent. We sent it hundreds of times."

"A picture," said Tsorl quietly, "and a way for a voice to be heard."

"A visual?" Sam was unbelieving, but he set a larger screen glowing. "There . . . and the channel open. Is that right?"

"Wait . . ." said Tsorl-U-Tsorl.

So we waited in our lighted corner of the incredible room, and after a few long moments while Sam became restless, there was a sound from the panel that made my neck hair prickle. A voice spoke faintly and was whirled away by the crackle and whine in the instruments. But it had spoken Moruian.

Sam was filled with excitement as he tried to make the voice clearer. Then it came in strong and bell-like.

"Hear me!" commanded the voice. "Hear me, Man family, out of your own silver ship. Hear me from your little toy pouch ship. Hear me for Escott Garl Brinroyan, your sib. . . ."

Sam fell back in astonishment and Tsorl leaped forward and replied into the speaking place.

"We do hear you. There are those in the mother ship who can hear and understand."

I had whispered all I could to Sam in the way of translation. Then the voice sounded again, quick and light, as if talking to another person we could not see.

"I was right. The scrying cup did not lie. Escott Garl's family have some tame islander that speaks for them!" Then more directly, "I have a message. I have not much time."

"First," said Tsorl-U-Tsorl. "Who speaks?"

I still whispered the words to Sam Fletcher, but he signed that I need not worry if I missed too much; the whole conversation was being recorded.

He went to Tsorl and said: "Tell them to press the visual contact . . . third red from the left on the lower bank."

He showed the place on the instruments before him and Tsorl spoke this back as clearly as he could in Moruian.

"I speak," said the voice. "I am the Maker of Engines. I am called Nantgeeb. . . ."

I could not help crying out, for the screen at Tsorl's left hand glowed into life, and at last, dimly, we saw the figure of the Magician. Nantgeeb sat in the tiny cabin of the shuttle: dark, long-faced; fine hair so dark that it could have been a wig swept to the shoulders; a band of green brilliants held the hair straight across the narrow forehead. Nantgeeb stared into the ship and into our minds with that powerful gaze that could blind and entrance the inhabitants of Torin.

"Who speaks?" demanded Nantgeeb.

"I do," replied Tsorl-U-Tsorl.

He did not say a name but pressed the panel so that his own face was shown to Nantgeeb, and we saw it on a smaller screen called a monitor. We heard Nantgeeb draw breath as the picture appeared.

"Give your message," begged Tsorl. "Where is Scott Gale? Is he safe? His family are eager for news."

"Show me them!" ordered Nantgeeb. "Where are these other Man creatures?"

Tsorl frowned and stepped away from the screen; he beckoned to Sam Fletcher.

"Nantgeeb will see you . . ." I told Sam.

"Tell him to speak softly and respectfully," said the Deputy, "for this Magician is a ruling spirit and full of vanity."

I tried to tell this to Sam, and he stepped into the range of the small screen. He bowed, then gave a human salute, placing his right hand against his forehead.

"Sam Fletcher, 12349, Captain, commanding the ship *Heron*, World Space Service/Satellite Station Terra-Sol XNV 34, Biosurvey Team One, Planet 4, 70 Ophiuchi A."

He uttered his full rank in this way, and then he said: "Captain Fletcher presents his compliments to Nantgeeb the Engineer. Please tell us anything you know about Lieutenant Scott Gale; you are speaking from the ship he piloted."

"By the fire, how shall we translate all that?" whispered Tsorl.

"Call it a formal greeting," I said.

"You do it, Yolo Harn."

"No," I said. "Nantgeeb need not see me at all; it takes too much explanation."

Tsorl stepped up and translated over Sam Fletcher's shoulder.

"Thank this leader," said Nantgeeb. "I can see that it is another such creature. One question as to his appearance."

She asked the question and Tsorl, growing impatient, translated it.

"Why is your hair growing white and why is there no hair on top of the head?"

Sam Fletcher could *not* control his impatience. He waved his hands and roared in a perfect display of the nature of Sam Deg. Then he said as politely as he could: "My hair turns white because I am getting old and I am going bald . . . losing my hair . . . because of an inherited baldness common to the males of my family and to many other males on our home world. And please tell the Great Engineer we are not here for a damned biology lesson!"

Tsorl translated all this with help from me; he was smiling.

"Oh, ask the Captain's pardon," said Nantgeeb quite simply. "Such questions interest me, that is all."

"What of Scott Gale . . . ?" asked Tsorl, taking Sam's place at the screen.

"He lives and he has made some noise in the land of Torin. Many people know Othoro Brinroyan, the Luck of Brin's Five."

"A mountain family!" said Tsorl. "So the fellow was saved by weavers on the Pentroy lands . . . I have often said he must lead a charmed life. Where is he now? Can he come to the island of Tsabeggan?"

"You know too much, but not enough!" said Nantgeeb. "What kind of an islander can you be?"

"Call me a sailor," said Tsorl warily, "a one-legged sailor who helps his friends. What news of Scott Gale?"

"He will come to Tsabeggan . . ." said Nantgeeb.

Suddenly the words and the picture were lost in a confusion of static. Sam rushed for the instruments and cursed as he tried to get back the signals.

"The link will not hold," came Nantgeeb's voice. "We have drained the power from Garl's flying machine that he mended, and it is almost gone. Beware . . . let Scott Gale beware of danger on the sea . . . I have seen it. . . ."

"Is it Pentroy?" cried Tsorl.

"Alert . . . ship . . . Scott Gale . . ." the words were whirled away.

"Nantgeeb—return to us!" Tsorl shouted aloud.

"This link fails," said the Maker of Engines, faint but clear. "But now I know who speaks!"

"What is the danger? Tell about Scott Gale; do not speak of me!"

"This must work to protect Scott Gale," said Nantgeeb. "I know you, Deputy. . . ."

The words were gone again and returned after a few pulse beats.

"You are dead, and I see another empty grave ringed with fire!"

Then Tsorl-U-Tsorl reeled back from the instruments with a cry, and all the lines went dead.

Sam flicked at the panel and played back all that had been said. Tsorl remained silent, his face deeply clouded, as I translated all to Sam as best I could. The voice of Nantgeeb was always clear, but the words, once we heard them again, were not clear at all. There were many things that could be taken two ways. "He will come to Tsabeggan . . ." or did that mean "He wants to come to Tsabeggan" or even "He will try to come to Tsabeggan." So I battled on with Sam, slowing the words and playing them back until we came to the last speeches concerning Tsorl, where Nantgeeb called him "Deputy."

Before I could translate, Tsorl rose to his feet and limped to face Sam Fletcher. His manner had become urgent and oddly formal. He spoke in Moruian, not trusting his new speech.

"Captain Sam Fletcher, I must ask you to unpick the last few lines of that tape. I cannot for my life and honor have such words spoken anywhere on Torin."

I was able to translate, however clumsily; I knew what would follow.

"I can't do that!" roared Sam, his human voice making the Comcen ring. "Blue Hell, Yolo Harn, he knows I can't do that. What do a few words in Moruian matter?"

"These words concern the Deputy," I said. "Even I do not know what they mean. Nothing was said of Scott Gale. Please Sam, do as he asks!"

"I can't do it!"

Sam turned to the Deputy.

"This is my ship. No one else will hear or understand the tape."

"The small ship fell into Nantgeeb's hand!" said Tsorl angrily.

He turned aside and limped across the shining floor on his ring-walker.

"Please," I said. "Do this thing for Tsorl-U-Tsorl. He was a leader of our city, Tsagul. Now for no bad thing—

no crime—he is lame and has no friends except for your-self, Sam Deg, and Lisa-Child and Karen-Ru. He helps you. Please do this one thing he asks."

"You left out the best friend of all," said Sam kindly. "He has Yolo Harn to help him. Tell the Deputy I will do as he asks."

So I went and led the Deputy back to the panel, and Sam ran the tape again; when he gave the signal, the last few speeches were erased. Still they lived in my memory, and I puzzled over Nantgeeb's last words: "Another empty grave ringed with fire."

III

We went away from the ship and had time for another short sleep before breakfast. When we came to the camp again, the humans were all highly excited from the report of last night's message, and Karen was shining like the two suns. She had it fixed in her mind that Scott Gale was coming. I was not so sure and tried to lessen her hopes.

"But what does he mean by danger?" she asked, looking around at us as we all sat with our eating trays on the platform. "This Engine-maker, this Magician . . . what does he mean?"

I laughed and exchanged glances with Tsorl.

"Come on, Yolo Harn," said Karen, "I see you smiling. Have I said the name wrong, Nantgeeb?"

"Not the name, Karen-Ru," I said. "The Maker of Engines, Nantgeeb, is female. *She* spoke of danger."

"Is that a fact?" asked Sam. "I was doubtful once or twice, but I thought she was a young man . . . male . . ."

"Nantgeeb is not so young," said Tsorl. "I know a little of her history from my father who studied science. Once she was a leading house servant of Clan Luntroy."

"No clan of mine. . . ." I grinned, and the Deputy gave a laugh.

"I'm sick and tired of these private jokes in Moruian!" exploded Sam.

"All right," said Lisa. "We get the message . . . Sam Deg."

So with this kind of teasing talk we finished breakfast and went off to all kinds of tasks. It was the sort of island day that is hot and still, with a film of cloud over the Great

Sun; the sea had been peaceful all the time we were on Tsabeggan but now it was choppy beyond the harbor mouth. I put off my revision test with the Teaching Machine, took a specimen bag from the blue tent, and went off toward the foothills to gather fruit. There was a large ogodan or green-hat tree just ready for the harvest below a certain rock pinnacle, and I wanted to get to it before the weljin and the flame-birds.

It was a steady walk up a gentle slope through the forest with the trees and vines separating into their natural layers. Here the lace leaves thinned out, here a bright green shrub began to appear on the forest floor, here the mountain redwoods became more numerous. I came to the tree and found the weljin there before me, several families of them. I shooed them away, and they went to the top of the tree's high green canopy and pelted me, slyly, with over-ripe fruit.

I filled my bag and then sat still, hiding from the tree-folk. I wanted to get a good look at them. Karen-Ru insisted that they resembled her own species in that the females had no pouch. I fell into a dream of ages passing on Torin and the weljin producing distant sibs like Humans. I thought about the world of Torin and its animals. We kept fewer pets, it seemed, than Humans in their cities. We had no carrying animals—though there had been some kind of thick-skinned beast that warriors rode on in very distant times.

Before the weljin came down again, I heard someone hurrying through the forest toward the tree. I thought from the noise it must be one of the humans. I called out, "Hello," and received a long, breathless: "Nahoo . . . Be silent!"

Tsorl-U-Tsorl was climbing toward me; I went forward to help him. He looked wild and strange, and I saw that he carried a good deal of our gear from Little Fish Cove strung about his body. He even had a blanket strung about him for a cloak although the day was hot.

"Deputy, what is this? Why have you left them?"

My first thought was that he had quarreled with Sam Fletcher. Or perhaps the Deputy was so full of his dark, private thoughts that he had turned hermit.

"I am not mad, Yolo Harn," he said, reading my thoughts.

He held out Sam Fletcher's small one-eyed seeing-glass

"Look to the harbor," he said.

"A ship! Has their Scott Gale come then?"

Tsorl sat in the shade of the ogodan tree surrounded by the odds and ends he had brought; he had a strange, defeated look. I stared at him, wondering, and as I went to climb on a rock with the seeing-glass, a new sound echoed about the island. It was an unusual one but I had heard it before . . . the high hooting call from the chimney of a steam vessel.

I moved around the rocky shelves until I had a perfect view of the harbor of Tsabeggan, a pond of still water within the old Tsatroy stonework on the headland. A ship had just entered the harbor, and I saw at once that it was a Mattroyan steam vessel. But this was neither the *Ullo* nor the *Telve,* the two big working trade ships that had made the fortune of the Merchant of Itsik. This was his famous ship-of-honor that some called his folly, his silly fancy-work ship. This was the *Esnar,* the Little Sun, puffing into the quiet harbor with its funnel mast shining, its rails decked with colored cords, its rigging twined with good-luck skeins and silk lilies and banners.

My first thoughts were ones of pride and joy for the whole land of Torin. Mattroyan, the Merchant, had somehow found Scott Gale and now he was bringing the human home to his family. Karen-Ru would be united with her dear partner, and all the many-colored threads of Torin and its people and the things they had made would be displayed for the humans. I lifted the seeing-glass and stared at the decks of the *Esnar,* seeking a human among the others. And I saw instead an armed troop of Pentroy vassals, black messengers of the Great Elder's power, surrounding a thin grayish figure, magnificently dressed. There was even a large Pentroy banner at the masthead and at the bow that I had missed among the colored skeins. I felt as if a black cloud had blotted out the sun.

I walked slowly around to the tree and sat upon the ground beside Tsorl-U-Tsorl, hanging my head.

"You saw?"

"Pentroy. And one among them that must be Ammur, the High Steward. Would the Great Elder be there too—below decks?"

"Tiath would never venture so far from the continent."

"Why have they come?" I burst out. "Have they brought Scott Gale? Was this the danger Nantgeeb meant?"

"I don't know, Yolo Harn, and I dare not stay to find out."

I knew with an inner shuddering that he was right; he could not be seen by Ammur or it would mean his death. My next thoughts were of our poor friends. What did the Pentroy intend for them? I knew they would greet the ship with delight.

"The Pentroy will not harm them," said Tsorl. "This is not an attack—it is a peaceful visit. We do not know how things stand between Scott and the Pentroy. He may have become the friend of the Great Elder."

"Is that possible?"

"Of course," said Tsorl. "What better way to control the new power these humans bring? Fair words and fancy-work presents. It is not Tiath's way, but perhaps he has done it."

"We must stay out of sight . . ." I whispered.

"Do you think the vassals will know you?"

"No. I doubt that very much. No vassal who had served time on Itsik would be sent on a pleasure trip like this."

"Yolo Harn, you are the one person on this world, the one Moruian, who speaks reasonable human speech."

"I am still far from perfect."

But I knew what the Deputy meant. I could not leave Karen-Ru, Lisa-Child and Sam Deg at the mercy of the Pentroy. I looked sadly around at the forest and heard the twittering of the tree-folk and the flap of a flame-bird's wings. Far, far behind my eyes, perhaps, I thought of freedom once again. I sat for a moment with the Deputy, and we arranged a place for leaving message skeins in the lower forest. Then I gathered up my bag of ripe fruit and went down the hill, heading back to camp. I seemed to hear the sweet voice of the Teaching Machine in my head: *"You must go back."*

8

The Ningan's Web

I WENT BACK FASTER AND FASTER once the decision was made and arrived at the blue tent breathless. What I saw made me want to laugh and cry. In place of the three friends I saw every day there were three new persons. Sam, Lisa and Karen had taken the time while the ship approached to dress in fresh clothes. Lisa and Karen had silk overalls, in that blinding white that the looms of Earth manage so well, and Sam was very fine in a uniform of white, blue and gold.

"Yolo . . ." Karen was bright-eyed. "Look—do you think he is coming?"

"Who are they?" asked Sam. "Is Scotty with them? Was Nantgeeb telling us about this visit?"

"I have heard of the persons who come on this ship."

I had the first hint of the terrible difficulties that lay ahead. How could I explain even a part of the things I knew and feared from Ammur Ningan and the Pentroy vassals?

"Come on!" exclaimed Sam Deg. "These are your folks, Yolo Harn. Moruians like yourself. Cheer up, don't shut your eyes. Where's the Deputy? We want him on the platform. . . ."

"No!" I shouted. "The Deputy cannot be seen by these people."

Lisa and Sam looked at each other then, and Lisa laid a hand on my arm.

"We don't want to get mixed up in any quarrels, Yolo," she said. "Will you translate for us? We come in peace— that's the main thing to say. We come in peace, and we want news of Scott Gale."

Karen who had been watching the ship come closer came running in.

"Sam, they're docking. Can we help?"

I stood helpless, pulling leaves from my hair.

"I must clean up," I said. "Then I will help with the speaking."

"Yolo . . . ?"

Sam Fletcher looked into my face earnestly, and I knew what he feared.

"I will not run away," I said.

I ran down the paths between the domes and the labeled grasses until I came to the sandhills and so to Little Fish Cove. Tsorl had left my own possessions; so many of them came from the humans that I was suddenly ashamed of living so completely on their bounty. I splashed my face with water and dragged my plaited hair into some sort of order. Then I cast off my good tunic of prison gray and put on the T-shirt over my short breeches. It was beautifully white and closely woven with two sleeves, and had a ring of green leaves for the planet Earth painted on the cloth. I was a creature between two worlds, a Moruian half in human clothes. As I turned back to the camp where the bright flags of the *Esnar* fluttered at the old dock, I caught a glimpse of my precious boat in its place among the reeds. Stay till I come, I told the boat, we will sail again together.

As I came through the grass trails, I saw that the ship had docked and the gangway was going down. I hurried to the platform and stood behind the others. We could hear the voices of the crew making all fast, but these were the only voices. There was no sound of music, no landing songs. The ship looked like a pleasure ship, but it did not sound like one. I saw the Pentroy vassals lining the rail in silence; on the high bridge an omor flashed a finger sign before a leather mask-helmet. The averting sign. They were all afraid.

The humans were talking excitedly but in low voices, almost whispering, as if the silence from the laden ship had affected their spirits.

"Shall we wave or make any sign?" asked Sam.

"Place your hands on the chest for 'no weapons,' " I said.

A green mat rolled down the gangplank, and two of the tallest vassals came down and stood to right and left. Then came a young house servant in gray and green carrying a large hamper of presents, a "wish-basket" tied up with colored cords. Then at last came the Pentroy High Steward: an old straight-backed creature, not tall but accustomed to command.

Ammur Ningan wore a jeweled pectoral over a straight gray robe; the sunlight flashed on black and yellow stones mounted in silver; there were rings on the stubby hands. In one hand she held a tall staff tipped with metal, in the other a sheaf of willow paper. Pens and skeins dangled at belt and wrists; I remembered the Deputy's description: "the scribe of scribes."

The vassals were coming from the ship; I was keeping count: there were thirty of them. More Pentroy than I cared to see in one place and more of an army than was often seen in the whole of Torin. Ammur kept her eyes fixed upon the humans on the platform; she paced slowly forward across the grass and the old cobblestones and stilled the little murmur of Moruian voices with a movement of her staff.

She cried out in a strong singsong voice, "In the name of the Great Elder and the Council of Five I bid good wind, greeting, peace and all bonds of friendship to beings called Man."

Sam Fletcher stepped forward and bowed, but before he could reply or even discover what had been said, the Ningan bowed in his direction and continued in a loud voice: "See—it appears peaceful. Fetch my chair. Do you see any weapons? Officers, any weapons to be seen?"

I translated all this in a low voice to the humans.

"She speaks this way because she has not seen me."

"Step forward, Yolo," ordered Sam. "Come here beside me."

I preferred to wait. Perhaps I hoped that the Ningan would become more rude and high-handed, knowing that the humans did not understand her speech. A vassal unfolded a writing chair of wood and carpet cloth with a platten built to one side and the Ningan settled upon it, eyes still fixed upon the humans. When she was seated, Sam Fletcher bowed again and spoke.

"We have no weapons," he said. "We return your greetings. Captain Sam Fletcher, First Officer; Lisa Child—"

The Ningan turned about angrily as an officer whispered in her ear.

"Where? What?" she exclaimed. "An Islander? Are you sure?"

At last the long yellowish eyes—which were in fact short-sighted from years of scribe's work—rested upon myself. I walked between Sam and Karen, bowed to the Ningan and went down the steps of the platform.

"Fetch it," said Ammur harshly.

An officer with an arrow skin-sewn on its upper arm was upon me in two strides; I stood my ground. As the creature's hand clamped down on my shoulder, Sam Fletcher lost patience and let loose his human voice.

"Now wait a minute!" he roared. *"Let her alone!"*

All the Moruians cringed; Ammur rubbed an ear; after two pulse beats she blinked and nodded at Sam Fletcher. With a thin, upcurving smile, she beckoned me. I stepped up and stood beside the writing chair; I saw that the thin, mirthless smile had netted her face into hundreds of wrinkles.

"What are you? And what are you doing with these strangers?"

The tone was not harsh, but there was behind it a world of threat and power. There were few common folk on Torin who would not come when the Ningan beckoned. I looked at her and prepared to lie. But her yellow eyes did not see farther than my face and perhaps even that was shadowy to her. The Maker of Engines might have looked deeper; it would have been difficult to lie to a Diviner.

"I am Yolo Harn, sailor out of Tsagul," I said. "I was washed overboard from a salt boat, Excellence, and came in the Round Current to this place. The humans found me."

"Salt boat?"

"The *Gvalo* out of Tsagul."

It was indeed a salt boat . . . the one on which I had traveled to Itsik.

"What was that you called these devils?"

"Humans, Excellence."

"Do they have weapons?"

"I have never seen one in all the time I have been with them. They are scholars and come in peace."

"Do they use fire and metal?"

"Open flames never, but metal yes. More than we do."

"Why do they give you this tunic and have you close to them? Are you their servant?"

"Excellence," I said, "I have their speech, and I can stand between your Excellence and the Humans and tell what each one says."

The Ningan stared at me in silence for as long as ten pulse beats, and although I am no Diviner, I saw that this simple fact had altered all her plans. It was completely unexpected. What might have happened if there had been no Yolo Harn, no "sailor" on Tsabeggan? I guessed later that some of the Ningan's rituals would have been unchanged, but after a show of greeting there would have been a quick seizure of the "devils." As it was, she tried to turn my presence to her advantage.

"So be it," she said. "Do this faithfully, by the North Wind or the spirit Telve, my young sailor, and you will earn the favor of the highest in the land. Present your humans to me."

So, with the backs of my legs trembling a little as if I were facing up to a sea-sunner, I stepped into the open space between the platform and the Ningan's chair and spoke in Moruian in a loud voice.

"These present return the greetings of the Great Elder and the Council, and they are called Captain Sam Fletcher, the leader, and Lisa-Child, the First Officer, and Karen Schwartz, the scholar, of the ship *Heron*, flown from the planet Earth in the void to the land of Torin."

"I greet them," said Ningan. "Tell them I am Ammur, High Steward of the Pentroy Clan and the personal envoy of the Great Elder Tiath Avran Pentroy."

I did this clumsily enough, for we still had not worked out many Moruian titles, and expressions like High Steward and Great Elder came out as Best-Helper-in-the-House and Tall Oldest.

"Tell the envoy we are all eager to hear news of our fourth member, Scott Gale, who is on the continent of Torin," said Sam.

This went easily enough, and I saw the eyes of Karen-

Ru, pale blue and brimming with anxiety. The Ningan gave a long sigh.

"So we come to it," she said in a silken voice. "The main purpose of this visit to the island of the Nearest Fire. Escott Garl is indeed known to the Council. He lives. He has gone freely among the people of Torin."

I brought out every phrase as best I could, hardly daring to look at my friends, feeling myself more and more a shadow, a gray box, a voice-wire.

"Now the Council have sent this ship, the *Esnar*, to bring the humans once again to their friend Escott Garl."

"Ask the envoy why he did not come himself?" Sam's voice was controlled.

I translated the question, and saw the pattern of wrinkles alter on Ammur's furrowed brow. But before she could reply, the winds sprang out of their sack or, as Sam might say, all hell broke loose. The Pentroy vassals had edged along the screen of trees dividing the two halves of the camp and they had seen the great silver ship.

One officer, old as Tsorl, with gray hair wisping his chin, fell down screaming in a fit; others shouted and tumbled over each other. They blundered off the paths crushing the fragile domes underfoot and sending the seed nets flying. Still others, braver than the rest, chanted to avert fire-metal-magic and rushed into the ship's clearing, keeping their distance and raising their parade spears in attitudes of defense as if to ward off the ship if it sprang at them. The few who really kept their heads tried to bring order to the troop and shouted to the Ningan for help.

The Ningan jumped up; she did not speak but signed to the officer marked with an arrow, who blew a loud series of blasts on a roarer, a kind of wooden trumpet. Sam rushed to the end of the platform and shouted, holding up his hands in what he believed were soothing gestures.

The Ningan suddenly clamped a hand on my own wrist and cried sharply in my ear, "Is it safe? Have you been close to that great heap of metal?"

"Yes, Excellence, it is perfectly safe."

The roarer was blown a second time, and some sort of order was restored; the vassals stood panting and trembling.

"Stand true! The ship will not harm anyone!" called the

Ningan in her singsong voice. "Stand true, you cowards, or you will be on a charge!"

"Tell the Ningan she may inspect the ship at closer range," called Sam.

"Tell the leader I will walk a little closer," she replied.

"Yolo," called Karen-Ru faintly, "tell them to keep to the paths."

I told this to the Ningan, with reasons, and she passed it on to the troop. The cry went up: "Keep to the paths. Protect the seed domes and pouches," and the vassals, hulking creatures that they were, began to tiptoe about.

The Ningan, who made up their lack in courage and wit, strode proudly beside Sam Fletcher down the ranks of the vassals and came to the clearing. Behind I paced with the tall officer; behind again came Lisa and Karen. I looked back and saw that they were not without fear of the troop of vassals, but they concealed it well and walked proudly along the paths.

I glanced at the person beside me; it was, I saw, an omor, perhaps the largest and toughest of the breed that I had ever seen in my life. Beside her I looked like a stripling. The expression on her broad face was watchful, even amused. As we passed the last vassals, drawn up, she called an order and a couple of them broke ranks and set off toward the *Esnar*. She had ordered a watch set.

"Good officer," I said, "what is your name?"

"Meetal Gullan, First Escort to the Envoy. What is that cloth you're wearing?"

"Some kind of flax."

"Well, you have had a good post here if their food is fit to eat, sailor."

"Believe me," I said, "they are all kind and good—not devils."

"I know that already. They are creatures of flesh and blood."

Meetal grinned, showing a gap where a tooth was missing. I was not soothed by that name. Gullan means "Sevener" or "One-of-Seven"; at some time Meetal had been bound in Gulgavor, a seven-fold bond, to carry out some dangerous task for the Great Elder, her Liege.

Meanwhile, the Ningan had come up within arm's reach of the ship; Sam gave the word, and I walked the length and breadth of it with the pair of them, translating clumsily, for there were no words for even the outside of such a vessel. I borrowed from flying machines—which I knew imperfectly—and from ships of the sea. Ammur took it all in and knotted nervously on a long skein that hung at her wrist.

"Ask the Captain how many of his people are needed to fly this ship?"

"Tell the Ningan that it will fly with three of the crew."

"What air can one breath inside such a vessel?" inquired the Ningan.

"Tell the Ningan our air is stored and purified and its supply kept up from the green plants in the sun rooms."

So I went on translating; it sounded like magical nonsense; no one on Torin commonly associated green plants with fresh air. At last the Ningan turned aside and squinted at the great sun overhead and passed a word down the line of vassals. The young house servant in gray and green came running into the clearing, knelt before the Ningan and opened the lid of a wooden coffer so that she could inspect the contents.

"What is that?" whispered Karen. "What is the old guy doing?"

I could not help smiling.

"It is her traveling clock," I said. "She is telling the time of day."

"I will sit privately with these humans," announced Ammur. "The vassals can make camp in their companies."

The order was given, and the vassals settled in their duty fives along the edge of the harbor, well away from anything the humans had made. They were shown where to pick fresh fruit on the western reaches of the clearing. Three sailors from the *Esnar* set off to the south along the old Tsatroy road carrying nets and axes. Woodcutting detail. The Mattroyan steam vessels burned wood or burning turf from the blackswamp lands in the far west. I could not see them go without a twinge of fear, thinking of Tsorl, hidden in the forest, but I knew that he was far away.

Ammur entered the blue tent, and when she was satisfied that it held no dangers, allowed two vassals and the house-servant to settle in her writing chair and the wish-basket of presents.

"Now please . . ." said Karen-Ru when the visitor was settled, "Yolo, ask the last question again. Why has Scotty stayed away? Is he sick?"

I asked, and the Ningan fidgeted sadly before making her reply.

"Scott Gale went about on Torin freely. He was permitted to do so by the Council of Five and the Hundred. It was planned that he should come on this journey and the Great Elder put this vessel, the *Esnar,* at his disposal. But before we set out a sickness came upon him. . . ."

"What sickness?" demanded Lisa. "Is he injured? Is he so sick he cannot even write a letter?"

I translated all these things uneasily because I thought the answer was suggested always by the question. It was too easy for the Ningan to agree, as she did, with a proper show of sadness and regret. I felt more and more certain that she lied; I looked beyond the wrinkled face and caught the eyes of the young servant, pale brown eyes alight with intelligence and mischief. He was drinking in the tale with a very strange smile.

"Scott Gale has a strange sickness come upon him," said Ammur Ningan. "It is thought that he is mad. He eats very sparingly and does not recognize his friends among the Moruians. Above all he does not speak; he sits still and does not utter a word. He whistles for the servants to bring him food."

I was halfway through this story when I recalled where I had heard it before: this was a Moruian madness, the kind that had overtaken the old grandee Elbin Tsatroy. Yet the humans were ready to believe what they heard; all three of them burst out into talk.

"Some kind of schizoid state," said Lisa. "He tested well for stability, heaven knows, but he's been away from us for so long."

"Sam—we must go—let me go with them," begged Karen. "I can bring him around and have him brought back here."

"I don't know. . . ." said Sam. "Lisa, could he have gotten any new virus or drug from these people?"

"Sure," said Lisa. "Remember Tsorl mentioned a religious sect, the Twirlers, who used drugs for their rites?"

Their pronunciation of the name was imperfect, but it filled me with alarm.

"Do not say that name, Lisa," I put in quietly. "Please do not say the name of that other."

"Yolo, it's very hard to play this double game of yours!"

said Sam impatiently. "We're in great trouble with Scott Gale, you hear that? What is this with . . . your friend?"

"It is not a game, believe me," I said. "If it were once known that my friend were on the island alive, he would be hunted down and killed."

"Yolo," said Karen gently, "how do we know that is true?"

But her very gentleness and the strain of all the words I had been speaking made me angry.

"You don't know," I said. "You only know what I say. And I say another thing, the Ningan is lying."

"Speak again!" said the Ningan. "What have the humans to say to my sad news?"

So I translated her speech, and Sam answered.

"We are worried. Perhaps some of us should go to attend him."

"Such was our hope," said the Ningan softly. "The Great Elder has a keen interest in this wonder: visitors from beyond the stars. He has spoken with Scott Gale many times and learned all he could."

As I spoke this back to the others, there came a soft whirring sound. It was the Ningan's traveling clock striking a warning note in its coffer. She turned aside and consulted in a low voice with the young servant.

"Tell the humans that they will behold a mystery of our land. It is time. Obal is in the service of the Great Elder and he is a registered Witness out of the city of Rintoul."

I translated with quickening interest; I had never in my life seen a Witness used as a messenger. Sam broke in with brisk questions.

"A Witness? Those telepaths you . . . and your friend tried to describe? What will he do?"

"Another will speak through him," I said. "It can be done, Sam, believe it."

"It's very difficult for us to understand or to believe. Tell the Ningan that," he said.

"Tell the leader he must watch and hear, and his ears will be opened," said the Ningan in reply.

Obal had lost his look of mischief; his face had a still, dreaming look. He stepped from behind the Ningan's chair, and she began a series of ritual questions.

"Is there one who wishes to speak?"

"Yes," replied Obal in a clear voice, "Tiath Avran

Pentroy, Great Elder of Torin, will speak to the Man family, believed to be three persons, and to Ammur the High Steward, in the presence of all these persons."

"How shall they be known?"

"By the word of Ammur. . . ."

"All the hearers are present," said Ammur. "Where will you stand?"

Obal peered all around the tent and stood beside the wish-basket. His shoulders began to shake a little, his head came lower on his chest.

"Highness," he called in a long drowsy call, "Highness, you may speak. . . ."

Obal now entered a full trance; it was not a gradual thing: his muscles stiffened oddly and he slept, still standing, like a marsh bird. The Ningan spoke again.

"Highness. My liege."

There was no change in the Witness's set, sleeping face and she spoke again: "My liege . . . we are all here on Tsabeggan. . . ."

We waited, and the humans fidgeted a little and a shuddering ran through the body of the Witness. A voice sprang out of his mouth, strong, deep, resonant; I felt a prickling in the skin of my scalp.

"I speak. I greet the Man family in the name of the Five Clans, the Hundred of Rintoul and all the people of the Moruia in the Land of Torin."

The speaker said no name, there was only the voice issuing from another's lips, and from the first words I had no more doubts. Here spoke the Great Elder, here was indeed a wonder of Torin. There was a pause, and I whispered the translation to the humans, then the voice continued.

"I have spoken to Scott Gale and I will speak with all members of the Man family. You came unasked to this world; you bring engines and powers that must be used wisely; come before my face and explain yourselves."

Another pause. I had time to translate again; the humans looked strange; Sam was glum and embarrassed.

"Come in safety," said the voice of the Great Elder. "Come in peace in the ship *Esnar*. Ammur Ningan will obey my charge and bring you all to my presence. This must be done."

There was another breathing silence, and a sound from the Witness as if the Great Elder cleared his throat. The words burst out again and this time they were in the stranger's language, badly spoken but understandable.

"Hello. Well-come. Peace."

There was no more; Ammur waited, then pronounced a final response.

"Highness, we have heard and understood."

Obal the Witness slowly relaxed his limbs, the rhythm of his breathing changed and the lines in his face were gone. He slowly opened his eyes and rubbed them with his fingers, like a child coming from sleep. The Ningan nodded at him, pleased, and he wandered back behind her chair and sat on the floor of the tent.

The Ningan said nothing but looked expectantly at the humans.

"Go on Sam," murmured Lisa. "Say something. Say something polite."

"No reason to doubt that this Leader prepared the text," said Karen. "Why didn't he mention Scotty being sick?"

"Hell, how do we know who prepared the text," grumbled Sam. "Yolo, was the message very strong . . . you know, threatening?"

"No," I said, "not for the Great Elder, the ruler of Torin."

I could hardly control my disappointment. The humans had not been convinced even for a moment; they went on speaking among themselves about "trance" and "medium" and a "pretty crude performance from the kid."

"The humans have heard and understood," I said to the Ningan, "but they are not convinced of this wonder."

"No matter," said the Ningan gently and scornfully, "they are thought-blind. I must act as the voice of the Great Elder. I have the honor to set forth my charge. I must bring you safely to the presence of the Great Elder aboard the *Esnar*."

"Well," said Sam Fletcher, "what does she want?"

I smiled a little, I could not help it; we had made the joke so often in the camp. I was pierced with sadness because our dream was ending; we had all come back from the place-beyond-the-four-winds and now the voices of the world were beginning to strike at us through the mist.

"It is as the Great Elder said, through the Witness," I said. "Ammur Ningan is supposed to take you to her Leader."

My friends looked at me with their queer small eyes,

their bird's eyes, and turned their heads away, talking among themselves. At last Sam made another speech.

"Tell the Ningan we had thought of taking the ship to the mainland."

I had heard of the difficulties that were involved. It was hard to believe that the silver ship must make an orbit of the planet in order to fly to the continent of Torin; then there was the problem of a landing site and of the consumption of fuel.

The Ningan replied, "You will use fuel and must make a great circle in order to land again. Also, I pray, remember the panic the vessel would raise among our poor citizens— you saw how these strong ones behaved."

The source of her knowledge was not lost on the humans; it could only have come from Scott Gale.

"Come with us now," she went on, "and the Great Elder himself will help choose a landing site and return you all to the ship so that you may bring it to the mainland."

So I translated everything as well as I could. I felt the net that the Ningan was weaving around us, but I could do nothing. I was a mouthpiece, a Witness, who stands entranced and repeats the words of another speaker.

"We would have to break up this camp," said Sam, "and store our records in the ship. Ask the Ningan what assurance we have that we *will* be returned to the ship with our poor comrade Scott Gale."

"Truly," said Ammur, her face wrinkled with care, "I can only give my word and swear by the honor of Clan Pentroy and the Great Elder, whom I serve. I swear the Man family will be brought back to Tsabeggan and will be reunited with Scott Gale."

This was a solemn oath, and the Ningan struck an attitude when she gave it. The humans were impressed. The Ningan had by no means finished.

"Certain things can be shown," she said. "Obal has another skill—he is a musician. . . ."

Obal came forward and drew a pouch-pipe from the side of the wish-basket; he set it to his lips and began to play. It was a melody I had never heard before, but after a few notes the humans cried out in recognition.

"There," said the Ningan. "The song is from Scott Gale. Its name in our speech is "Een Turugan'—the Young Harper."

The pipe music changed, and the Ningan gave the

name of another song "The Cheerful Walker" and another "Sailing Home." Karen-Ru dabbed at her eyes.

"There is still more to be shown," murmured the Ningan.

She clapped her hands and Obal, from another side pocket of the wish-basket, drew out certain objects: a pair of white socks, a face shaver, a camera, a weapon called a stun gun. This was something I had heard of but never seen. Sam examined all the objects and commented on the weapon.

"Fused into the light setting," he said. "I wonder . . ."

"Ask the Captain if he possesses any other of those weapons?" inquired the Ningan.

"I have some weapons of this sort," Sam replied, "but they are locked aboard the ship and we do not use them."

The Ningan did not press the point but took out a fold of willow paper from the pocket of her sleeve; she handed me a silkbeam copy mounted on plaited wood. It had been made in bright sunlight of course and posed in traditional fashion, in profile with the hands held before the body as if the persons were walking. There were three persons in the picture: on the left, a tall handsome Moruian, on the right a younger one, probably an omor; the middle person, who had not quite held the profile pose, was Scott Gale. I gave the silkbeam to the humans, who bent over it eagerly.

"I know when it was made," I said. "They have won the Air Race. See the decorations on the platform? On the left stands Blacklock—Murno Pentroy—you remember, the one who makes jumps? The other Moruian must be Ullo Mattroyan, third place; child of the one who owns the steamship *Esnar.*"

Then quickly the Ningan pulled the long cord that held together the wish-basket, and it opened like a star-lily to reveal a wonderful profusion of colored cloth. The humans gasped with admiration; they saw the wealth of Torin.

"These are poor gifts," said Ammur, "and they cannot take your minds from the sickness of your sib, Scott Gale. But wear them and keep them as expressions of our friendship when you step aboard the *Esnar.*"

She gestured to Obal and to myself, and we began to display the gifts. There were three blue cloaks, woven of silk and wool floss and embroidered with cut-work sewn with brilliants. There were lengths of cloth in every weight, caps and sleeves and ribboned overboots and pouch-purses.

I would never have guessed the use of some of this finery if I had not seen the castoff gear of the grandees at Itsik.

"Thank the Ningan and the Leader for these beautiful things," said Sam, as they all handled the cloth. "We must make gifts in return."

Lisa and Sam went to the store cupboards, and I spoke to Karen.

"Will you go on this ship *Esnar?*"

"Some of us must go, Yolo."

"Karen, you must take care. . . ."

Then the human gifts were brought, T-shirts, socks, suit-liners, chocolate, and the Ningan accepted them graciously. She was plainly delighted with her own gift of ball-point pens and the plio-film used for mapping. I began to realize that even I had come some way toward trusting her, and I was sure the humans had come even further. I carried a T-shirt to the servant Obal and presented it to him behind the Ningan's writing chair. I knew that it was difficult for a Witness to tell a lie; it is part of their training. As I handed him the gift, I asked: "Have you seen Scott Gale?"

He had only to blink his eyes to confirm some part of what the Ningan had said, but he stared into my face un-blinking, bold, all shyness gone.

The Ningan knew when to let things work. She rose and repeated her request for all the humans to sail to Rintoul, meet the Great Elder and help Scott Gale. Then she went away to give out the presents and let the humans talk. They did talk, loud and fast; it was too much for me to understand fully. I could not make out what they in-tended to do. "Too many variables," Sam kept saying and I took it to mean, "Too many things we cannot know." They turned to me again.

"Yolo," asked Sam, "why are you afraid of this envoy?"

"Ammur Ningan has much power. She is First Helper of the leader; she brings life or death."

"Can we trust her word? That was a solemn oath she took, wasn't it?"

"It was," I said. "But I know that Tsorl would never trust her."

"Tsorl is not here," said Sam.

I knew then that he did not trust the Deputy; he saw the exile, the poor castaway. He had no real knowledge of the Deputy's former place at the head of our town. I felt angry and helpless, but I did not speak up; it was as if the mere presence of Ammur had made us sly and cautious.

"The ship is very safe," I said. "No one can get into it if the doors are locked. The soldiers are afraid of it. Let us all go into the ship and speak on the outside broadcast to the Ningan."

"Why should we do that?" asked Sam. "No, Yolo, it's far too threatening. We don't want to frighten these guys. We have to go along with this Ningan and get to see Scotty."

"Yolo," said Lisa, "whatever quarrel Tsorl had with these people it is not our quarrel . . . and it isn't your quarrel either."

"Please," said Karen. "Come with us to Rintoul."

"Yes," I said. "Yes, I will come."

I wondered if they would have me swear an oath, like the Ningan; in my mind I swore by the City of Tsagul. I must stay with them and try to keep them from harm.

Presently I went out and gave the word to the Ningan: the humans would sail on the *Esnar*. She was so pleased that even her eyes smiled. The time was past midday; for the rest of the time until the Great Sun set, we broke up camp and stored all the wonders of the place in the ship of the void, the *Heron*. It was a sad time for me, but the humans and the Pentroy "envoys" were lighthearted. I took some pleasure in the *Esnar*, which was a very fine vessel with a crew of seven Mattroyan sailors—fewer than usual because the vassals helped with the stoking of the boiler.

Since it was a pleasure boat, the cabins were spacious; there was plenty of room in the forward tower for the humans, in a fine room hung with striped silk. In the after section there were two more large sleeping places with hammocks and a small hold. It struck me that we should still be a little crowded for the voyage.

"Not so," said an old Mattroyan hand, doing duty as sailing guide. "Look there, young Harn . . ."

I saw that ten of the vassals, including the First Escort, Meetal Gullan, were settling down again on shore. They had made camp in the flattened place where the blue tent had stood. It was puzzling. I asked another question of the sail guide.

"Where do we sail from here, friend?"

"Secret orders," it grumbled. "Shouldn't read the skein

until the Ningan hands it out after we sail. But it's bound to be Rintoul . . . though maybe . . ."

"Where else?"

"Nowhere—mid-ocean . . ." said the sailing guide. "We might have to stand off the islands, that's all."

I was still puzzled, though the sailing guide did expect to go to Rintoul. I looked about for the humans and found them at the tree platform where Sam was taking a last reading of the weather. It was not as pleasant as it had been; a wind was rising and a mist came off the sea. I went and stood with them; they were wearing their new Moruian cloaks, each in a different shade of blue; they had all slung the folds of the cloak to hang down their backs in a most un-Moruian fashion. They had their kitbags, ready to go aboard.

"The guard?" said Sam. "Sure . . . the Ningan is leaving them to guard the ship, so far as I can make out. Only the poor guys don't like to stand too close. . . ."

It was time for the humans to embark. The young musician, Obal, played them aboard with his pouch-pipe, a medley of tunes from Torin and from Earth. The voyage took on something of the spirit of a pleasure cruise after all; the evening wind flapped at the flags and silk lilies. The *Esnar* was slowly building up its steam ready to sail when the Far Sun rose. I went with the humans as the Mattroyan captain, a fat fellow with something of the house-servant about him, gave a tour of the ship. The Ningan, who had not much interest in ships, sat in the chart tent on the high bridge and scribbled with pens of every kind.

There had been talk of a feast with Moruian food and delicacies from Earth, but no one felt too sure of a feast before trying the Great Ocean Sea. Lisa doled out pills to the humans, and they all sat in their cabin. I went on deck and made myself small in a corner by the after rail and stared at Tsabeggan. There was the old Tsatroy road, leading to the villa on the headland, where the setting sun would soon turn the symbol over the archway to living fire. There was the cone of the fire-mountain and the layers of the forest where Tsorl lay hidden. There was the Fish Cove, and the Little Fish Cove—I had taken up the tent but left the boat for Tsorl if he could use it.

I saw a vassal come running down from the headland at the harbor mouth; they had been keeping watch all day from the Tsatroy earth works, the remains of a watch-

tower. Now Meetal Gullan came from the camp and talked
eagerly with the watch. She ordered a third vassal to the
Esnar and then set out along the Tsatroy wall to the
headland herself. I watched these mysterious comings and
goings with only a shred of interest until I heard the Mattroyan crew grumbling. Lay back on the stoking? Delay the
sailing until setting of Esder? What a time to set out!

The gangplank was still down and there was still activity
on shore. I went back into the place where the camp had
been and walked on the paths a little to the east. No one
saw me. I dropped down into the tall grasses and crawled
until I came to the shelter of the crumbling Tsatroy wall
that led up to the headland. I crawled uphill the whole
length of the wall and came to the old watchtower. I lay
in a nest of vines hardly a body-length from Meetal Gullan
and the other vassals on watch. The Great Sun was hidden
behind the rock headland across the harbor mouth; the last
of the light was on the sea.

". . . to the southeast . . ." said the watch.

"Trader, from what I can make out," said Meetal. "Curse
this glass!"

"Ah, if this is your devil, Meetal . . . there's a haul for
you!" said the second watch.

Meetal Gullan laughed like a wolf.

"Yes, if this is Garl's ship—what was it called—we'll
have all four devils tight in our net."

"It was called the *Beldan*," said the first watch. "We
were told the *Beldan*. Spicewood trader."

"Should we tell the Ningan?" asked the second watch.

"Not yet, let the ship come on," said Meetal. "We're in
no hurry. If it makes harbor here, we'll take it. If it sails
roundabout through these cursed islands, we'll still be
waiting here on shore."

I eased back through the vines and bent my head so that
I could look at the darkening sea. I saw nothing to the
southeast but mist and water; then a light. It was like the
masthead light of a trader. I eased back farther and lay
flat, pressing my whole body against the warm earth of
Tsabeggan, as if to gain its strength. Scott Gale was not
mad, and he was not in Rintoul. The Ningan's story had
been lies from beginning to end. Scott Gale was coming
to Tsabeggan on the ship, out there in the darkness; he was
coming to find his friends, just as Karen-Ru had hoped.
This was Nantgeeb's warning: *"ship . . . danger . . ."* There

were two ships: one, this *Beldan*, the spicewood trader, and the other, the *Esnar*, a much faster ship sent by Tiath Gargan to catch Scott Gale's companions.

Yet, with all this knowledge, what could I do? Sam and Lisa and Karen were aboard the *Esnar*, fast in the Ningan's net. I did not know if they had a weapon among them. Worse than that—how would they believe me if I rushed back and raised the alarm? They were outnumbered; they could hardly fight their way off the *Esnar* even if I persuaded them to try. The image of the *Beldan* coming on steadily loomed in my mind. *"If it sails roundabout . . . through the islands . . ."* And suddenly I had the answer.

I crawled backward under cover of the old wall. The little darkness had fallen; the only light was from the *Esnar*'s riding lamps; the guards had no campfire. I bent low and sprinted along the paths to the sand dunes. There was Little Fish Cove and there in the reeds was my own boat.

9

Scott Gale

THERE WAS THE BOAT HIDDEN well out of sight of the camp; I took it in my arms and ran with it. I launched it into the dark waters like a swimming mat and flung my body down upon it. We glided out together, the boat and I, past the reef of rock that sheltered Fish Cove, and into the open sea. When the gliding motion had ceased, I pulled on the starter string and the small powerpack began to hum; I moved swiftly over the Great Ocean Sea. It was the time of the little darkness, the last rays of Esto had just faded leaving the waves black. I zigzagged about crazily for there was a heavy swell, and I strained my eyes to find that point of light from the approaching ship.

Suddenly the boat jolted as if it had hit a rock and I felt myself being carried to the south. I was in the Round Current again, and it was stronger than the powerpack on its first setting. I pulled on the string again and the noise altered to a sharper humming. The boat, as I steered it with my body, began to gain on the Current and to run more easily against it. I saw the ship, still a long way off, then the waves rushed over me and I came up gasping. Still the boat bore on, fighting in the direction of the ship. It was the beginning of a wind and wave battle as difficult as the running of the channel between Hindan and Steen. There was nothing to be seen around me but the foaming tops of the waves, the dark, moist air of the sea, and overhead the stars.

I drove on and on, breathing in the gaps between the waves like a swimmer and straining my eyes to penetrate the darkness. I thought I saw the ship once more and I drove the good brave boat on and on, the little man-made powerpack fighting against the might of the Ocean Sea as surely as the hefty equipment of a Mattroyan steam vessel. More than once the blunt nose of the boat flipped so high that it nearly overturned and I pressed down on it as hard as I could. I felt my strength going; I was tired and frightened. I saw myself collapsing across the boat, tired out, while it rushed out into the darkness without meeting the ship *Beldan*.

There was a sudden lull, a patch of calmer water, and I slewed the boat around, hanging arms and legs off it to act as a brake. A dark wall rose up from the sea about four body lengths away. I was so bewildered that for a moment I did not realize that it was the ship.

The *Beldan* was sailing at a steady rate toward the unlit harbor mouth of Tsabeggan. I had a sudden picture of the ambush in that quiet place with the Pentroy vassals falling upon the crew of this trading ship. I pressed forward on the boat in a long curving burst of speed and came to the ship's side. It towered above me churning water, and I stood up and beat with all my might upon the sturdy trader. I shouted aloud, and the wind and the darkness seemed to turn my voice into a whisper. I leaned down and twisted the string of the powerpack in such a way that a high screaming whine sounded through the night.

"Stop!" I cried. "Nahoo the *Beldan*! Alert! Danger! Pentroy on the island. Pentroy on the island!"

So I thumped and shouted, and my poor boat squealed and when I could do no more I saw heads above me at the rail. The ship staggered in the water as they began to heave to; Moruian voices spoke among themselves and shouted questions to me. I saw a ladder and a boat sling come down so I shut off my powerpack and waited.

An omor was climbing down, asking questions. I reached for her hand but the trader gave a lurch and connected with my head. I fell forward across my boat and lost my senses for a few seconds then came into a painful half-

waking state. I was being lifted, carried, dragged aboard.
I heard a voice through the mist of spin and tiredness and
it filled me with such joy that I fought off my wretched
bump on the head.

"Oh help!" I called in the human language. "Alert Scott
Gale. . . ."

There was light now on the deck and all the people I
could see were Moruians. Then the crowd parted, and he
came through: I saw him at last. Scott Gale was there,
dressed in a Moruian cloak; his beard had grown thick and
black, and his eyes were bright blue, bluer than the sky or
the eyes of his friend Karen-Ru. I looked another way and
made out a Moruian face filled with wonder. It was a young
male, almost a child, with broad square cheeks and bright
hazel eyes.

"Praise Telve and the spirits of fire," I whispered. "Scott
Gale . . . turn this ship back, sail around the shore of
Tsabeggan. The harbor is full of Pentroy soldiers."

"Vassals!" said Scott Gale.

"How did the Pentroy come to Tsabeggan?" he asked.

His voice was deep and resonant, like the voice of Sam
Deg. He spoke Moruian very well, but with a strong
mountain accent.

"They have come in a steam vessel, the *Esnar*," I said.
"The pleasure-ship of the merchant Mattroyan."

"Are my friends safe?" he demanded. "How are they?
Is Karen okay . . . Sam, Lisa . . . ?"

"They are fine," I said in English, "but they believe the
lies of the Pentroy."

"Who are you?" he asked. "Are you an islander?"

"No," I said. "I think my speech tells where I learned
Moruian just as yours does."

I caught the eye of the young Moruian, and he laughed.
There were good Moruian faces all around me and they
all smiled.

A round-faced "townee" said fussily, "Yes, yes truly,
Escott Garl, this young person speaks truly. We can hear
that she speaks in the accents of Tsagul, she comes from
the Fire-Town."

"My name is Yolo Harn," I said. "I am a helper in the
strangers' camp. I am a castaway."

Then Scott Gale questioned me again about all kinds
of things until my head swam, and the townee helper whose
name was Ablo Binigan broke in.

"Excuse me," he said, "but this Yolo Harn is tired if not hurt. Let us take her below to the sleeping hold and give her a reviving drink."

"Is the ship heading away from the harbor?" I asked.

"Yes," said Scott. "Mamor, our Captain, has changed course. Your warning came in time."

So I went down with Scott and Ablo and the young male whose name was Dorn. The *Beldan* was a comfortable, ordinary trading ship, not half so fine as the *Esnar,* the Mattroyan vessel. I drank my reviving drink in a big sleeping hold with hanging beds. Scott Gale was painfully anxious for his friends, and he took me through the strange story more than once.

"Thirty armed vassals?" he asked.

"A full thirty," I said, "but only ten remain behind, if the ship sails, under this huge brute of an officer Meetal Gullan."

"I know how this one came by its name," said Dorn.

So I first heard the tale of the Gulgavor who had joined together to capture Scott Gale for the Great Elder. They failed at first after some brawl by the fairground of Otolor, then they waylaid Scott, Dorn and this Ablo in the very streets of Rintoul.

"Meetal knows you are coming, Scott," I said. "She will crack your skull if she can."

"Not if I can help it!" said Scott Gale.

He looked dangerous for a moment, with a look I had hardly seen on a human face. I did not know it then, but there had been a death in the field by Otolor. Scott Gale had killed one of the Gulgavor by a blow with the side of his hand. In all the time I had spent with the humans on Tsabeggan, violence and fighting had played no part in our lives. We had argued, perhaps, and Sam Deg had shouted, and Tsorl had been cross and aloof, but none of us had thought of lifting a hand.

"This Ammur Ningan is a dangerous creature," said Scott. "I have heard about it from Vel Ragan, our friend."

"I know of this scribe," I said carefully, "for he comes from Tsagul."

"When will the *Esnar* sail?" asked Scott.

"Not until the setting of the Far Sun."

"And the Captain has secret orders . . . ?"

"They expect to sail to Rintoul or to lie off Tsabeggan," I said.

"Yolo," said Scott Gale, "what do you think the Pentroy plan is?"

"Tiath Gargan has said it himself, through the Witness Obal," I replied. "He will have your ship on the mainland in a place where he can watch it."

"I have heard the Great Elder speak," said Dorn with a shudder, "and I would not hear him again, not even through a Witness."

"Sam Deg would not believe," I said sadly.

Scott Gale began to laugh.

"Sam Deg!" he said. "That is a good name for Captain Sam Fletcher!"

He laughed and his laughter choked a little as if he were close to tears.

"I want to see them," he said angrily, clenching his fists. "To come so damned far and not to see those guys . . ."

He walked around the sleeping hold, and Dorn went after him to comfort him. Ablo Binigan fed me more medicine and urged me to lie back, to rest. Presently Scott Gale and Ablo went up on deck to speak with the Captain, and I fell into a kind of half-sleep with the rocking of the ship. I lay in this dreaming state for an hour or more, then was wide awake in the dim, salt-smelling hold. I was afraid and empty; the time in camp was over. I did not know what would become of me. Then I saw that Dorn Brinroyan, the mountain cub, was watching by my sleeping net.

"How long have I slept?"

"It is middle night and Esder is well up," he said. "We are still lying off Tsabeggan while Diver—Scott Gale— decides what to do."

We stared at each other warily in the dark cabin with only a small lantern containing a candlecone to give light.

"Tell me how you found Scott Gale," I said.

So he began to speak, slowly at first, then with real spirit and excitement. Dorn was a good storyteller; the tale he had to tell is well known on Torin through his telling: everyone has heard of Othoro Brinroyan, the Luck of Brin's Five, and of his adventures. Even players have taken up a version of this strange tale and carried it about the towns and villages of Torin. But I am proud that I heard it that strange night in the hold of the ship *Beldan*, when we had one or two more adventures before us.

"Now," said Dorn, when his tale was done and I had

thanked him for it, "tell me something, Yolo Harn. How long were you in the camp of the other humans? How long did it take you to learn their speech?"

He sounded full of interest, maybe a little envious; Dorn had the instincts of a scholar. I thought of my struggles with the Teaching Machine and laughed sadly. I would have gone on the wretched thing all over again just to have that time, that time of learning and peace and friendship over again. I told him all about learning Basic English.

"If we come out of this cave-in," I said, "you can have Scott Gale put the metal cap on your head and turn on the sleeping light. If I took forty camp hours, you might take fewer to learn the speech."

"What is a cave-in?" asked Dorn.

"It is the miners' word for a bad time. Maybe you call it a tangle," I said. "I am rested now. Is there anything to eat?"

I had had a thought while we were speaking and I knew one thing that I must do, but it did not frighten me too much. Dorn gave me some sailors' fare, sea cake and a little tot of thin tipsy mash, while he went to fetch Scott Gale. When they came down the ladder, I saw that Scott wore a blue zippersuit like the ones Sam and Lisa and Karen wore sometimes in the camp. I saw him as a member of the team, the Navigator: Scotty, whose guitar hung in his sleeping place in the blue tent. He completed the Bio-Survey Team—in a way he was their Luck too; they had been unhappy without him.

"What will you do?" I asked.

"I thought of risking a confrontation," he said, "of talking to the Ningan."

"No!"

"No . . . I will not try it," he said. "It's too dangerous for the others."

"They have no weapons; they cannot fight their way off the *Esnar*," I said.

"Well, perhaps they fight better than you think, Yolo Harn," he said, "but I agree that they are outnumbered."

"Scott Gale," I said, "I am going back on my boat. I will see them. I will sail with them on the *Esnar*."

"Would you do that?" he looked at me thoughtfully.

"Whew!" said Dorn. "Go back to that Ningan? Go and visit Tiath Gargan? You are brave, Yolo Harn."

"I must do it," I said. "I cannot leave them without a Speaker."

At this moment a heavily built Moruian came down the ladder and said his name to me. "Mamor Brinroyan!"

The Captain of the *Beldan* had the same face as Dorn, but old and scarred. The family bond was made clear between all these three: Mamor, Dorn and Scott Gale, their Luck. They sat together touching each other on the shoulder in the common family sign of recognition. Then Mamor leaned forward from the round bench where they were sitting and began to speak of Tsagul. I slipped from my sleeping net and sat on the matted floor of the hold to answer him. He had lived in Tsagul once when he was young, it seemed, and his uncle had been a glider pilot. Between the two of us, we knew the old place pretty well. I had spoken a good deal before I realized that Mamor was checking my story. I drew breath to steady myself: there were only these three in the hold, and I trusted them.

"Friends," I said, "I will tell you how I came to Tsabeggan as a castaway. It is a story I have not even told to my friends on the island."

So I told them of my crime and my imprisonment and how I came to Itsik. I fought against my own shame in the telling.

When I came to the journey on the muck raft, Mamor slapped his leg and cried, "What a yarn! What a sailor you are, Yolo Harn! I would have you in my crew!"

I felt comfortable, having told so much, but I had still said no word of Tsorl-U-Tsorl. I missed him as much, even more, than I missed the team. I needed his advice, his ruling on all that had happened; I thought of him hobbling about on the island. Yet his secret meant so much to him that I could hardly blurt out his name, bring him to life again, even before these persons of good will.

"Scott Gale," I said, "I must go back. How will you handle these vassals who lie in wait?"

"I will secure the ship," he said. "Everything follows from that. Mamor will bring the *Beldan* to that beach where your raft lies, below the old Tsatroy villa. We won't attempt a hand to hand fight between this crew and the vassals."

"But that ship is a fortress," put in Mamor. "If your friends have locked it, how will you come into it again?"

Scott Gale caught my eye, and we both smiled.

"Yolo Harn knows the secret," he said.

"There is a door-control, a sesame box on the outside of the ship," I said. "It is hidden behind a panel. It is for an emergency: if the crew of the ship get accidentally locked out of their ship on a strange world."

"Oh, the great air ship!" cried Dorn. "Will we fly in it, Diver? Will we fly the round of Torin?"

"You are too bold," I said. "I am a miner from Tsagul, but the metal of that ship is too much for me. I fear it almost as much as the Pentroy vassals. It is larger than the *Beldan* and fierce as a fire-mountain. Yet there is one Moruian who does not fear it."

"Who can that be?" asked Scott Gale. "Do you mean Nantgeeb?"

"Well perhaps that is such another," I said, "but the Moruian I mean is on Tsabeggan."

"Another Moruian on the island?" he asked.

"Truly," I said. "I am reluctant to say his name, but he came with me from Itsik. He has committed no crime and is no friend of the Pentroy."

I saw Mamor and Scott exchange glances.

"This sounds like a certain leader," said Mamor, "but it cannot be so!"

"It is impossible!" said Scott. "The Pentroy have made many enemies. Vel Ragan's old liege . . ."

"What?" cried Dorn. "Is this the one she means? Is it Tsorl-U-Tsorl?"

So the name was blurted out anyway, but they did not see my face.

"No, it cannot be," said Mamor. "Dorn, we did not tell you, but word had come from Vel Ragan before we sailed. The Deputy of Tsagul is dead. He lies in a nameless grave on Itsik—Vel Ragan has seen the place by now."

Dorn reacted strongly to this news. He had never seen the Deputy, but he must have had some attachment to the idea of such a leader. He looked angry and as if he would weep.

"You should have told me," he said. "I am not a baby, four years shown. I did hope that Vel Ragan and Onnar the Witness would find their leader again, at Itsik or some other place. Tsorl-U-Tsorl. It is a proud name. Did you know him, Yolo?"

"I have heard him speak many times," I said.

I held out a hand to Dorn in the gesture that means,

"Do not weep . . . be comforted," and when he clasped my fingers in acknowledgment I drew him closer to me and whispered.

"I heard him speak this same day on the island!"

Dorn drew back, eyes wide with astonishment.

"Then they are wrong!"

"Tsorl is alive," I said. "I dug his grave myself. Vel Ragan mourned over it for nothing. For a bunch of bara stalks sewn in a sack."

Scott and Mamor stared in unbelief.

"Tsorl-U-Tsorl . . ." said Scott Gale. Then he burst out in the human language: "The old devil must lead a charmed life!"

I laughed then.

"That is exactly what he has said about you!"

So I added the rescue of Tsorl to my story and told what he had done on the island and how I left him at the last, hidden in the forest by the ogodan tree.

"There is no one easier to kill than a dead person," I said at last. "The Deputy is still in danger . . . Ammur Ningan would swat him like a honey-bug. Please find him."

"I promise," he said, giving his version of the Moruian sign for a promise.

"Truly, the winds must have protected this fellow," said Mamor shaking his head.

"Say rather the fire-spirits," I laughed, "for he is a citizen of Tsagul!"

I thought of that time when Tsorl-U-Tsorl stood before the Tsatroy villa at the setting of the Great Sun and hailed the spirits of fire.

We climbed on deck again, and I checked my good boat. Scott Gale was very restless, striding the deck and staring at the dark bulk of the island, silvered on its heights when the clouds parted over the Far Sun. The *Beldan* had out its sea anchor, but it was drifting slowly to the south in the edges of the Round Current; I was actually a little closer to Tsabeggan than I had been. Scott Gale sat with me in the waist of the ship.

"This is the most difficult part, Yolo Harn," he said. "I don't think you should tell Sam or the girls that you have seen me. If I know Sam, it would make him try to leave the ship at all costs . . . they might all get hurt."

"But if there is a real chance?" I asked.

"Then tell them. They could secure the ship and tell the Ningan to go to hell."

"Scott Gale," I said, "will there be much fighting . . . wounding . . . when you go ashore . . . ?"

"No," he said solemnly. "No . . . I'll do my best."

"Tsabeggan is a good place," I said. "I would not have it accursed . . . stained with blood. Have you heard of a place called Sarunin?"

"Why yes," he said, "yes, I have. Vel Ragan spoke of it as we sailed down to Rintoul. The fire-clan, the Tsatroy, committed suicide there. What really killed the army? Some kind of plague?"

"Red-wither," I said. "Summer plague. The only purification for such a sickness is burning."

"We have a cloak in the family . . . in the Brinroyan family . . ." he said. "It has the insignia of the fire-clan. It was made for the old Highness Elbin Tsatroy. I wore it at the Bird Clan Air Race."

"Well, you are under her protection then," I said, as cheerfully as I could.

"Don't be afraid, Yolo Harn," he said, smiling. "We will all come out of this net. Tsabeggan will not turn into a battleground. Let me give you a letter for the team."

"No," I said. "Give me rather some words that they will understand as coming from you."

He thought for a few moments then laughed sadly and said, "Tell them 'Corrigan sends his love.' "

He coached me in the strange word a few times until I knew it. We went to the rail; it was time for me to embark. Scott Gale's blue eyes were very bright; Dorn stood beside him to comfort him. The boat went down in a sling and everyone pressed around me for a farewell. I climbed down to the boat, tugged on its string, and veered off toward the island. I waved to the *Beldan* and saw Scott Gale in his blue suit leaning over the rail. Then I set my face toward Tsabeggan and went off into the misty half-light of Esder under cloud.

It was not such a battle as before, but it took some strength and concentration to get the boat back to the island. I found myself on a stretch of rocky shore about a weaver's mile from Little Fish Cove. I bent down, dragging the boat under cover and thought I saw light through the trees in the direction of the harbor. I was shaken from my travels, and I had a strong sense of danger growing upon me.

I moved slowly toward Little Fish Cove, then the light of two, three torches picked me up and I heard shouts. I ran back into the darkness to my boat . . . the Pentroy vassals were out looking for me. I heard my name called and other jeering names they called me: "The Runaway," "The Telling-Bird." I knew that I must let myself be caught, and that they must not know where I had been. There was nothing for it; I released the valves on my poor boat and with a sad hissing sound it crumpled into a bundle of wet plastic around the powerpack and I thrust it well out of sight under the bushes. Then I ran through the trees in the direction of the Tsatroy road.

It was easy to let oneself be caught; I blundered out before a second search party of three vassals and was grasped firmly by Meetal Gullan herself.

"Stupid little muck-eater!" growled the omor. "You have given us trouble!"

I said nothing but found my strength; the old violent strength I had used in prison. I twisted from her grasp and landed several good blows before I was held hand and foot and dragged toward the campsite. Meetal shook a fist the size of a crushing hammer in my face.

"The Ningan will deal with you—"

"Then hold your hand . . . *vassal*," I said boldly. "She wants me to be able to speak."

Meetal dropped her hand at my word. Shouts went up as we came to the *Esnar* at the dock: "Found! Found! Call off the search!" I had not expected this reception; the Ningan seemed to value my efforts as translator. I knew that I must have this one thread of bargaining power, but as I came to the ship and saw that spare, gray figure, I was afraid. I could see none of the humans. My captors half carried me up the gangplank, across the deck, where the vassals and sailors were stoking again. I was shoved up the ladder to the bridge where Ammur Ningan sat on her writing chair. The moment I was released I struggled up-right and faced her. There were torches about and in the light her long eyeslits shone red like those of a wild beast.

"You have wasted my time," she said in a thin, whining voice.

She gave a signal, and the *Esnar* was made ready for departure. Meetal and the members of the land party went ashore. I stood on the high bridge wih the Ningan in a little circle of quiet; Obal stood watching and a couple of other Pentroy vassals.

"You were needed here," said the Ningan. "You ran off. Why was that, I wonder?"

I made no reply; the Ningan gave a sharp, controlled movement with her right hand, and I felt a cruel stinging blow on my cheek. Her whip was made of thin, black grass rope; its handle was made of bone.

"Speak up!" said the Ningan.

Again the whip stung my cheek in exactly the same spot; the pain was sharp, but I knew that the skin would be no more than reddened. At the same time I knew that the whip could be made to split the skin, to take my eye out, if she willed it. Still I made no reply, there was nothing I could say.

"Well, the answer is known to me!" hissed the Ningan. "I know very well why you ran off . . . *Cub Dohtroy!*"

She nodded to one of the vassals, who climbed down from the bridge and went into the luxurious fore-cabins. I heard the humans coming up, their heavy boots on the ladders. Sam, Lisa and Karen all were ushered out to stand beside the Ningan's chair, and she bowed and smiled and made polite gestures to them as she had done before.

"For heaven's sake, Yolo—where did you get to?" said Sam.

"Look—we need you . . ." said Karen. "We don't want to take you if you would rather stay, but it is so difficult . . ."

"Were you looking for . . . your friend?" asked Lisa.

I saw them there, my true friends, and I thought of Tsorl and of Scott Gale and all that had passed. I could have sunk down on the deck and wept for fear and weariness and the things I knew and could not tell.

"Don't speak!" ordered the Ningan. "We will see how good a translator you are."

She rose up and addressed the team formally.

"I, the High Steward of the Pentroy, have some bad news for you concerning your helper, Yolo Harn."

There was nothing for it. I could not tell them any more or less than she wished. The gangplank was up and the ship had enough steam to edge away from the dock. Vassals were strung along the rails; the whistle on the tall mast-chimney blew merrily and puffs of smoke came from its mouth. To hint at my meeting with Scott Gale and the lies of the Ningan would make my friends angry and confused. They could not escape. I threw back my head and translated as exactly as I could.

"Yolo Harn is an escaped prisoner. She was sentenced to ten years for wounding a fellow mineworker. She was sent to the settlement of Itsik, the place for badly behaved prisoners."

So they heard my shame for the first time and I saw the faces of my friends clouded with pity and embarrassment. Sam was able to put in a few words.

"Is this true?"

"Yes, Sam, it is all true," I put in at the end of one of Ningan's speeches.

"Oh, Yolo, why didn't you tell us!" said Karen.

The Ningan hissed for silence when she spoke.

"This runaway must not stay close to our honored guests. It will be treated as a prisoner."

Sam cleared his throat.

"Tell the Ningan that you . . . that Yolo Harn has helped us very much . . . we need her services. . . ."

He burst out: "Damn it, Yolo. You shouldn't have made a break for it."

I translated the first part of what he had said and added quickly to him: "Please Sam . . . do as she says. . . ."

"Yolo Harn belongs to us," said the Ningan. "We can use her speaking when it is necessary. After all, you will soon be able to speak to your friend Escott Garl."

I translated it all and felt the Ningan's eye upon me. I was suddenly more frightened than ever. Did she know where I had been? Did she suspect that I had found out her lies?

"Enough!" said the Ningan. "Not another word."

Her hand moved, and I felt the black string of her whip curl around my throat. I heard the startled exclamation of the humans; Sam began to protest, but Lisa touched his arm. It was the first violent act from Ammur Ningan, the first real threat that they had seen.

"Take it below!" ordered Ammur.

The vassals led me down, right across the deck, past the boiler to the crew's quarters. I looked back and saw the Ningan talking to Sam, Lisa and Karen, ushering them back to their cabin. I saw that we were sailing out through the harbor mouth, past the old Tsatroy tower; I took a last, long look at the shore with the glitter of the silver ship among the trees and the spark of a candlecone at the camp of Meetal Gullan. I saw the misty sea before us, silvered where the Far Sun shone through cloud. Then I was below decks and pushed into a dark, salt-smelling hole at the end of the sleeping hold.

I heard the sea moving and gurgling all around me as I sat on the rough planks. I thought of the Pentroy vassals and the crew of the Mattroyan ship and wondered which one of them had known me as Cub Dohtroy and betrayed me to the Ningan. It was something I never found out. I tried not to think of the looks on the faces of my human friends. I had disappointed them.

The *Esnar* traveled very fast, much faster than a sailing ship or even the larger Mattroyan vessels, *Ullo* and *Telve*. I did not see my friends again for the whole of the voyage. My trip was not as uncomfortable as it might have been: the Mattroyan crew let me come out of the little punishment hole and walk about. The Pentroy vassals who were supposed to guard me knew about this, but turned their heads aside. They knew the Ningan would never set foot in the hold.

The Mattroyan sailors were puzzled, easy-going persons. They were being paid double, triple for this single voyage and they were pleased by this and by the wonders they had seen. I wondered what would become of the humans and of myself. I felt sure Scott Gale had control of the island of Tsabeggan and of the space ship *Heron* by this time, but I did not see clearly how this would help my friends. I could not see the Great Elder's plan, but by now I knew where we were going.

On the morning of the third day, before the rising of the Great Sun I was woken in my punishment hole and allowed to clean myself up. The Ningan had sent down a fresh Earth T-shirt and a brown cloak; evidently she wanted the tame Speaker to look fine. I appeared on deck, and there were Sam, Lisa and Karen clustered by the rail. They were in good spirits, pleased to see me but rather bewildered. A procession was forming up below on the dock and the vassals were urging my friends to go down and take their places.

We began to call to each other.

"Yolo, can you stay with us? Are you okay?"

"I'm fine! They want you to march in procession, Karen!"

"But where are we?" boomed Sam Deg. "That Ningan has gone on ahead. Is this . . . surely this isn't the city we've heard so much about?"

"No." I laughed. "No, this is not the city." I looked at the docks, the neat compounds, the shining bara trees beyond the stockade; I snuffed the foul air.

"We have come to Itsik!"

10

The Great Elder

THE REASON FOR OUR COMING TO ITSIK was to be seen right there at the wharf. There were two vessels tied up besides the *Esnar:* one was a sturdy rounder: a strong little boat with a paddlewheel and sails, the other was a barge draped in black. It was the barge of the Great Elder, and although Dorn Brinroyan had pictured for me this sinister conveyance threading the waterways of the Troon, as a ship it was unimpressive, barely seaworthy. It had been dragged down the coast from Rintoul by the little rounder. But the banner at the masthead with the Pentroy device of three knots made me cold and apprehensive.

It was sunrise; I looked around at the cargo sheds and the deserted wharf. The inhabitants of Itsik were afraid of the Strangers, and they hid or stood back, mumbling and peering. High on the wall of the largest wharf building was a table of numbers painted in fish-gut blue: I saw that one and twenty fives of fivedays had passed since the New Year, plus two days. There was a star on the calendar and a scrawl representing a bird: we had come to Itsik on the eve of a festival. Tomorrow was Mid-Year, the so-called Darkest Day, when Esder shone in the constellation of the great bird, Vano. In Rintoul and the northeast, this is the

Festival of the Four Winds, a time for kite flying, but in the west, along the Datse and in Tsagul, this is the Festival of Wind and Fire. I remembered the delicious whiff of burned leaves and candle fat in the streets of Tsagul. I looked about for Gwell Nu but could not make out the skinny frame of the Healer.

We grouped on the dock: humans, vassals, interpreter, more vassals. Suddenly, as we marched off to the beat of a clapping stick, a voice rang out: "Ghost of Eenath, ain't that Cub Dohtroy?"

There was a scurry and rush; all those who had been hiding in the cargo sheds to get a look at the "devils" tumbled out. I was hailed on all sides; I felt a sad bubble of laughter rise up and I waved freely. The sight of a fellow prisoner, long since given up for dead, was as exciting to the poor folk of Itsik as beings from another world. In fact my presence convinced them that the humans were harmless. They came out of the sleeping houses in their raggedy finery and lined the route of the procession. It was a chorus of, "Hey Cub . . . Nahoo Yolo Harn . . . are your devils tame? What can we say to them? Did they steal your soul? Can they fly?"

"Peace, friends!" I called. "Say to my new masters, 'Welcome.' They are good folk and come in peace. Yes . . . sure, I ate well! Fresh fish, not a dish of leather-stew. No, I'm flesh and blood, no spirit!"

Even the vassals, who seldom had the experience of marching in a friendly crowd, took it all in good part. Sam and Lisa and Karen had some idea of what was going on, and they waved to the crowd. The word of greeting went from lip to lip and together with the sign for averting evil, it became from that very hour the way to greet the humans. They got Well-Come and Vill-kim everywhere they went upon Torin.

So we came over the first and largest compound cheerfully enough and I was relieved when we left it. I had half believed that we might be stowed away in the Special Compound, off to the right beside the quiet hump of the sickhouses. There was still no sign of Gwell Nu, and I thought of her sleeping or tending a difficult case.

There was no work going on in the compound we had just passed: the tannery and the refinery were shut up. It was the same in the second compound: the bara plantation was empty and still, the houses of the warders were silent.

On the larger house of Boss Black hung a fresh Pentroy banner; I wondered idly what kin he was in terms of blood to the Great Elder. They were more or less of an age, but one was of the half-blood, his mother a house-servant, not a grandee. Perhaps they had run together in the houses of the grandees as children. There had been a time when I would have trembled to go into the presence of Boss Black, the so-called "Elder of Itsik," but now I was bound for the presence of his noble cross-cousin, and I feared the encounter much more.

Part of the stockade between the second and third compounds had been rebuilt; the officer in the lead rapped on the tall double gates of wood and painted hides and they were flung open from within. The third compound was really no compound at all, for it had only a light fence or two separating it from the red road and the dry and dusty countryside. Once it had been a pleasant place, for Itsik, with a few more houses for the warders, redwood trees to hold weavers' tents and pens for the old wool-deer. Now there was hardly a tree to be seen, the weavers had gone and the animal pens, leaving something like a grassy field.

The black tent spread so far and reared up so high that it cast a shadow over the world. It was five, ten times as large as the humans' blue tent and of a richness that I hardly knew existed. We speak, on Torin, of the curtain walls of stone buildings, where the stonework is wrought to resemble cloth. Here were the real curtain walls of a ruler of Torin, tent-cloth thick and soft as fleece, falling in folds so deep that a child could hide in them. The edges of the folds were worked with silks and dark brilliants, and the borders, where they trailed upon the ground, were weighted with graymetal chain, chased with leaves and symbols.

The roof dipped and shone in the morning light; it was made of glazed cloth so that rains would run off. At its points and angles appeared the pointed ends of the tent poles, like giant lances, tipped with more precious stones set in graymetal. The tent was ten or fifteen sided; it was hard to know its true shape unless one flew over it. On the entry wall were hangings with the emblems and colors of the Five Noble Clans of Torin, which even I knew by this time. Three Knots in black, gray and green for Pentroy, star and spindle in deep red and white for Galtroy, flax flowers in blue, green and yellow for Luntroy, flower and gourd in brown, orange and white for Dohtroy, a bird's head in greens and yellow for Wentroy. In a space above these entry panels, there were whirling suns and stars in flame-red, orange and blue: the colors and emblems of the Fire Clan, Tsatroy, which is no more. Tiath Pentroy was taking no chances with the spirits; he paid homage to them all. I prayed, as we drew up in sight of his tent or traveling palace, that the fire-spirits would protect me and my strangers.

The place was busy and bustling; on the low wooden steps of the great tent, carpeted with green, there stood a few personages in colored silks, furs and brilliants who could only be grandees. House servants stood about; there was a smell of warm food. In the center of the steps stood our companion, Ammur the High Steward, full of pride and glory for bringing back the strangers. There was a spatter of cheering and applause as the procession arrived. As we drew up before the steps, I was able to slip by the guard and stand with Sam, Lisa and Karen for the first time.

". . . Montezuma . . ." Karen was saying. "Or maybe the Persians, Cyrus, Darius . . ."

"What is that?" I asked.

"Old rulers of Earth," whispered Lisa, for we all spoke in lower voices in this place. "They had magnificent tents, palaces."

"This beats all, I think," said Sam Fletcher.

"Sam," I whispered boldly, "we have not much time. I must speak to you, and you must believe my speaking but not show anger or fear."

"What is it?" he looked at me seriously.

"All is not as the Ningan said. I know it. You are something like prisoners."

"Where is poor Scotty?" asked Karen, pulling Sam by the sleeve.

They both saw my face change at her question.

"Yolo!" she said. "Where is he? What do you know? What have they done with him?"

"He is safe," I said.

But I could say no more. There was a sudden blast of music; the guard of vassals stepped back leaving us alone before the steps and the Ningan began to speak.

"Let it be seen," she cried in her loudest singsong voice,

to still the clamor of the grandees and the harps and pipes alike. "Let it be seen that I have fulfilled my charge and returned to the Great Elder, my liege, these Man Human Devils, who were nested in the island of Tsabeggan. They seem to be intelligent and peaceful, more peaceful than their other companion, Escott Garl, who stood before the Council. They are conveyed here by me in good order and condition; there is nothing to fear from their strange looks. They are ugly, especially the ones with the bulging chests, and you will observe that one of these two has a dark skin color. But there is nothing to fear from these creatures whatever their strange looks: they have no mind powers, they cannot fly without their large silver ship, which is on the island under guard. They do not carry weapons. They speak well enough but in their own tongue, and they have found a Moruian runaway, some outcast from Tsagul, and taught it their speech. It can stand between us and tell what is said."

I had already been doing just that.

"Tell her I wish to speak," murmured Sam.

"By all means," replied the Ningan. "This one with the hairy face and the head with less hair is the leader and its name is something like Sarm."

"We greet the people of Torin," said Sam pleasantly. "We notice certain differences in their appearance as they do in ours. The Ningan came to us on the island of Tsabeggan and invited us, with solemn oaths, to be the guests of her master, the Great Elder. It is certain that we come in peace. We long to see our fourth member, Scott Gale. We were told he is among you."

There was a noisy murmuring from the grandees on the steps as I translated this.

"You see?" cried the Ningan. "The hairy one speaks well."

"You have been doing a lot of fair speaking yourself, Ammur," remarked a youngish grandee with a sleeve-knot in Galtroy colors. He bowed and nodded to the humans who all bowed in return.

"Really," said an old creature dressed from head to foot in crimson silk, "I can't see that we can speak through this common slave they have here. How do we know what the devils say?"

"Dear Mother Leeth," said a sweet-voiced person in

fantastically colored silks and a blonde wig; "I am sure the Speaker tells what they say and what we say, too."

"Welcome to the mainland of Torin," she continued, looking at the Humans. "We were once done a service by Escott Garl. Let us be friends."

"Perhaps this noble person could tell us how it is with Scott Gale?" asked Sam.

"Alas, I do not know," returned the Highness. "I last saw him at the Council in Rintoul. He may be in that city still."

"Enough, Highnesses, I pray," called the Ningan. "Exercise time is nearly done. I must complete my charge and bring them to the third chamber."

"Ask the Ningan where the Great Elder is," said Sam with a touch of his usual impatience. "Are we to meet this ruler?"

"He is taking his morning exercise," said Ammur Ningan. "He is yonder in the wilderness across the red road with his team of training servants and skippers."

The grandees pointed and spoke among themselves. We saw that the attention of the company before the tent had been directed not so much at the procession the Ningan had made but out into the brownish land beyond the road. We could just make out small dust clouds and figures where the Great Elder was running and jumping with his servants.

"Take the devils to the third chamber," said the Ningan.

The last of her courtesy had gone. The vassals hustled the humans and myself through a panel into the huge black tent. We crossed a passage lit with daylight through white silk overhead and came to a quiet round room lit this time with candlecones under glass shades. It was thickly carpeted and very fine with cushions and flowers in a water frame and wicker chairs. The hangings were of silk and of wool; the silken panels were softly colored, the woolen ones thick and black.

"Right!" said Sam. "Speak up, Yolo. What else do you know?"

"I know we must be careful here, Sam," I said, not looking at the walls. "Don't look about. There are guards behind the black panels."

The three humans sat down warily, trying to be unconcerned and relaxed upon the silken cushions. They still carried their white kitbags. I was caught by the strangeness of the scene.

"Quickly then . . ." said Lisa.

"Scott Gale is on the island of Tsabeggan," I said. "He is not mad or sick."

Karen gave a cry and put her hands to her lips.

"Why . . ." she said. "Why did this Ammur—"

"I can guess why," said Sam, grimly. "What I want to find out is: how do you know, Yolo Harn? Tsabeggan? What is he doing back at the island?"

"He came on a ship, the *Beldan*," I said. "The Pentroy soldiers were watching—remember—at the headland. You were all aboard the *Esnar*. I heard Meetal Gullan say that the ship was coming. I went out in my own boat and warned the *Beldan* of the danger."

The shock was very bad; Sam rose up, almost shouting.

"*For God's sake!*" he lowered his voice with an effort. "You're trying to tell me that you *saw* him and said nothing?"

"Could you have got off the ship?" I pleaded.

"All that stuff about being a runaway . . . Yolo, what are you playing at?"

"I am a runaway," I said. "Could you have left the ship, Sam?"

"Yolo," said Karen, "did Scotty give you a letter or anything?"

"Yes, he did," I said, feeling worse than ever. "But with the journey it has gone away. There was a name . . . something like Ko-gan . . . Ko-gan sends his love. . . ."

"I don't believe you," said Karen. "That is some kind of word you made up. It has a Moruian ending like Ningan or Forgan. I don't know where you got this fairy tale."

She touched Sam on the shoulder, and all three of them whispered together. Then they stared at me seriously, concerned and kind.

"Yolo," said Lisa, "if you've been forced to tell this story by the Ningan so that we will go back to the island, please drop the play-acting. Don't lie. We're friends."

"I don't lie," I said. "I lied to the Ningan about being a sailor, but that was all."

"You were on this ship with Scott Gale," said Sam, with the air of one taking a child through a wild tale to prove how silly it is. "You *came back* . . . and let yourself be caught . . . and said nothing to us . . . and returned to this old prison of yours, this Itsik we're in."

"It was as we planned on the ship," I said. I was beginning to lose heart. They would never believe me; my story did sound fantastic, the reasons that had seemed so good were feeble. Worst of all I had forgotten the message. "Scott was very sad not to come and meet you. He thought of speaking with the Ningan. He decided to secure the ship and defeat the ambush of vassals. He feared for your safety and for loss of life if a fight started there and then. Besides he had others to think of."

"Which others?" asked Karen.

"His family and the crew of the *Beldan*."

"His family?" said all the humans together.

"There were two of his Moruian family on the ship," I said. "The Captain and a young male. Scott is their Luck. The Luck of Brin's Five. Tsorl explained the custom to you, remember?"

"Did you cook all this up with old Tsorl?" asked Sam. "Yolo, we don't know what game he is playing."

"Karen-Ru," I said sadly and desperately, feeling that I might shame myself here in the Great Elder's tent and shed tears. "Remember the sea-sunner. You wouldn't believe . . . but it was true."

"The sea-sunners exist," said Karen. "But I'm not sure I believed that story you and Tsorl had about meeting one."

I turned aside and walked to the other side of the room and sat on a cushion. I shut my eyes and thought I would die of their unbelief and lack of trust. I thought of the time when Len Alroyan, my foster sib, had refused to recognize me aboard the salt boat *Gvalo*. Sam called in a soft, soothing voice like one speaking to a naughty child or a mad person.

"Hey, Yolo . . . what are we supposed to do? What is supposed to happen on the island?"

I could not answer. We sat in the beautiful round room and heard the voices of the grandees and servants chattering and laughing through the tent walls. Close at hand we could hear the vassals on guard in the walls of our room stirring, shifting their boots. When I had been sad aboard the salt boat, the Rope Ward, my handsome sailor, had suddenly come to comfort me. Now I heard the humans utter a gasp and I felt a light touch on the crown of my head. I remembered where I was—had the Elder come?—and I flung back my head in fear.

I looked into a pair of eyes hardly on a level with my

own as I sat on the cushion. It was a dwarf: a sturdy, muscular, smooth-faced creature in rich clothes of leather and thick silk. On the front of its tiny tunic was embroidered the name *Urnat;* I had heard enough of the clan gossip that was spoken on Itsik to know that this was Urnat Arvan Pentroy, the Luck of the Great Elder's own five. It was admired and feared by the Pentroy servants and vassals.

"Hello! Hello!" said the dwarf Urnat "You hear that? I'm a Speaker too."

He spoke in a bold childish voice and laughed at his own joke.

"Cheer up, Telling-Bird!" he said. "Stand between little Urnat and the devils. I think I will choose one for my Luck—what do you think of that? The Luck's Own Luck. What, has the wind stolen your voice?"

"No," I said. "Good Wind, noble Urnat. Where is your noble sib?"

"Jumping rope," said Urnat. "I am more skillful than he. I am a dancer. Look here! Tell your devils to look!"

Before I could say a word, he turned three somersaults and executed a complicated dance figure on the carpet. The humans, somewhat mystified, laughed and clapped their hands. Urnat bowed to them.

"Is that their way of showing pleasure?" he asked.

"Indeed it is," I said. "They appreciate your art."

"Go along," he squeaked. "You do not flatter well, you are untrained. I am used to thick and shameless flattery, like bean soup. Present your masters."

So I made the introductions, and Urnat had me lead him to the humans. He bade them remain seated and went all around them tweaking their clothes and their hair, patting Sam's bald place.

"Yolo," said Sam through set teeth, "the little guy is awfully cute. Is he some kind of court dwarf? An entertainer? Can we send him away?"

"Sam," I said warily, coming back into an area of unbelief, "I have said his title. He is part of the Great Elder's own family: an adopted Luck. He is close as the Elder's child or his brother. We can't send him away like a servant."

"Speak back, speak back! No secrets!" cried Urnat, and I spoke back an edited version. I found that I was learning flattery very quickly and that it was an art I despised.

"Ask his highness where Scott Gale is," prompted Lisa.

"That is the prettiest one," said Urnat, staring at Lisa, "but I prefer the one with child's yellow hair. Ka-ren, you called her. Are you sure it is a female?"

I replied to him and put in Lisa's question.

"Good question!" laughed Urnat. He turned a somersault with pure glee.

"Obal is even now trying to get through to Tsabeggan," he said. "Poor music-maker. What a heaviness for my poor friend to be a Witness."

I spoke this back and hoped the humans got even a little of the sense of it.

"Why is it such a heaviness, noble Urnat?" I asked.

"To link in mind with Tiath is fine," said Urnat, "but who would link in mind with a leatherhead like Meetal Gullan? I am sure it damages Obal's head for days. He cannot play for my dancing."

I spoke back some of this, and Sam ventured a question.

"We find the idea of a Witness difficult to believe. Why is the servant Obal trying to 'link' with a guard officer on Tsabeggan?"

"What other way to reach so far?" returned Urnat. "You devils may have engines for talking far away, but we have none. Birds are used and flying machines and runners. The voice-wire reaches as far as its wire can reach. But we also have mind powers, and some have them in special measure. We speak through Witnesses. It is swift and private."

"That is most interesting," replied Sam, "but it is not quite what I meant. What message is expected from the island of Tsabeggan?"

"Clever! Clever!" cried Urnat. "That one *is* a ruling spirit, hair or no hair. He thinks I will give out secrets."

Then he danced off around the room and ran up to the black panels one after the other kicking at the concealed guards so that they cursed or groaned. It was cruel and also funny; none of us could help smiling.

A guard officer stuck his head into the room and said wearily, "Highness, leave us in peace. We are on duty!"

Urnat's foolery turned the sinister, hidden guards back into ordinary vassals. When he had grown tired of his dancing and showing-off, he came and stood before Karen-Ru and looked at her with an adoring face. He took off a copper amulet that hung on a thong around his neck and put it into her hand.

"Ah, my dear devil . . ." he said. "She is a sweet-faced creature. Tell her the amulet will not hurt her, although it is metal."

Karen thanked him and felt in a pocket of her kitbag. She drew out a little drawstring bag of sky-blue silken cloth, a specimen bag, and gave it to Urnat. She put it into his small hands in their leather half-gloves and asked in a gentle, pleading voice, "Please . . . where is our dear friend Scott Gale?"

Urnat blinked his yellow-green eyes; he had the sense of the question before I spoke it back. I kept the tone as best I could and translated "our dear friend" as "our dear sib."

The dwarf turned aside, clutching the little silken bag, and said in distress, "Tsabeggan. Gullen has him in the net again!"

Then he bounced off and was gone as suddenly as he had come, through one of the tent panels. I spoke back his last words. I did not add to them. Outside the grandees were chattering more loudly than ever and the music playing. The humans talked anxiously among themselves.

Suddenly outside the tent there was an utter silence, no more voices, no more music. Only the humans went on talking beside me, but I did not try to stop them, I was too busy listening to the silence. A voice spoke inside the tent, once, twice; each time the silence rolled back. The guard officer in our wall gave a soft light whistle. The silence hung over us like mist; even the human voices fell silent.

A middle-aged male strode into the chamber wiping his hands and his neck with a bunch of amyth leaves. He wore a black tunic, simple in cut as my old prison gray, a circle with one shoulder free; his leather boots were dusty. His face was striking, all its features exaggerated to the point where he looked the pattern of a grandee: pale skin, lipless mouth, high-bridge nose, narrow as the beak of a bird. His brow jutted like a cliff over long eyes, the look called "yadorn" or "three-eyed"; the eyes were light brown; their power and concentration was immense. He stared at the humans and nodded, panting from his exercise; he was smiling. Sam, Lisa and Karen rose at once from the cushions and stood at attention.

"Hello! Well-Come!" said the Great Elder.

He flung aside the amyth leaves and sat in a wicker

chair, not taking his eyes from the humans except for one sweeping glance in my direction; I bowed my head.

"Welcome indeed," he continued in Moruian. "I am sorry to interrupt your studies on the island of Tsabeggan, but these islands are part of the land of Torin. For the present I have charge of all this land and all the people in it."

The accent and resonance of the voice were plainly those that we had heard from the Witness Obal. I wondered if Sam and the others were more convinced. Tiath stopped short in his speaking, raised one long hand in my direction without turning his head. I translated at once, and he went on smoothly when I had done.

"We are the only thinking creatures on this world. From the green ice of the North, the home of the North Wind, throughout the length and breadth of the continent of Torin, from the homes of the flax people in the far west to the salt havens in the east; throughout all the islands and the lands below the islands and the blue ice of the southern sea, there are no other races. There are creatures of legend —spirit warriors, sea weavers, devils—but none of flesh and blood. We are the Moruia, the weavers, and our most ancient writings and skeins tell how this world, Torin, was hung in the void for the use of the Moruia and of the Tsamuia, the fire-people.

"Now you have come unasked to this our land, and I can see your coming, your powers, your silver ships, your weapons and engines, as a threat of change and of violence. If you wish to stay, you must be ruled by me and fly the large ship to a place I have chosen."

Sam Fletcher had been following closely—and in truth I translated slowly enough—and now he replied, "We greet the Great Elder in the name of our Space Service and of the people of Earth. It was never our intention to do anything but make a first study of the air and plants and animals of Torin. Change and violence are far from our thoughts. Scott Gale, our navigator, was separated from us by an accident. Please tell us where he is at this time; then we will be able to make plans concerning the ship."

When I began to speak this back in Moruian, the Great Elder threw me a look and gave a single yap of laughter.

"Child of Tsagul!" he exclaimed. "The voice and accent of the Fire-Town. Proceed!"

When I had done, he lay back in his chair reaching for a cloak that lay to hand.

"Did not my Ningan tell you his sad history?" he asked.

"We would like the Great Elder to tell us plainly: where is Scott Gale at this time? We must see him," replied Sam.

I spoke this back to Tiath and wished with all my mind that he would not lie. At least he did not give back the Ningan's tale again.

"At this time?" he repeated, with a hint of scorn, even playfulness. "I say this truly, Man. I do not know where your sib Scott Gale is at this time."

"The Ningan swore solemn oaths in your name that we should be reunited," said Sam. "Nothing can go well between our team of scholars and you, the ruler of the great land of Torin, unless we know the whereabouts of Scott Gale."

"I have said I do not know," said the Great Elder dangerously. "But perhaps there is word. Come . . ."

He held up a hand, and Ammur Ningan swept into the room. She had changed her clothes and was more finely dressed than ever in baghose of black and silver and a green half-cloak. But her finery only marked her out as a servant; Tiath, her liege, had no need of trappings.

"Ammur," he said, not looking in her direction, but smiling, with his eyes still fixed upon the humans. "Did you lie and take false oaths in my service?"

I translated this, and Ningan's reply.

"Perhaps I did, Highness."

Then Tiath and the Ningan both laughed aloud.

"Where is Scott Gale?" demanded Sam angrily.

"I have already said that I do not know!" said Tiath, turning from laughter to coldness in an instant. "Do you know, Ammur?"

"I had hoped to get through by this time," she replied, "but the Witness cannot contact Meetal Gullan."

Tiath raked Ammur with a hard glance then, and the Ningan wilted a little in her rich clothes.

"Well then, we must say that no one quite knows where Scott Gale is . . ." said Tiath. "You must be patient, Man."

Then Sam Fletcher lost patience entirely, and before I could get the words out he cried: "I protest! Be damned to you . . . you have lied to us. We came in peace to the islands and then to this meeting. *Where is Scott Gale?*"

His voice filled the tent room, and the Great Elder exclaimed angrily: "You see? They're violent!"

He made a sign before Sam had finished speaking, and two guards armed with net and short spears burst from the black panels nearest Sam and came at the humans. What followed surprised me. Sam gave a loud terrifying shout and felled the guard with the side of his hand. Lisa seemed to crumple a little as the second guard, an omor as large as Meetal, came within arm's reach, then she twisted up, struck down the spear, and hurled the guard easily to the ground with a thump that shook the tent. The other guards burst from their panels—I felt one at my back—and stood warily, ready to attack the embattled humans. I stood still and shouted with all my might in Moruian and in English:

"I know! I know!"

The Great Elder raised his hand and all movement was arrested. For the first time he looked at me, let his eyes rest on my face.

"Fire-brat!" he said.

"I know that Scott Gale is on the island of Tsabeggan," I said. "I know he came there in the ship *Beldan*. I went to this ship in a boat from the Human camp and warned him of the trap set by the Ningan. This is the reason Meetal Gullan cannot speak, the ambush has failed."

Then I turned to Sam, Lisa and Karen, knowing that I would not be able to get many more words out. But my memory had not failed this time. I said in their speech, "See how the Great Elder believes me. Scott is on Tsabeggan. He sent this message: *Corrigan sends his love.*"

I saw Karen mouthing the word silently, "Corrigan . . . Corrigan . . . ," then she covered her face with her hands.

Sam burst out: "Okay . . . okay, Yolo . . . we're sorry. . . ."

Tiath looked at me again.

"Take it!" he said. "Let it's mouth be stopped!"

The guard seized me, and I felt the folded net at my throat. Everyone believed me at last. Tiath gestured, and the Ningan came close to him. He reached up one hand and took hold of a heavy chain about the High Steward's neck and twisted it cruelly until she rested on her knees by his chair.

"Your web was not strong enough," he said in a terrible soft voice. "I have been ill-served."

I saw the faces of the humans full of fear and loathing. They knew at last how the Great Elder might use his power. This was his trusted servant and an old female, much older than the Great Elder himself: to ill-treat her in this way was for them especially brutal.

The Great Elder let the Ningan fall to the ground and gave a sign to my guard.

I was marched toward the door panel when suddenly the Great Elder called out: "Wait! Bring back the Speaker. . . ."

He leaned forward wearily in his chair and passed a hand over his face. He spoke in a moderate voice, ordering the guards to retreat; he reached out a hand and let it fall on the Ningan's gray head. She drew back and stood once more behind his chair, stiff and proud as before.

"Tell the Humans to sit down," said Tiath. "I will speak further. Then they can rest."

I translated promptly if a little hoarsely.

Sam Fletcher replied: "I am sorry. My temper is short. We are tired, and this place is strange to us."

"I will have the ship," said Tiath. "I must know where the ship lands if it flies to the mainland. To this end I brought you here and hoped to seize Scott Gale."

He spoke at last without reserve; he simply told his will.

"The situation has not changed so much . . ." he went on. "Scott Gale knows you are here. Is it possible that he could fly the ship alone?"

"The ship flies itself!" said Sam. "If Scott wanted to fly to the station—the sky-town around the planet Derin in your system—he could do so, though it would be very difficult. But to launch, orbit, land in a place he had not surveyed from the ground—that would be even more difficult. He would need at least one trained helper."

"He has none," said Tiath flatly. "I know of few Moruians who would set foot in such a vessel."

"The members of his . . . family?" suggested Lisa.

"They are mountain weavers," said the Great Elder, with a first suggestion of a smile, as if he took some pride in Brin's Five. "A bold, stubborn family, puffed up with their special destiny and their Luck. Born and bred on my own lands to the north. But they are not flyers. They know nothing of engines."

"Don't you have any people of this sort on Torin?" asked Sam, catching my eye.

"Very few," said Tiath easily. "What do you say, Ammur? Who are you thinking of?"

"Your own cousin perhaps," said Ammur, fawning and smiling.

"Young Murno?" Tiath laughed. "He is a fool. His teacher might do it . . . the damned magician."

"Nantgeeb," said Karen-Ru. "Is the magician called Nantgeeb?"

"So your young fire-cub has told you of Nantgeeb," said Tiath. "I wonder what a picture of Torin you have received from this Speaker. Yes, Nantgeeb might help to fly that ship. And there was one proud spirit who bore a great name from the Fire-Town—do you remember, Ammur?"

So we had almost come to the name I feared, and to my surprise the Ningan shuddered and stepped back as if putting a safe distance between herself and the Great Elder.

"Who was Deputy of Tsagul when you were last there?" demanded Tiath, casting his eye upon me once more.

"The Deputy was Tsorl-U-Tsorl, Highness!" I replied.

"A great scientist!" said Tiath. I could not be sure if he said this to tease Ammur.

"Shall we meet this person?" asked Sam quietly. He gave no sign, even when he heard the answer. I saw how well humans could conceal their feelings; even quick-tempered persons like Sam Deg could, if they tried, give nothing away.

"He is dead," said Tiath. "Tsorl-U-Tsorl died here on Itsik; he lies yonder by the Special Compound."

He sighed briefly.

"Scott Gale will stay till we come," he said. "Now go to the house prepared for you. It is the Eve of a great festival."

"May the Speaker, Yolo Harn, be lodged with us?" asked Sam.

"No!" put in Ammur Ningan. "It must go beyond the stockade."

She bent down and whispered to the Great Elder. I wondered if she would be revenged on me. Tiath shrugged, and the Ningan said in her familiar singsong tones.

"The traveling palace must be purified. Only guests and members of the Great Elder's household may remain.

Diviners have come from the ancient temple at Windrock for the ceremonies."

She gave a sign, and the guard stepped up behind me again and obediently clamped the folded net about my poor throat. I was marched through the corridor and back into the harsh daylight. I gasped and choked, and the guard released me.

"Great Wind!" it said. "Your devils can fight well. I thought there would be trouble. . . ."

I saw that it was a youngish male vassal; by its speech it came from the north.

"Where will my masters be lodged?" I asked, more hoarsely than ever.

"See . . . there. The double-round house."

I saw that it was a spacious house that had once housed two families of warders; it did not look like a prison.

"And where are you taking me?"

"Special Compound," said the guard. "You've come up in the world."

We passed out of the shadow of the black tent and crossed the quiet second compound where a few prisoners were making faggots for the festival cook fires. In the main compound there was some holiday activity: the paths were being swept cleaner than ever; there were food troughs and a small kite-flying tower being assembled. A number of the prisoners waved and shouted greetings to me.

"No tricks," said the guard nervously. "Be a good fellow. . . ."

"I'm sick," I croaked. "If I can hardly speak, maybe your damned rope is to blame."

"Only doing my job . . ." he mumbled, marching me as fast as possible to the Special Compound. "You saw how it was in there."

"I'm sick," I repeated. "When you've put me in my hut, fetch the Forgan from the sickhouse yonder."

"Perhaps I will, at that."

So I was left alone in a small round hut built of redwood logs set into the earth, with a flat wooden roof of split logs like the lid of a cooking pot. I lay on a heap of bara straw; there was a leather water bag on the center post and a wooden waste bucket by the floor drain. Elbin Tsatroy had gone down to death in such a place; Tsorl-U-Tsorl might have burned with fever in this cell. Presently the bar was lifted on the round door and Coth came in, the Doh-troy sick aide.

"Yolo Harn," he said between smiling and weeping. "Yolo Harn. She knew that you still lived."

I sat up trembling.

"She has gone," he said. "Gwell Nu is dead. I am Forgan of Itsik now."

Then I wept aloud, and he wept, too, and we sat keening for our dead friend.

"How did it happen?" I asked slipping the cordial he had brought for my ruined voice.

"Twenty days after your escape, she came down with a chest rheum. She was immune to everything else."

"She was a great Healer."

"She spoke of you," said Coth, "and saw you come to the islands."

"Yet here I am again, back on Itsik. It is Mid-Year. If I had stayed put, I would be out of time . . . ready to go back to Tsagul and serve the rest of my sentence . . . nine whole years with time off for good behavior. I don't know how I will ever come out of this cave-in."

"Fluff and rubbish," said Coth more cheerfully. "I have heard all about you. You will never be a common prisoner again. You are the Speaker."

"And the rest of my sentence . . . ?"

"Find your way to some goods or credits, and you can buy yourself out of time if you get back to the Fire-Town," he said. "How was it in the islands?"

"I have seen wonders."

"Gwell Nu spoke of other things," said Coth. "Things I had half-guessed. I am a citizen of Tsagul, too."

He turned aside and looked out from the narrow window slit over the graveyard of the Special Compound.

"About five days after Gwell Nu died—no, she does not lie here, she is in the common place beyond the bara planta-tion. . . . About five days after she died there came a grandee from Tsagul; I think it was called Paroyan Doh-troy."

"Tilje Paroyan?"

"That may be. She was making a pilgrimage to the Windrock Temple, so it was said. There was a scribe with her who had a scarred face, and a younger female, a Wit-ness out of Tsagul. The Highness brought presents to Boss

Black; she could not be refused much. I saw her stand here
in the Specials' burying ground with her servants . . . by
a certain grave."

"The grave of the Deputy, Tsorl-U-Tsorl," I said. "He
lost a leg, do you remember?"

"He was on the Council when I was last in Tsagul,"
said Coth sadly. "I might have spoken to that Highness—
given some hope to her—but I only knew what Gwell Nu
said in her last illness. Besides I have never spoken to a
grandee. I am only a citizen like yourself, even if we are
lumped together into Clan Dohtroy in this place."

"It was best to do nothing . . . to know nothing," I
said. "I do not know how things will turn out. There are
still some who need our prayers. Today in Tsagul it is
Stiporu, candle-night."

"Think of old times!" he said. "Look from your window
when it is dark, and I will send out candle boats and a fire
balloon for all who need the help of the spirits."

He gave me food and more medicine. It was hard to
believe, but Coth had served ten years and would never
leave Itsik. He had killed his own sib in a drunken brawl
and barely escaped hanging. He was a former cook-shop
owner in Tsagul, a sober, gentle, strong-armed fellow with
a gift for healing.

When he had gone, I sat and pondered on the nature
of the Moruians and of the humans as well. I heard the
cold, hooting voice of the Great Elder, and the boom and
roar of Sam Deg; I shuddered at the way humans could
fight. I thought of violence, breaking out like a grass fire
among humans and Moruians alike. Who controlled it
better?

I ate my dish of leather-stew and lay on the bara straw
trying to draw the threads of my life together. I thought of
Morritt and Old Harn and the streets of Tsagul; I thought
of the island—my good, green island of Tsabeggan—where
in some part of my mind I would learn and play forever.
Then I fell asleep and slept for the rest of the long day
before candle-night and dreamed only a simple, kind dream
of sailing on a calm ocean with one who could have been
the Rope Ward from the salt boat *Gvalo*.

I woke in the darkness, the so-called "long darkness"
that precedes Mid-Year; there were no fire ceremonies in
the main compound of Itsik. Presently I went to the

window-slit and looked out over that gray place reclaimed from the sea. Beyond the graves at the edge of the lagoon, I could see a few flickering lights. A single balloon of willow paper rose up like a ghost and blazed high in the air. The candles that Coth had launched on their rafts of bara leaves floated off into the darkness. One by one their flames were quenched by the sea.

11

Festival of Wind and Fire

MID-YEAR WAS A PERFECT SUMMER DAY, the sky was clear
and pale, there was a good breeze for the kite flying. The
tannery and the oil-works had been closed down for five
days, and the stench of Itsik had diminished at last. The
festival itself was bound to be a poor and simple thing
here in the first compound, or so I told myself when no
one came to open my door or bring me a bite to eat. All
I heard for hours was distant movement and a murmur of
voices. I felt well and strong, and my voice was healed;
I tried it out with a few songs and shouts, but no one heard
or took any notice. I prowled the tiny cell and did some
of Sam's morning exercises—he had always been disgusted
because I could do more pushups than he could, but I saw
no sense in it.

At last, toward midday, when I was very hungry, the
door was lifted off my hut and there was a weatherbeaten
male in black leather and an almost-new wig who grinned,
giving off a whiff of fresh tipsy mash. His face was doubly
familiar; he was deeply tanned from an outdoor life, his
wrinkles were deeper, but there was the craggy brow, the
high-bridged nose, the harsh mouth. Only his hands were

strong and broad, not the hands of an aristocrat; otherwise he was the Great Elder's twin.

"Come along, Cub," said Boss Black. "The good folk of Itsik are calling for you."

I stepped out, puzzled, and found a party of guards dressed in the colors of every clan waiting for me.

"Don't look so scared!" said one. "We ain't going to toss you in a blanket. They want you for the lucky kite flyer!"

They gave me bean bread and a fiery gulp of tipsy mash and explained the custom as we walked from the stockade into the main compound. Every prisoner of Itsik was there; it was like a gathering of the ghost clans. They were a strange, orderly mob, ranged in rows around the food troughs as if they hardly knew how to rejoice. There was the wooden tower—twice the height of a tall weaver—and on its platform rested a large kite, a winged box that must be flown for luck and to avert the winds' bane in the coming half-year. A lucky kite demanded a lucky kite flyer, and a female who had returned from the dead seemed a good choice.

The cry went up for Cub Dohtroy as we approached and willing hands reached out to put me on the ladder. I had never flown such a large kite in my life, but I had to admit that, within reason, my luck had been very good indeed. I climbed up into the wind and waved to the crowd.

"How shall I do this thing?" I cried. "Give me good advice!"

There was no lack of this. I saw that my ropes were in good condition as Boss Black settled himself on a green-covered platform by the stockade. There he sat with his five and their children, playing the Elder. He blew on his roarer for the flying to begin, and I raised the kite as I had been instructed. The wind on the small tower was strong, and I nearly sailed away with the damned kite. This was the luckiest thing the watchers had ever seen, and the cheers rose. The kite rose too, steadily into the wind as I played out the cord. It was a fine feeling, the kite was well balanced and rode on the wind like a live creature. I tied it off on the rail of the platform and accepted offerings of food and water.

There was a sound of clappers and pouch-pipes; the gates of the stockade were opened, and a vassal ran to Boss

Black who blew on his roarer. The Itsik warders opened up a pathway and a cry was raised: "More Luck! Great good fortune!" A procession came into the first compound; the prisoners stood amazed at the amount of luck they were receiving this day.

First came the musicians, then a middle-aged female in strange antique robes: one of the Diviners from Windrock, as I guessed. She carried a dish of ceremonial fire that burned blue and green. Part of the ceremony of Mid-Year was the quenching of fire in water, and she meant to carry this fire to the harbor of Itsik. Behind the Diviner walked a tall omor in gray and green for the Pentroy household, and on its shoulders rode the Luck of the Avran Pentroy. Urnat was dressed fine as ever and in high spirits.

"Luck! Luck!" he squealed. "I've brought you my own kite and a Lucky Person to fly it!"

The kite was carried by two servants: it was beautifully made, a great blue and yellow bird. The kite flyer, with a house-servant all to herself, was Karen-Ru.

My head reeled at this chance; I began to feel the day was really a lucky one. Hands reached out again, and soon they were both on the platform beside me.

"Yolo!" cried Karen. "This is crazy . . . what are we supposed to do?"

"There, you see!" said Urnat. "Speak to my Ka-ren, Telling-Bird. I brought her here because she was asking after you. At least you are not hard to find."

I passed this on to Karen, and she smiled sweetly on Urnat who bounced for joy.

"Watch this platform, Urnat Avran!" I said. "Hold still, Highness. . . ."

Up came the splendid Pentroy kite, and I got its strings right and helped Karen to raise it to the wind. It flew readily, but it was difficult to control and went swooping over the heads of the crowd, who cheered and whooped in mock fear. Urnat would have taken the strings, but I could not let him; I had a vision of the Pentroy Luck being carried off by the winds. So we stood on the platform laughing and struggling with the kites like children. Down on the ground the Diviner and the musicians had reached the wharf: a cheer went up as the fire was quenched in the sea. Karen-Ru flew her kite skillfully now, and I unleashed my box kite; the two kites soared together high into the pale sky of Itsik, as if to call down on these poor folk a blessing of which they had not dreamed.

The sound was like distant thunder; I heard and did not hear it in the laughter and cheering. Then there came a string of small explosions, not much louder than a clapping board or a skin drum. Still no one paid attention. Then there was a base note, a humming that began to seep into our heads, like the fumes of tipsy mash. I saw Urnat Avran, whose hearing was very keen, shake his head and knock at his ears to make the humming go away. Then, far out over the ocean, there was a fierce boom that echoed eerily over the sea and land. I saw Karen's hands jerk and tremble on the strings of the bird kite.

The noise of the crowd stopped for an instant then redoubled as everyone asked, "What was that?"

The sound came again. It was a sound absolutely new; it fell upon the ears of everyone on Torin for the first time. It was like thunder; it was like a huge rock striking the ground; it was a wrenching and tearing apart of the air as if the winds had gone mad. The base note grew stronger; Urnat screamed aloud and rolled on the platform covering his ears. I looked into Karen's blue eyes, we stared at each other like two creatures in a dream. I took the strings of both kites and tied them to the rail. The sound grew and changed and pressed down on Itsik like a hard hand. I stared upward shading my eyes and saw a patch of radiance slip away from the side of the Great Sun and begin to come down.

Karen snatched up the Luck of the Pentroy and held him like a child, covering his head with her cloak. We clung to the rail and watched the crowd below turn by slow pulse beats from a horde of ragged prisoners, their faces upturned, their mouths gaping, into a single creature, mad with fear. I looked for the Pentroy house-servants, who might have taken the dwarf and helped us down, but they had already gone. The crowd was bent down, crouched, all heads were covered; there was a blind surge outward, to left and right. The noise of the crowd was a wailing, windy sound of terror; I shouted aloud, and my voice was absolutely lost in the sound from above and the crowd's noise.

The tower rocked and swayed; I turned to the ladder and then saw the movement coming that would unseat the tower, and at the last moment, I jumped to the ground. I landed on my feet on grass, which was luck by itself, and I felt panic-stricken creatures brush past me on either side. I struggled back into the crumbling wreckage of the tower and looked for Karen-Ru. The noise overhead had changed again.

Karen was not hurt, but she was tangled in the struts of the fallen tower reaching vainly toward something that lay on the ground. I crawled from beneath the little shelter of the wreckage and snatched Urnat's body from under the very feet of the crowd. I crouched beside Karen and wrapped him in my cloak. She pointed, and I knew that the sound was no longer directly overhead but moving over the second compound.

The crowd had opened up a way for us, a way that no one else wanted. We ran toward the sound, we ran to the stockade and through the gate into the second compound. The new gate was open up ahead, and I had a glimpse of vassals; I steered Karen into the bara plantation. I looked up and saw it for the first time, the ship of the void, the ship *Heron,* high, high in the air, hovering sun-bright and crushing Itsik with its sound.

"Where?" I shouted. "Where will it land?"

"Up ahead . . . by the road . . ." said Karen. "Is he hurt? I think the little guy is badly hurt. . . ."

We sat under a tree, and I unwrapped my cloak and looked at Urnat. His color was bad; my cloak was drenched with his blood, all from a cut on his arm. I went to work with a stone and a white scarf from Karen-Ru. I knew the wound must be stitched, but I had the bleeding stopped. As I worked, we saw three or four Pentroy vassals, the only ones who had kept their heads, come running from the dreadful noise and commotion of the first compound. They shouted to the gatekeepers, and I thought I heard the words "Luck! Luck!" and "The devil . . ." Then they went through and the gate was shut.

"The gate!" said Karen. "We must get through. . . ."

"I know a way," I said.

Beyond the new part of the stockade, at the end of the tall, old palings, there was a leafy tunnel into the third compound. The prisoners had used it when they trafficked with the bush weavers for extra food. We crawled through and found ourselves in a stand of tall grass. The third compound looked deserted, with signs of panic—chairs and flower-frames overturned on the steps of the black tent, food wagons tumbled on the grass. As we watched, a few house-servants scrambled up from beside a fallen wagon and showed us where everyone had gone. They raced to the tent and burrowed under the outer folds. Still the ship descended and a wind sprang up and whirled all over the roof of the Great Elder's tent.

Karen tried to leap out of the grass and run forward, but I pulled her back. We went on, crouching. The silken curtains at the entry to the tent were wrenched aside and Tiath came out in his ceremonial robe. He hitched it over his arm and came down the steps with his eyes fixed on the ship. Behind him, in formation, walked the black-clad vassals following their liege. Tiath strode on until he came to some spot upon the ground where he felt the limit of safety was reached and there he stood. The vassals, fully armed, wearing their mask-helmets, came on in ranks until the ground outside the tent was black. There was no word, their words were lost in the crushing roar of the ship descending.

"Where are Sam and Lisa?" mouthed Karen in my ear.

"He has them fast," I said.

Karen watched the ship come down; her fists were tightly clenched, she whispered in her own language. The ship was so bright it deceived the eye: it grew large, then dwindled, the dust clouds obscured it. It moved, it hovered with sliding movements, it seemed to sing and twang in the dry air. With a frightful roar it swung half upright, and flames burst forth from its vents. The vassals cried aloud and cast themselves flat on the ground. The flame became two, three sharp jets of fire that charred the ground in a neat circle as they had done on Tsabeggan. Still it came down; the noise was like the roar of the fire-mountains that had split the world. It came down and down, and set out struts and projections, and I raised my head a little to mark the place where it came to rest. The ship settled in a cloud of dust and dwindling flame exactly across the red road that runs from Rintoul to Tsagul.

And of all the company of the Pentroy, there was only one who greeted the ship standing upright and that was the Great Elder himself. He stood as close as anyone could stand. Behind him the vassals crouched and trembled and burrowed their faces into the earth. A little runnel of fire came close to him along a thread of dry grass, and he stamped impatiently with his boot and put it out.

A thick woolly silence rolled back; we were all half deaf. Something moved on the ship: the silver boom with the microphones came out and swung toward the Great Elder. One or two vassals, braver than the rest, leaped up and hurled their spears so that they clanged against the thing. But Tiath waved them aside as if he knew its purpose.

A voice came out of the long silver branch, and I looked at Karen, but she gave no sign of recognition. The voice was speaking Moruian.

"Tiath Pentroy," said Scott Gale, "where are my team. I've come to get them."

"You have certainly played the Spirit Warrior here today, Escott Garl," said Tiath with bitter scorn. He spoke into the microphone on the boom and his voice sounded far and wide.

"You have driven a lot of prisoners out of their wits," he said. "You have shown the weakness of my guards. You have played with wind and fire!"

"Where are Sam and Lisa and Karen?" asked Scott Gale. "Bring them out!"

"I have two of them fast and I will keep them," said Tiath. "The smallest one was in that place by the sea where you caused a riot. You were too high in the air to see the havoc; we heard the crashing and screaming. My own Luck was in that bad place. Perhaps you have stolen the luck of the Avran Pentroy. What will you do now? Kill us all with a storm of fire and prove what I have said from the beginning?"

"Damn you!" said Scott Gale. "What about Meetal Gullan, that brute from the Gulgavor that you set upon me again?"

"It is my creature," said Tiath, "and it does my will and so must you if you wish to see your friends again. This is the land of Torin, you come unasked, I owe you nothing."

"You owe me something, Gargan!" said a new voice.

Then for the first time, Tiath showed fear; he stepped back from the boom. Then he leaned forward again and spoke in a shaking voice.

"Who speaks? What devil's work is this?"

"You owe me my life," said the voice. "You even owe me my left leg."

"Tsorl . . ." said the Great Elder, and the microphone sent the name echoing about.

"We are coming out," said Scott Gale. "Keep your guards back. I don't want to hurt them."

The doors opened, and the ramp went down with a sigh. Scott Gale came out first, wearing his space suit, a man, a stranger flown from the void, just as Brin's Five had first found him on Hingstull Mountain. His helmet was off, and he had clipped back his thick, black beard. Behind him came a figure hardly less strange, also wearing a space suit and with two legs. But it was Tsorl-U-Tsorl, the former Deputy of Tsagul, and he still limped upon his ring-walker.

"Bring out my friends!" said Scott Gale. "Where are they?"

Tiath swung from side to side as if uncertain what to do; when the vassals scrambled up, he motioned them to keep back.

"You see me, Gargan," called Tsorl-U-Tsorl. "I am alive . . . I have not withered away."

"I see you, Deputy," said the Great Elder, shrill and nervous. "What do you want of me? Shall I admit that I did not want you dead?"

"Shall I believe it?" cried Tsorl. "Prove it by bringing all these people, strangers and Moruians alike, to a Round Mat. Today is Mid-Year: we have had wind and fire enough. Let us have a Speaking Chain like the Clans of old."

"Always the politican!" said Tiath. "I will consider your proposal, Deputy. Keep close to your ship, Escott Garl. You have done enough damage."

So he turned on his heel and began to walk back briskly to his traveling palace, his face twitching with strain. He brushed the vassals away from his path.

"Now!" I said to Karen.

We sprang up out of the long grass. Karen gave a loud cry and she ran, ran faster than the wind, faster than the startled vassals on the edge of the landing place, who reached out to catch the white figure. She ran and came straight to the arms of Scott Gale, and he held her close in a human embrace.

Tiath turned back with a furious shout at the vassals, and I raised my voice.

"Highness!"

I stepped among the vassals, and they crowded in on all sides, but I lifted up my voice again. They saw that I held in my arms the pale, limp body of Urnat Avran, the Luck

of Tiath's family and they shrank back, making me a path.
I came to the Great Elder, and his gaze raked over me like
fire.

"Urnat?" he said.

"He lives," I said. "I caught him up after the kite-flying
tower was destroyed. But his arm wound must be stitched
at once."

There was no softening of the Great Elder's face as he
took the dwarf's body, but his long hands, his grandee's
hands, curled most lovingly about the little creature and
smoothed its dusty hair. He spoke curtly to an officer who
took Urnat Avran and ran into the tent calling for the
Healers who traveled with the Great Elder and his court.

"You have saved my luck," said Tiath in a flat, angry
voice. "What was I supposed to do in return?"

I shook my head.

"No . . ." I said. "That was not in my thoughts."

I could have asked for Sam and Lisa, but something
held me back. I had saved Urnat because he needed saving;
I had already used the poor dwarf a little to make sure that
Karen went free. I could not barter one life for others.
Tiath stared at me; his hands sketched the sign of "Thanks."
He went up the steps and into the tent with his ceremonial
robe trailing in his wake. I went warily among the vassals,
some of whom gave me a greeting, and came at last to the
place where the ship stood.

I went toward them—Tsorl, Karen, Scott Gale, feeling
shy and unkempt. But as I arrived, two more very strange
figures tumbled out of the ship and down the ramp. One
was Dorn Brinroyan, the other Ablo Binigan; they wore
space suits—Dorn's did not fit very well—and they could
scarcely speak from the excitement of the journey. So we
all stood together and laughed and shouted in the strangers' language and in our own. I went to the ship and laid a
hand on its warm silver skin and found that I had not a
thread of fear left for it. I loved it for bringing my friends.

Tsorl was in good health and spirits.

"Deputy, how do you have two legs?"

"It is the magic of a pressurized suit, Yolo Harn. This
leg is a balloon, nothing else."

Now that the excitement of our first greetings had worn
off, we all stood by the silver ship in a different mood. The
weather had turned around a little, as if the elements themselves had been upset by the ship's landing; the clouds had

thickened overhead, and the day was not so warm. The vassals spread out in their companies in a half-circle; there were only six of our number, two humans and four Moruians standing alone in that black half-circle. We all thought with anxiety of Sam and Lisa, imprisoned inside the vast traveling palace. Scott Gale suggested that we go into the ship, but Tsorl urged him to stay outside.

"It will frighten the vassals," he said. "They will think we are going to fly away again. They have their courage back and might make a rush."

So Scott and Ablo went into the ship and brought out a blue tent, and we set about making a camp beside the ship *Heron*. We made ourselves more comfortable and had food to eat, but our spirits were low and our tension increased. As I took my turn standing watch outside the tent in the late afternoon, a pair of guard officers called to me.

"Hey, Telling-Bird. We have a question for Escott Garl Brinroyan."

"Come forward," I said. "I'll fetch him."

When Scott came out, the two vassals came a little nearer and put their question.

"You may not know her," said the smaller officer, "but this here is Alloo Gullan. We want to ask about Tsabeggan —about the party of guards left there. . . ."

"Escott Garl," put in the one called Alloo, "what has come to Meetal and to the rest of them? They drew this thread, this duty. Have the winds taken them?"

"I know you, Alloo," said Scott Gale in the voice of one who speaks as easily as he can with an enemy. "I remember every one of the Gulgavor that was sent against me. But you need have no fear. None of the vassals on Tsabeggan were killed or even badly hurt. Meetal has a sore shoulder, nothing more. There was some work with the stun guns."

"Praise the North Wind," said Alloo humbly, making the gesture for thanks.

"I gave them a choice," said Scott. "They might have flown back to Itsik with this ship *Heron*. But they would not do it; they ran off into the woods."

"By the fire, I don't blame them," said the smaller officer. "Come on, Alloo. . . ."

He touched his big companion on the shoulder, and they went back to their ranks. The Great Sun set and the long darkness returned while we sat talking quietly in the blue tent. Scott Gale had found his guitar, and he was teaching Dorn Brinroyan to strike the notes. Karen sat beside them, and Dorn looked at her very often in wonder. He was not quite sure that she was female until she made a certain remark, which I had spoken back to him. She had scolded Scott Gale for bringing Dorn on the spaceship. "What would his mother say?" she had asked.

Suddenly Ablo Binigan, who was on watch, came rushing in and told us something was happening. We listened hard and heard a familiar singsong voice.

"Ammur . . ." said Tsorl. "Now what is afoot?"

Then we heard another voice, loud and clear, and we all rushed out into the darkness. A wide path had been cleared between the black tent and the ship; Ammur Ningan stood on the steps, and vassals were carrying torches. Down the path walked Sam and Lisa; they walked without an escort; they were free. Sam carried a large green message skein. They came quickly, as if the Great Elder might change his mind, and were received into the blue tent. Then the four humans spoke and laughed as loudly as a dozen grandees. Tsorl read the skein, and it was the order for a Speaking Chain to begin in two days.

"Why has the Old Strangler done this?" he asked. "Is he learning sense? Is he superstitious?"

No one knew the answer. Some thought it was because Tsorl-U-Tsorl had returned from the dead. Some thought it was a hint for all the humans to fly away again. But I always believed that the Great Elder sent back Sam and Lisa because his Luck was saved and nothing asked in return.

12

The Speaking Chain

WE SAT IN THE BLUE TENT on the day after Mid-Year. I
was as happy as I had been since I saw the *Esnar* sail into
the harbor of Tsabeggan and bring the world of Torin to
our camp. There sat the humans, the whole of the Bio-
Survey Team together at last; to right and left were their
friends and Scott Gale's young sib and Ablo Binigan, who
counted himself as an outclip of Brin's Five. There sat
Tsorl-U-Tsorl, and I sat by his side. The talk flowed
sweetly and naturally, and everyone who was able translated from one language to the other so that nothing was
missed. It was the end of the adventure.

"No one has been killed," said Dorn Brinroyan. "No
one has been hurt . . . though there are some bruised vassals on Tsabeggan."

I did not like to disillusion him, so I said nothing. There
were broken bones among the prisoners in the first compound; Tiath Gargan had not been so much changed: he
had found the two house-servants whose duty it was to
guard the Luck, Urnat Avran, during the procession. He
had hanged them out of hand.

"Gentle Friends," said Tsorl, "we have a Speaking Chain.

It is a very old thread and a long one, but it is better than nothing."

"Okay," said Sam, "I see this as some kind of palaver. We are going to discuss a landing place, a more permanent landing place for the ship. We talk, Tiath Pentroy talks—"

"Sam Fletcher," said Tsorl, "this is Torin. *Everyone* talks."

"You mean anyone can have a say?" put in Karen.

"If they form a Speaking Five and follow the ritual," replied Tsorl.

"Wait!" said Scott Gale. "Does this chain overrule the Council of Five or the Hundred of Rintoul?"

"It can," said Tsorl. "It is an older thread than these."

"Itsik is an out-of-the-way place," said Scott Gale. "Tiath was keeping things secret from the other Clans by coming here with his court."

All the Moruians smiled.

"Truly, Escott Garl," burst out Ablo, "it will not be a secret very long."

"Diver," said Dorn, using another of Scott Gale's Moruian names, "the news of the ship and of the Speaking Chain are already spreading over the land!"

Indeed I could feel the threads of communication spreading over the land of Torin like a web. Trading vessels had taken the news from Itsik harbor, the Diviners had sent thought messages to their Temple inland, runners had been sent to Rintoul, and I knew that Tsorl had personally sent a runner—the servant of a Merchant who happened along—back to Tsagul. The news was passing from lip to lip and from mind to mind all across the continent.

"All right," said Scott Gale, teasing his young sib a little, "*everyone* will come, and *everyone* will speak!"

"What a lot of speaking-back, translating, in the two languages that will mean!" exclaimed Dorn.

I could not hold back a loud groan.

The first meetings of the Chain were impressive: the large central chamber of the Great Elder's tent was made ready with a raised mat—which the Humans called "the Round Table"—and wicker stools. Panels were folded back overhead, and we sat under the open sky. The two Diviners, male and female, from the Temple at Windrock, made a solemn dedication to the Four Winds and the Spirits of Fire.

The Five Clans of Torin had the right to speak first, and

there were two clan leaders on these first days, Tiath Avran Pentroy and the old female, Leeth Galtroy. She was a proud and stupid old creature from the first, who found fire-metal-magic in the very fastenings of the human clothes. When these two speakers had made a beginning, Scott Gale presented the humans as a speaking five who wished to make a new link—this was the rule. The first days passed in ritual and expressions of goodwill from the humans.

On the fifth day, a flying machine came from the east containing two Luntroy grandees: one young male named Jethan took his place at the Round Mat as the representative of the clan. He did seem not a bad fellow and disposed to hear the humans out, but I was still glad that I was not his clan's vassal.

On the eighth day Captain Mamor sailed the *Beldan* into Itsik harbor from Tsabeggan, four parties of Merchants from Tsagul arrived along the red road, ten families of bush-weavers set up camp in the plain, and Guno Deg, the Wentroy Elder, a ferocious person, arrived on the back of a runner. She took her place at the Round Mat supporting the humans in everything.

On the ninth and tenth days there were fifteen "new links" in the chain including Merchants who asked permission to build a new road around the spaceship, the Town Council of Otolor offering a permanent landing place for the ship on their Fairground, and a family of shepherds from the Datse who insisted that the ship had scattered their wool-deer.

On the twelfth day a mother and two young children, accompanied by a Harper, arrived in a hired boat from Rintoul. Brin's Five was reunited, and they put a new link into the chain to testify to Scott Gale's good and peaceful character.

On the thirteenth day, Tilje Paroyan Dohtroy came from Tsagul and took her place as the representative of her clan; with her came the scribe Vel Ragan, who had a scarred face, and his Witness Onnar. This was a sign for great rejoicing—Tsorl-U-Tsorl had his friends about him again—and also for bitter fighting on the Speaking Chain. Tiath Pentroy felt that his opponents were gathering against him.

On the fifteenth day there was a long backlog of twenty-two new links including a party from the village of Thig, east of Rintoul, who requested that the ship fly away at once because it had injured the fishing out of Thig Port.

On the sixteenth day the Round Mat was set up in the open air, and the sound system from the ship was installed —with many averting signs and averted eyes. I believed that it had been permitted because Tiath Pentroy, like everyone else on Torin, loved the sound of his own voice and the louder the better.

On the seventeenth day there was one extra link. Yolo Harn headed a speaking five of the Interpreters, including herself and Scott Gale and Tsorl-U-Tsorl, insisted on shorter hours and payment in credits from all new links, else their words would not be translated.

On the eighteenth day a break in the chain or rest day was called. I slept for the whole of the day from sheer exhaustion, and so did my fellow translators, the Deputy and Scott Gale. Brin Brinroyan, that tall and clear-eyed mountain mother, took us all into her tent and fed us herb drinks and would let no one come to us. Yet they still came, and some came and paid credits for links already spoken; we woke up rich with credits earned from our labors, which Ablo was collecting in a kitbag.

On the nineteenth day, Tiath Pentroy called for a clearing of the threads. He wanted to know exactly what we had been talking about all this long time . . . and in fact so did I.

It was generally agreed, by now, that the humans had come in peace to the land of Torin, but it was also agreed that a spaceship was a very different thing from a lone human, as Scott Gale had first appeared. The ship must be settled in some place, if the humans wished to remain on our world and pursue their research. There were hidden threads here: some wished secretly or openly for the humans to leave, to fly away. Others, possibly including the Great Elder himself, wanted them to remain and give their bounty of knowledge to the Moruia.

Four places had been set forth as possible landing sites: the precinct of the Windrock Temple, inland; the delta island of Curweth-beg, hard by the city of Rintoul; the Lebbin field, by Tsagul on the Datse, and the Fairground of Otolor. Two of these places were held to be unsuitable as landing places: the Windrock site was too dry, the Fairground too highly populated. The island of Curweth-beg was a fine site; both Scott Gale and Tsorl had seen it;

the Lebbin field was equally good, perhaps even better. But one place brought the ship very close to the realm of the Great Elder, and the other took it away from him to our despised city of Tsagul. If it came to a vote of the Five Clans it was expected that Pentroy, Galtroy and Luntroy would vote for Curweth-beg; Dohtroy and Wentroy, somewhat reluctantly, would vote for Lebbin. In my dreams at night in my various sleeping places—on the ship, in the blue tent, in the tent of Brin's Five, in Sam's round guest house—I had the nightmare that the speaking would never end. We would be here talking from dark to dark and under the light of the Far Sun until the weljin grew into humans.

I was surrounded by good friends, more than I had had in my life, but I was somewhat alone again. Tsorl had his companions; the proud Dohtroy Highness had looked on me as kindly as she could, but she saw me for what I was, a miner of Tsagul. Vel Ragan was a fine scribe and he understood my story, but there was a thread of jealousy in him for anyone who came too close to the Deputy. The humans were one unit, and they were strained among themselves with the effort to understand the world of Torin. They could not get used to Scott Gale's bond with Brin's Five and were put out when he slept in their nomad tent.

I talked best and laughed with Dorn Brinroyan and his two younger sibs. Narneen Brinroyan, about nine or ten years shown, was a Witness; she was a sweet and sensible child for all that, though there was some rivalry between her and Dorn. Tomar, the baby, was half a year shown, at the most active stage . . . climbing, prattling, making puddles. I had never had much time for little children—Dorn had five times the motherly feeling that I had. Perhaps I had deliberately turned aside from such things because I had planned to become an omor—and might still be one, for all I knew at that time. Yet there could have been no more loving mother than my own Morritt, the former "mountain-mover." I grew to like, even to love that little wretch Tomar—I liked to feel the weight of him as I picked him out of some mischief and carried him off, struggling, on my hip. There is plenty of hindsight in such things, but one thing I do remember.

Tomar disappeared one day, and Narneen and I went looking for him. He had gone into the ship *Heron*—a forbidden place—and found his way to the food store in the cargo hold. We sneaked up on him. He stood in a shaft of sunlight coming in through the open cargo doors, a Moruian baby, a mountain child, skinny and brown in a breech cloth.

He stood before a shelf of food cartons and cried out a magic word, "Sock! Sock!"

It was his word for chocolate. He stood well away from the shelf, and as we watched, the cartons fell slowly in a great wave, all around him. It was too much; he sat down on his bottom and began to cry. Narneen went and snatched him up, scolding gently. I tidied up the cartons; I even gave him some chocolate. Yet we both knew, Narneen and I, what we had seen.

When we were out in the sunlight again, Narneen drew a single letter in the dust of the red road and said, not looking at me, "Don't tell Dorn. Don't tell anyone."

I made the fingersign for a promise. The letter she wrote was for the sound "J"; it signified the word "jarn" or "jayarn" meaning something like "three-handed." The power of jarn, of moving objects from a distance without touching them, is very rare and wonderful, much more rare than the power of a Witness. Those who have this power go on to become Diviners. I held my breath when I thought about it. Clearly the family of Brin's Five had been touched by destiny and much could be expected of all its members.

One night after the threads were cleared on the Speaking Chain, I sat with Dorn before the blue tent. We were in the midst of a large, strange camp: the Great Elder's tent rose up before us, the tents of weavers and visitors were all around, the merchants had set up way-stations in the desert land on their new bypass of the red road. Gangs of porters with their loads of metal passed through regularly on their way to Rintoul. We had sentries of Pentroy vassals at a good distance from the ship, which loomed pale and shining, even in the little darkness. We sat and stared at the empty speaking place, the Round Mat, its bright colors fading into the dark. A figure approached from the Dohtroy tent in the plain.

"There is my good Fellow-Speaker," said the Deputy. "Take heart, it will not take long now. The rope of the catapult is wound up. We will fire the stone and it will land in the right place."

"Deputy," I said, "what will you do? Have you planned all this?"

"Not all," replied Tsorl-U-Tsorl. "Destiny has woven threads into the work."

So he went on into the ship, and we heard Sam Fletcher welcome him, saying that the maps seemed very good.

"That is a ruling spirit," said Dorn. "What has Tsorl-U-Tsorl behind his eyes this time?"

Next day it was the turn of Clan Dohtroy to open the chain, but Tilje Paroyan rose up and said in her lazy, deep-toned voice: "I will waive my turn for a red link in the Speaking Chain. . . ."

This was something quite new, but the humans already understood it: a red link was a link with the dead, a speech on behalf of some group who could speak no more. Tiath Pentroy was suddenly alert, hooding his eyes like a great bird; Leeth Leethroyan Galtroy fretted; Guno Deg and Jethan Luntroy whispered together. Tsorl rose up to speak, and it was my turn to speak back in the human language.

"I have a new site to set forth for some who can speak no longer, whose rights and history have been neglected and forgotten. I propose that the ship *Heron* be flown and settled in a place a little to the west. It is a fine site, better than any we have discussed. It is within the influence neither of the city of Rintoul nor the Fire-Town, Tsagul. I propose the valley of Sarunin; I speak for Tsatroy . . . the Fire Clan."

It came to the Round Mat like a bolt of fire. Old Leeth made the averting sign with trembling fingers; the other grandees spoke in hushed voices. The name went about like a hot wind blowing: "Sarunin . . . Sarunin." I thought of that strange, unblessed place, that pleasant valley, and knew that here was, perhaps, the best site of all.

Tiath Avran Pentroy burst out, "It cannot be. The place is accursed!"

"It would make an excellent site, Highness . . ." said Sam Fletcher.

"The place could be purified, cousin," suggested Tilje Paroyan.

"Who would do it?" said Tiath. "Can we call back poor Elbin Tsatroy's silent spirit?"

"If we knew where she lies," said Tsorl-U-Tsorl, "and who brought her there."

There was a moment of heavy silence. All the grandees

knew where Elbin Tsatroy was buried, and they also knew that it was Clan Pentroy that had brought her there. Just as Tiath had put the Deputy to wither away in captivity and then denied that it was his will, so Tiath's predecessor, as leader of the Pentroy, the old Highness Relrin, had shut up the last mad relict of the once-mighty Fire Clan.

"That could be an insult to my honored dead," said Tiath. "Even you, Deputy, must own that Sarunin is accursed."

"It *is* an excellent place, Cousin Pentroy," said young Jethan Luntroy. "Should we give it some thought?"

"No!" said Tiath. "No! I forbid it. We have challenged the powers of wind and fire too much!"

"Will you forbid our thoughts then, Tiath?" cried Guno Deg.

"Hold your tongue, old spite!" snapped Tiath. "You have snarled up the chain already with your monstrous prejudice. Pass on to other links. . . ."

There were not many other links that day, and the last was Brin's Five again; they requested a hearing for their sib Roy Turugan, the Harper. Scott Gale took his place with Brin's Five and brought out his guitar. I showed Harper Roy where to stand for the sound system, and he struck his harp; the harp and the foreign instrument blended beautifully. The piece was entitled "Sarunin: the Last Battle." It was late afternoon, summer in Itsik but autumn in the north; the light was strong and golden, dust rose, there were more than a hundred spectators near the Round Mat. From the first ringing notes, the Harper captured all his audience—grandees, humans and common folk alike.

First the Harper sang of the dispute between the clans Pentroy and Tsatroy over a large estate in the north on the Datse, at the border of the Pentroy lands. He told how the dispute could not be settled and the two clans gathered their vassals and their free supporters into two armed hosts. He told how the Tsatroy warriors came to their land farthest west, an unnamed green valley on the old road to Rintoul, and how the Pentroy marched to meet them. But the Last Battle was no battle at all but a sacrifice, a descent into ashes.

As the Army of the Pentroy came along the old road, they saw smoke rising and loud keening filled the air. A herald stood in the way and hailed them to stand still, not

to come any closer. Then she sang in a loud, wild voice
of the pestilence that had stricken the army, how they had
died, how the place had come to look like an old battlefield
of the clan wars, with fires and burial mounds for the slain.

Then the herald charged those who heard to remember
the deeds and leaders of Clan Tsatroy. It was a song of
leave taking, and for the first time the listeners knew what
the Tsatroy leaders intended. So presently the herald was
done; she returned to the valley; there was one great shout
and a torrent of flame rose into the air "like the bright
hair of Telve."

The Pentroy leaders of the host ran up to where the
herald had been standing and looked into the valley and
beheld the silken tents all aflame and the Tsatroy grandees,
old and young, standing in the midst of the flame without
uttering a sound. And the watchers were filled with pity
and with terror at the sight. Then when the fires were
burning low, there came a storm overhead with thunder
and lightning and a rain dropped down, fell hissing among
the embers "like the tears of Ullo." So the green valley
was blackened and accursed and became Sarunin, the place
of ashes.

Lastly the Harper told of the great grief of those few
Tsatroy remaining, how the spirits took Elbin's children
Tell and Geran, and how Elbin wandered through all the
land of Torin. He ended dramatically, "Remember the
sacrifice of the Tsatroy leaders" and unfurled for all to
see that marvelous old cloak of his own family's weaving,
which showed the emblems of the Fire Clan, the suns and
stars whirling over the golden silk.

Everyone was lost in admiration for the tale and for the
performance of the Harper and the accompaniment of
Scott Gale. I stood behind the Deputy's stool and heard
Scott Gale chuckle as he took his place beside Tsorl-U-
Tsorl.

"What are you doing, Deputy?" he asked in a low voice.
"I know you had the Harper weave in this skein. Why all
this propaganda for the Fire Clan?"

"That is a useful word," said Tsorl, his face betraying
nothing. "Propaganda. It might win us Sarunin."

I felt the hair crawl on the back of my neck; I knew that
something was being wound up, and I was afraid and excited. Tsorl called me aside as I ate supper in the blue tent
with Ablo, Karen and Lisa.

"It is time you paid a visit to Urnat Avran," he said.

"I went already, with Karen-Ru. He is almost well again."

In fact, the dwarf was quite untamed by his accident; he was as full of bounce and cruel mischief as he had ever been. Dorn Binroyan did not know how Karen and I could speak to such a creature; he had had a beating from Urnat once and could not forget.

"Go again," said Tsorl. "I need to send a skein in the utmost secrecy to the Great Elder. You will give it into the hand of Ammur herself, no other. This visit will be your excuse to come into the family quarters of the traveling palace."

I hesitated; I had no wish to face up to the Ningan ever again. Then I saw that Tsorl, far from being the smooth politician, was deeply troubled.

"What I must do is more difficult than I had imagined," he said. "Do this errand for me, Yolo Harn."

"I will do it then."

I helped myself to some chocolate from the supplies of the ship *Heron* and brought it to Urnat Avran. Luck was with me. After I had had some time, a cheerful visit even, with the dwarf in his chamber, listening to Obal's music and hearing Urnat's patter, I came upon the Ningan in a corridor. Her look was preoccupied; she was in and out of favor with her liege; she took the skein without a word.

When I came out of the tent, I found that darkness had fallen; the Deputy was waiting for me beside the ship.

"You must do another thing," he said. "You must witness a certain transaction. This is more secret than death, more secret than our escape."

"I will do it, Deputy."

"Meet me at the setting of Esder, before the rising of the Great Sun, in the second compound."

I slept in the blue tent that night because it was easier for me to leave my place without waking anyone. I wondered very much at the Deputy's actions; I wondered why he could not use his older comrades for these strange comings and goings. But I put my trust in Tsorl-U-Tsorl; I remembered that trust and belief were fragile things. I rose up in the last hour of Esder and stole away into the bara plantation through my own secret way.

The Deputy came through the trees, and I thought he

might have spent the whole night here, alone with his thoughts; his face was as dark as the tree shadows. He set off, and I followed him. We found a guard holding open the gate into the first compound; I followed still, and we came quickly to the sickhouses and passed them. We came to the Special Compound and to the graveyard beyond it, that gray, forlorn strip of land reclaimed from the sea.

There was another guard officer by the gate of the Special Compound, but the graveyard itself seemed to be empty. The Deputy went first to the grave of Elbin Tsatroy and stood above it, leaning on his ring-walker. Then to my surprise he brought out a candlecone and a little metal firebox to make homage to the dead as it was done in the Fire-Town. I took the candlecone—which was a real, precious, waxy cone from a candlecone tree, not a cheap imitation made in a mold—and waved aside the firebox. I had in my sleeve pocket matches, the useful fire-making sticks that came in the field packs of the ship *Heron*. I knelt down and set the candlecone in the old earth of the grave and set it alight with a match. I set the little burned-out torch of the dead match in the earth, too.

The Deputy turned aside then and went to stand by the grave that was empty, his own grave, still bearing the faded red skein woven by Gwell Nu and a second skein of red silk that must have come from Tilje Paroyan. As we stood above this grave, two figures moved from behind the huts and came slowly toward us. They stood at the other end of the grave: one was Tiath Avran Pentroy, the Great Elder himself, and accompanying him, as I accompanied Tsorl, was Ammur Ningan.

"What have you to tell us, Deputy?" asked Tiath. "You have set a name on this skein that I have not seen except in the records of the old Highness Relrin."

"Let Ammur, your steward, speak the name and how it stands in the record," said Tsorl in a strange, determined voice.

"I wove the records myself," said Ammur. "The name is Orath Sorell, a young teacher and scholar employed by Elbin Tsatroy; tended the two children, Tell and Geran; supposed to have run off with other house-servants after Sarunin. Yet there was a doubt . . ."

"Where was Elbin at this time?" asked Tiath with keen interest.

"Wandering," said Tsorl and Ammur together.

Tsorl fell silent, and let the Ningan continue.

"Wandering in the north," said Ammur. "The Highness was stricken with her madness long before the so-called Last Battle."

"If times had been more peaceful for her clan, Elbin's madness might have been called no more than waywardness," said Tsorl.

"Did you see her then?" asked Ammur. "She would hardly utter a word."

"Some hermits take a vow of silence," said Tsorl.

"She would not order her affairs!" said Ammur indignantly. "She would take no part in the land dispute or the preparations for battle. She showed little grief at the death of her own children."

"There was a reason for this," said Tsorl. "I can tell a little about that sad time."

"I was but two years shown at the time of the Sarunin disaster," said Tiath. "Where do you get this stuff? You are the same age as myself."

"Your pardon, Highness," said Tsorl, "I am seven years younger than yourself. . . ."

It was hard to believe; Tsorl-U-Tsorl looked old and weatherbeaten in comparison with the Great Elder.

"Speak up, Deputy!" cried the Ningan. "What of Orath Sorell? Did you see him or his kin? Do you know where he lies?"

"I will weave all the threads together," said Tsorl heavily and reluctantly. "It was a thing I swore never to do all my life long, but I will do it. Orath Sorell, Teacher Sorell so-called, was neither a vassal nor a house-servant, he was a citizen of Tsagul. Yet his devotion to his two charges, the young Highness Tell, a female of fourteen years, and her younger male sib Geran, was very deep. The fortunes of the Fire Clan were at a low ebb before they decided to go to war. . . ."

"I'm glad to hear you say it," put in Tiath. "Pentroy has been blamed for their ruin."

"The Pentroy and the Dohtroy clans both had a hand in the fall of the Tsatroy," said Tsorl bluntly. "Tsatroy was a poor clan with shrunken lands; it was the relict of the old warrior clans who guarded the Fire-Town and had little interest in trade or mining. Its five branch families lived crowded together in the Old Palace. Elbin was far away on her wanderings when the foolish decision to take up arms was made. Sorell held back the two children in her name, else they would surely have marched off with their cousins.

"When the news came of the plague and the sacrifice at Sarunin, it was the signal for the few remaining servants to die or to desert the accursed clan. Orath Sorell and his two pupils sat alone in the palace, surrounded by the bodies of the dead and the empty coffers that faithless servants had plundered. He sent word to Elbin Tsatroy. . . ."

"How did he do that?" put in Tiath sharply.

"The young Highness Tell was a Witness," said Tsorl with perfect confidence. "She was able to link with her mother. Then Orath Sorell took the children and a little silver that he had put by and fled up the Datse to a farm that was his own inheritance from a grandmother."

"Took the children?" asked the Ningan, plucking the Great Elder by the sleeve. "Took the children. . . ."

"Before he quit the palace, he made two graves, two empty fire-stone graves like the one we stand at now," said Tsorl. "He knew that even the most foolhardy person would not risk disturbing the rest of a member of the accursed Tsatroy clan. He raised the white cairns of stones above them and left a skein mourning the children's death from a fever."

The Ningan reached under her cloak and brought out a skein of white silk.

"This is a copy from memory," said the Ningan. "The original is locked up in Rintoul."

She put the skein into the hands of the Great Elder, who read it to himself, his long fingers moving impatiently over the knots. He did not take his eyes from Tsorl's face. I sat by the empty grave listening to the strange yet familiar story as if in a dream. The Deputy had thrown back the new cloak that he wore and stood there in his old red tunic and his leather vest; he set his hand upon the metal armband that had been wrought from Elbin Tsatroy's metal candlestick. I noticed that his hands, though dark and work-stained, were long and fine.

"Elbin Tsatroy came to Sorell's farm and saw her children several times," said Tsorl. "The poor child Geran did not thrive—he died three springs later. In the fourth spring after Sarunin, when Tell Elbinroyan was eighteen years shown, she made a pair marriage with her dear friend and protector, Orath Sorell. She bore and pouched one child—a male."

"This is presumption and madness!" cried the Ningan. "A male child—born five years from Sarunin—seven years younger than the Great Elder. Tsorl-U-Tsorl, your records are vague but they are set down. Child of a farmer at Trill Fall . . ."

"Yes?" said Tsorl.

"Trill Fall—a farm upon the river Datse. . . ." The Ningan's voice trailed into silence.

"The little family lived on in that peaceful place," said Tsorl, "and Elbin came by now and then and blessed them. She had no thought that they should ever return to the world or live in any other way. Tell Tellroyan, the heir of Elbin, took ill and died thirteen years after Sarunin, when her child was eight years shown. From that time Elbin's madness deepened. It may have been a kindness for the Pentroy to restrain her—but hardly in such a place as this."

"This cannot be proved—this is all dream-spinning!" cried the Ningan in a shaking singsong.

"Not much can be proved," said the Deputy, "yet there are a few threads. . . ."

He gestured to me, and I sprang up. He unclasped the broad band of metal from his forearm and pressed on its underside. From a hollow in the worked metal, he took a piece of silk, which he unfolded carefully and put into my hand. I saw that it was embroidered in black, a series of interlocking lines and circles upon the fine purple-brown of the old silk.

"This family skein was embroidered by Elbin's own hand," he said.

I took the piece of silk, and Ammur Ningan came to receive it from me; she gave it to the Great Elder, and he examined it in silence.

"I cannot understand . . ." said Tiath softly, "I cannot understand why such a wonder would be kept hidden. It might have brought friends and followers."

"These can be earned by other means," said Tsorl.

"This is a skein, then, showing the descent of the elder branch of Clan Tsatroy, from mother to mother for several generations," said the Great Elder. "It bears the name of Elbin and of Tell, her heir, and of that child, born in exile. . . ."

"I will say it once," said Tsorl, "though I break my own covenant. I will say it once only and never again, of that you may be sure. I am Tsorl Tellroyan Tsatroy, of Tell's family and Elbin's blood and the distant mothering of Telverel, Sebbin and Tsarn!"

The Great Elder lowered his gaze; he refolded the piece of silk and returned it to the Ningan, who brought it to me. I placed it in Tsorl's hand, and he set it back in his armband.

"You have no heirs," said the Great Elder flatly.

"None. It is finished. Clan Tsatroy will never come again," said Tsorl.

"Yet you have spoken. . . ."

"There is one living who can lift the curse on Sarunin," said Tsorl. "The ship *Heron* can have a neutral landing place."

"How shall this be done?" said Tiath.

"Let it be your will," said Tsorl, almost smiling. "That should be enough."

"By the fire," burst out the Great Elder, "I have been troubled all my life by know-alls like yourself, by hotheads and fools . . . by the hot breath of Tsagul and its fire-metal-magic. A Citizen can dare much—it is but one person; it can be voted in and out of office and can lay down its burden. A clan member who chooses to serve Torin must do all. . . ."

"There is still a choice," said Tsorl. "A clan member can idle its life away in wandering or flying or playing holdstone. As for fire-metal-magic, it is a thread so strained that it must break. We have fire and we have metal, and we pretend not to use them: this is mere foolishness."

"Don't lecture me . . . *cousin!*" said Tiath angrily. "See that your creature speaks no word out of place."

Then he stepped back and made the sign of greeting from one grandee to another; the Ningan bowed; Tiath Pentroy went striding out of the graveyard with his steward after him. We were left alone in the light of the Great Sun just rising, turning the eastern sky to gold. I stared at Tsorl in wonder, and when he looked at me I could not meet his eye. He was a grandee. Yet he seemed no different; he had hardly lived the life of a grandee. He was still the Deputy and the prisoner I had saved upon the raft and the scientist who dared to fly in the ship of the void and learn its secrets.

"Deputy . . ." I said, "Tsorl-U-Tsorl . . ."

"I am still that person." He smiled.

"What of Nantgeeb? She saw some of this: *an empty grave ringed with fire.*"

"This magician knows many of the secrets of Torin," he replied. "She is well-informed, I guess, about the doings on this long, silly skein, the Speaking Chain."

"Dorn Brinroyan always hopes that she will come or send Blacklock, the hero, in his flying machine. . . ."

"Nantgeeb has had the sense not to meddle and to annoy Tiath even further. She will come again when the humans are settled in Sarunin."

"Will it be a good place for their camp? Will they make another fine place like the camp of Tsabeggan?" I asked. "I often think of that time in the islands . . . in Car-Der-Vanuyu, the Place Beyond the Four Winds."

"What was that you called it?" asked the Deputy.

When I repeated the name, he turned to me and set a hand on my forehead, smoothing back my hair.

"Yolo Harn," he said, and I saw that his sharp black eyes, the eyes of Elbin Tsatroy, were full of tears.

"You are indeed a child of destiny," he said. "How do these thoughts come into your head? That was the name my mother used for our farm at Trill Fall. Car-Der-Vanuyu. A place of peace and learning and delight, far from the world. . . ."

"There are many such places," I whispered. "We find them from time to time, if we have good fortune."

"Come now," said Tsorl. "Keep silent about my family. It is an old thread, no more. When I am dead, perhaps it may all be set down."

So now it is set down. For time has passed since that morning in late summer on Itsik, and of all who stood in the graveyard, I am the only one left alive.

II

The Speaking Chain wound swiftly to a close. The Great Elder gave it out that day that Tsorl-U-Tsorl, former Deputy of the Fire-Town, had volunteered to lift the curse on Sarunin, to go alone into the valley and perform the necessary rites. No one wondered much at the decision.

Once Tiath had withdrawn his objections, everyone voted for the new site.

Ammur Ningan, working swiftly, as became the scribe of scribes, had prepared a perfect net of rules and regulations for the humans once they set up camp in the valley. Contact with Moruians was not forbidden, but it was limited; friends and helpers of the Bio-Survey Team were given a special identifying skein. For other Moruians there were the popular guided tours and picture shows concerning the Planet Earth. Vassals of every clan took turns patrolling the borders of the valley and its small harbor so that human artifacts were not brought out.

The humans paid in credits and in common things such as timber and fish for any work they had done or goods they purchased. Scott Gale was rich from his Brinroyan family and the goods they had all won in the Bird Clan Air Race. He purchased the freedom of the Itsik prisoners who had been injured on Mid-Year Day, and they became helpers in Sarunin.

The ship *Heron* rose up in its terrifying power and was gone from the red road at Itsik; it came down again in the valley, where a place had been prepared for it. And the valley was still called Sarunin or sometimes Heron-Hoo—Heron-call or Heron-shout—for the great noise of the ship. There was no uprush of scientific knowledge or fire-metal-magic, as some had feared; the humans were contained and controlled, and Tiath Pentroy had his way still.

Last Threads

THERE CAME A DAY IN SPRING, after the New Year, when everything had been put in order. I stepped out of my tent in the valley, Sarunin, and looked at the ship and the new building sites, and the stands of redwood trees. I remembered that I had to take a load of thatch faggots to the dock so I loaded up a barrow. Ablo Binigan came to fetch me as I was unloading.

"Go to the eating platform, Yolo Harn," he said. "They are keeping breakfast for you."

Sam was there, Lisa was cooking egg-pasty, Karen came up with Scott Gale: they had been taking the weather readings from a platform in a new tree. I sat with them, and we talked of ordinary things and made jokes, just as we had done at first. Tsorl-U-Tsorl was not with us; he was resting in Tilje Paroyan's villa at Deerfold Ponds, near Tsagul. The day was a special one; Sam stood up and began to make a speech of farewell. Then he stopped.

"Oh Goddammit, Yolo . . . what can we say to you?"

He gave me a hug and turned aside and blew his nose noisily.

"Good-bye, Sam Deg . . ." I said as bravely as I could. "I will come again."

Then they all came to me and gave me presents: a new blanket, a word-book, an embroidered cloth vest from the Brinroyan looms, a precious wind-finder or compass in a leather case. Karen-Ru and Scott Gale walked with me up the gentle slope of the valley to the red road. A few sleepy vassals came out of the place the humans called a Customs House and waved me through without a search.

I stole a glance at Karen on one side, small and slight, with the childish streaked hair that I had seen in the forest on Tsabeggan. I looked up at Scott Gale, tall, black-haired, black-bearded. Their two human voices rang out; I had a moment of complete astonishment. How could this be? How could these beings be here and how could I have become their friend, so that we were sad at parting? We clasped hands then, and I turned and walked off without looking back, along the red road to Tsagul.

I turned my thoughts entirely toward the Fire-Town. I had a scroll and a skein in my vest asking for a full pardon and signed by numerous dignitaries including Tilje Paroyan, Tsorl-U-Tsorl, Guno Wentroy and Boss Black. Better still I had credits earned by translating to buy my freedom, and I knew that Vel Ragan would be waiting at City Hall to help me.

So I walked on in perfect spring weather along the red road and behind my eyes a strange thought grew. "Uvoro . . ." said the wind as it stirred the dry bushes by the roadside; "Uvoro . . ." cried the bird wheeling high in the sky. Freedom. For even with people we love, even with interesting work to do, there are debts to be paid, promises to be kept. We cannot feel complete freedom. It is a lonely thing.

I paused on a hill, out of sight of Sarunin, and looked to the south. I could just see a line of light beyond the coastal valleys and low hills: the Great Ocean Sea. Then far away, coming from Tsagul, I saw a dust cloud. I waited and saw that a party of people was coming toward me; they did not look like porters or merchants. In fact as they came closer I blinked and rubbed my eyes. There were five, seven of these folk, and they wore flax kilts. I stood and looked at them as politely as I could, and presently they hailed me.

A tall female with skin-sewing on her forehead bowed and said, "Good wind, young traveler! Perhaps you can help us?"

"Good wind, gentle friends," I replied. "I will help you if I can. Have you passed through Tsagul?"

"No," said the Leader. "We crossed the Datse above the Fire-Town. We come from the Far West. We have heard that a strange being has fallen to the ground, and that there is a Speaking Chain. . . ."

Inwardly I laughed with delight. I bowed politely and replied, "Truly, my friends, you have come a little too late. But there are beings called Humans come to this land, and their camp is just a little way along the road at the place called Sarunin. Go there and observe their wonders . . . it is quite safe. Ask for the Moruian helper, Ablo Binigan, who arranges guided tours and shows pictures. Say that Yolo Harn sent you."

They questioned me a little further, and then went on their way. So in two days and nights, camping by the roadside, I came back to my home town, the old, dry, workaday city of Tsagul. I went straight to the City Hall on the third morning of my journey, and Vel Ragan already had my pardon in his hand.

"You have a friend, Yolo Harn," he said. "A third of the sentence was already cancelled."

I could not think who this friend might be, but I suspected that it was Tsorl-U-Tsorl. I did not wait to make inquiries at City Hall. I thanked Vel Ragan and paid him for his trouble. Then after a few hours enjoying the sun on Market Round, I set off out of town to the north. I was heading for that particular place on the Datse canals, just beyond the city, where Morritt had her work. She had described the house—a gray roundhouse with a small-leafed redwood in the front yard, a weaver's mile from the Lebbin lock. So I walked on, through the warm streets where the children sang, watching an occasional glider overhead that told me I was home again. Some time after midday I saw the tree and the house. Two or three children ran about and stopped to stare as I came up. A female, old and stout, stood digging beside the small gray roundhouse; it was Morritt.

She turned, peering from beneath the brim of her sun hat, then she threw down the digging fork and came toward me. We did not speak, we could not; I held her close and wept. It was Morritt, my true sib and my dear mother. Other persons came from around about, and everyone spoke of Morritt's child coming home "from the sea," as they politely put it.

Something in the face of the eldest child made me ask suddenly, "But whose house is this?"

"Do you not know?" asked Morritt, wiping her eyes. "It is the home of Tenn Tennroyan. He is much better now, back on half-time at the New Cut as a Tally Hand."

Then I knew how my sentence had been lightened; it had been worked out in lieu of credits. Morritt had given all that she had to give, her own strength; she had been working for the overseer's family all this time, to help set me free. She had heard nothing of my escape from Itsik, but this was not unusual; the prison authorities waited a long time before a prisoner was given up for lost.

"Come indoors," said Morritt. "They are not bad folk at all. No one thinks harshly of you."

Yet I felt humble and ashamed. What use was it to be a child of destiny and to have adventures by sea and land if it was somehow at the expense of one I loved? I paid some credits to the Tennroyan family and was able to shake Tenn, the former overseer, by the hand and take Morritt back to the city. But I could not talk much of my travels and the wonders I had seen until some time had passed and we were settled again in a half-house on Tin Lane. Morritt was pleased and proud when I did tell her of my adventures; we spoke of Old Harn, how he would have relished the tale, and lit candlecones to his memory. What pleased Morritt most of all was the fact that I had come back so soon.

I did not go back to the mines. I had lost the taste for them. I went down to the dock and shipped with the fishing fleet as a deck hand. I worked on one ship, then another, and earned the right to wear a sailor's cord around my neck. It was very soothing to be a private person again: never to speak in public, never to be marked out as the Speaker. I missed the Humans very much; I fretted for them so often that Morritt urged me to sail or walk to Sarunin and pay them a visit, and I planned to do this at Mid-Year.

Every so often we visited the Deputy, Tsorl-U-Tsorl, settled again in his lodgings on Canal Prospect, a retired politician, nothing more. He gave it out that he had lost his leg following an accident with a flying machine. He was one to attract legends; presently it was known that he

was a friend of the Strangers at Sarunin, he had flown in
their ship, he had flown to the stars and back again. I had
walked with him alone in the grounds of the Old Tsatroy
Palace, and I felt that nothing could be as strange as the
real history of Tsorl-U-Tsorl.

Spring had worn into summer, and not long before Mid-
Year I was walking on the dock one morning when someone called my name. I turned, and it was the Rope Ward
from the salt boat *Gvalo*. I knew his name now, Ogaro
Dyall or Dyall the Rope Ward, because I had asked among
the sailors. There he stood, tall, handsome, with his dark
red hair in a long plait and his eyes green as the sea. We
stared at each other, and I felt a smile on my face that
would not go away; I was so pleased to see him again. For
the pair of us it was suddenly springtime.

We knew a thread that should not be broken, and we
have seldom been parted since that time. That first winter
we put together our credits and bought our first boat, a
tiny rounder called *Ubin* or *One-Fish,* and we sailed to
Sarunin wharf, which was like coming home again. Dyall
has often complained that, for a waif, a Child of the City,
I have too many families. He, for instance, has only one,
a decent Five who still live and multiply in the village of
Thig, beyond Rintoul. He is one of the Silly Fishers of
Thig who have gone down in the skeins of Torin as the
askers of foolish questions.

This is the end of my part of the story. It has taken me
a spring and a summer to write it down, and the reason I
have stayed away from the sea and from Dyall, my dear
partner, for so long is one that might have surprised me
most of all, if I had thought about it on Itsik or on Tsabeggan. I sit here in a tower of the so-called New Academy
by Rintoul, on that island Curweth-beg, wearing a vented
robe. One drink of the watten cup does not make an omor,
and I have proved this twice over. My elder child, six
years shown, is sailing with her father to Tsagul to see
Grandmother Morritt. My second child lies heavy in my
pouch in the last days of his milk sleep. He stirs and kicks
and opens his eyes; when I tickle him with a feather pen,
he grasps it in a well-formed hand.

Dorn Brinroyan has the room overhead in this new
stone tower; I can hear him pacing about between his desk
and the window, which looks to the north, to the mountains
where his life rose. I might have had a room with a window

that looked toward the sea, but the sea is always in my
mind and so are the islands; I do not need to be reminded
of them. My window looks over the delta lands toward
the east; in the far distance I can see the blue-brown hills
above the Salt Haven. Flying machines come in from the
east—when Blacklock comes to the rooftop landing place,
there is noise and laughter and everyone takes a holiday.
I have a seeing-glass on my window ledge and I sometimes
look toward the Eastern Retreat and summon Nantgeeb
in a small voice. "Come on, Magician, tell us your part of
the story . . . I have told my secrets . . . you know
much more. . . ." But I do not speak very loud, even in
my mind; I think that Nantgeeb hears all and smiles and
one day she will answer.